Chris Petit is a film-maker and writer. He lives in North London. *The Psalm Killer*, his most recent novel, was published by Pan in 1997 to great acclaim.

Praise for *The Psalm Killer*

'*The Psalm Killer* is an example of the genre near its best. *Gorky Park* with something to spare; well worth anyone's weekend'
Guardian

'In the tradition of Thomas Harris's *The Silence of the Lambs* . . . one remains haunted by *The Psalm Killer* . . . a deeply satisfying and sophisticated thriller which approaches the Northern Ireland conflict with the intelligence it deserves'
Financial Times

'Disturbing, lurid and amoral . . . an epic thriller'
Daily Telegraph

By the same author

THE PSALM KILLER

CHRIS PETIT

BACK FROM THE DEAD

PAN BOOKS

First published 1999 by Macmillan

This edition published 2000 by Pan Books
an imprint of Macmillan Publishers Ltd
25 Eccleston Place, London SW1W 9NF
Basingstoke and Oxford
Associated companies throughout the world
www.macmillan.co.uk

ISBN 978-0-330-47489-4

1 3 5 7 9 8 6 4 2

A CIP catalogue record for this book is available from
the British Library.

Typeset by SetSystems Ltd, Saffron Walden, Essex
Printed and bound in the UK by
CPI Mackays, Chatham ME5 8TD

Visit **www.panmacmillan.com** to read more about all our books and to buy
them. You will also find features, author interviews and news of any author
events, and you can sign up for e-newsletters so that you're always first to hear
about our new releases.

PART I

CHAPTER ONE

—Did you close my eyes? I often wonder what happened. Was it you who found me and was I still beautiful? I do not know how it came to this. But here we are, after all, and I cannot tell if I am loving you or hating you. Both, I guess. What happened to Paolo? He must be grown by now and gone to college. You know I never stopped loving you, that is why I am writing. Some love never fades.

You must be surprised reading this. I can see your face as clear as ever, and your first reaction – it can't be, not her. Did you say a prayer for me in all those years, think of me just a little bit? I am different now from how you remember, but not so much. Then you do not look the same either, short hair. I saw you in a magazine. You have haunted my dreams for so long, now it is my turn.

On the good days my love for you overflows. Other times love is so cruel and I think, wait a minute, when I remember what you did, you should suffer too. Into each life some rain must fall. I cut out your picture. I am looking at it now. There's a sorrow in your eyes. Is that because of me or do you never think of me at all? Am I just the past to you? And if you are thinking,

'She can't come back,' do not bet on it. One of these days you will find out – Love to love you, Leah

Did you ever see a big star cry? This one did when he read what she wrote. 'How can I get a letter from a dead person?' he asked Youselli.

Like a lot of famous people the man had a big head, physically as well as in the mental sense, Youselli noticed. They were standing in a fancy panelled library out in the man's Long Island residence, a second or even third home that would cost Youselli several working lifetimes of his cop's salary.

Till he saw the man cry Youselli had never thought about how songs were always full of crying – not just this man's songs, everyone's. To be fair, he was not really crying after reading the letter but there were tears in his eyes, and Youselli thought, 'It sure has spoiled your party.' He remembered the old song, 'It's My Party (and I'll cry if I want to)'.

In the background servants came and went. The man's wife had told him there would be a lot of celebrities, as though he had never done security before. Recently the hiring of cops for celebrity security had become such a fashion accessory that his captain turned a blind eye because it gave the department access to a wealthy address list for fundraisers.

What he could not figure was why the wife had shown McMahon the letter at all after the fuss she had made on the phone that morning about keeping it secret. 'I don't want him upset. Just find out who's sending them,' she had said, like they were coming from around the corner instead of Los Angeles. Youselli had wondered then if the wife was insecure. Face to face, he was less sure. In the flesh she was something else, as snazzy as an Italian contessa. He had heard she and McMahon led pretty much separate lives, she in Manhattan while he partied out at the house. Close to, Youselli could see that the hard living was taking its toll on McMahon despite the work of orthodontists and clinics. He was still star skinny and had all his hair but Youselli wondered about face lifts.

McMahon read the letter again while Youselli looked at the envelope, an everyday brand and self-adhesive, which meant no saliva trace. As for getting hold of where McMahon lived, the internet was full of listings of famous addresses. The typeface was a regular font, almost certainly from a standard computer.

McMahon made a helpless gesture with his hand and said, 'I don't understand, it makes no sense.' Youselli's impression was that McMahon was a phony, using pauses like an actor. Maybe he had played too many big stages and that made it hard for him to do close-up work without resorting to exaggerated mannerisms, like the way he raked his hand through his shampoo-commercial hair to signal bafflement. Youselli had never seen such silky hair not on a girl.

McMahon finished the letter and appeared so upset that it took him several attempts to produce a coherent summary of the letter's meaning. It referred, he finally said, to an incident that had taken place in France fifteen years earlier, when a teenage American girl named Leah had died in an accident while looking after the young son of a fellow band member, now also deceased.

'What kind of accident?' Youselli asked.

'She died in a fall at Mickey's house. Mickey and Astrid were with me and when they got back she was lying at the bottom of the stairs.'

Youselli thought the story sounded conveniently vague. 'Who was the girl?'

'She came to look after Mickey's kid, Paolo.' McMahon spoke like he was issuing a press release. The band had been renting French chateaux that summer, gypsying round Europe to avoid British tax. Youselli watched the wife watching her husband and thought, he is not going to say anything in front of her. He wondered if big stars jerked off.

Big party, rich man's party, rich man's house, Youselli thought as he watched the chauffeured limousines arrive. Trees high as the house screened off the world outside, their dusky green in smoky contrast to the brash lit-up rectangle of azure, the rich man's pool. The rich were so predictable, he thought. He could bust them for the load of fancy dope they were pretending wasn't in the back room. Youselli stuck his hands in his pockets and gave a smile to the wife that went unreturned while McMahon charged around, suddenly energized. Youselli told himself it was another night for the three wise monkeys: see nothing, say nothing, do nothing, and play the dumb cop.

Youselli had made sure security was tight. He had

men on the gate and in the grounds with walkie talkies. His base was the secure room under the stairs, which amounted to a closet big enough to sit in. It was like the inside of a large safe, steel-lined, with a fax and phone – the last line of retreat from whatever unimaginable horrors the famous lived in fear of. Youselli had a man in there checking the CCTV monitors that screened the exteriors. Youselli spent the early part of the evening watching the guests arrive on the screens, like they were on regular TV. A lot of names, a lot of faces and a lot of people dressed like pirates, too many tall women for his taste, and a couple of celebrity photographers snapping away. It was like the Seventies never went away, Youselli thought, plus he had not realized there were still so many smokers.

The catering staff were dressed as slaves and the prettiest waitress rolled her eyes at him whenever she passed. A steady flow of guests – but only the elite – kept disappearing into the room Youselli wasn't supposed to know about and came back out animated. The door was guarded by private security. Youselli asked the wife about the extra muscle. She told him it was the standard arrangement for her people to mind the cloakroom. Youselli could not resist a grin, trying to decide which of the impossibly well-heeled guests was going to run off with a bunch of coats. The wife shot him a snooty look that said he was insubordinate.

Before the party got too wild she made a pretty speech about all the great things her husband was about to do, including write his book. The book involved the biggest deal ever signed for any star's memoirs, she proudly told her guests, and it would be the one that pulled no punches, she assured them, written by the man himself and not one of those as-told-to jobs. Youselli thought McMahon looked less than happy at the prospect. Maybe he was one of those musicians whose brains had been fried by drugs. Maybe he would be needing a ghost after all.

After the speech Youselli checked the grounds. He took O'Dowd, who complained his shoes pinched.

'You should swap them with Christopher Walken's,' said Youselli. 'His look comfortable.'

He had noticed Walken, taller than the rest, in a sinister dark suit that fitted his movie image, and shoes that did not, the rattiest pair Youselli had seen outside a building skip. Stars like Walken he had no problem recognizing. Lesser known faces hit him after a time lag. So many famous people in the room, it was like a waxworks museum.

From across the lawn the party floated like a ship in the night.

'How old's this guy?' O'Dowd asked. 'I mean, giving him a sled.'

The wife had made McMahon the presentation at the end of her speech. O'Dowd was right. A child's sled was not the easiest thing for one adult to give to another in public, regardless of its particular history. It must be nice to have so many toys, Youselli thought. He had counted four vintage cars in the garage.

They crossed from the edge of the lawn into the undergrowth. To their left was a summer house and by the light of the moon Youselli could make out the silhouette of a couple banging away at each other. Beyond, the water of the sound gleamed like oil. He wondered why the wife had shown McMahon the letter. He tried to picture the woman who had written it. When he got back to the house he would fax a copy to the shrink they used for assessment of hostile mail.

O'Dowd wanted to stay and watch the activity in the summer house, which was reaching its noisy climax. O'Dowd was so predictable, thought Youselli. He felt inexplicably flat, maybe because nobody was going to stand up and make speeches about what a great guy he was, and no one was going to write to him.

Guests with reputations to protect had gone early or retreated to private rooms. Youselli did not stop to ask himself what was going on in half of them. From time to time he heard applause from behind closed doors. Meanwhile the rest of the party disintegrated into an incoherent mass of squirming bodies, more or less upright on the dance floor and horizontal by the pool.

Youselli's eyes watered from the smoke. 'What are you doing after the orgy?' asked O'Dowd.

O'Dowd was one of those people he felt embarrassed standing next to, with his sneaky little grin, like whatever he said was the funniest thing. O'Dowd was short with weight trouble and had body hair like an animal pelt, Youselli knew because he had seen him once with his shirt off. It didn't take a lot of brains to see that his aggression was a form of defence. Not that the insight made Youselli any better disposed.

'Fucking Village People,' said O'Dowd.

Youselli wished he could have a drink. He tried to calculate the cost of keeping four hundred people in booze. He doubted if he knew four hundred people, not counting criminals.

O'Dowd was on about the sled again, worrying away at his initial question. 'Why'd she give him the sled, it's not like they got kids?'

'It's a movie sled,' said Youselli. The party had reached that stage when everything became stretched. 'A famous old movie sled.'

The concept appeared beyond O'Dowd.

'Remember Lassie the wonder dog?' asked Youselli.

O'Dowd frowned then nodded. 'In the movies?'

'Well, this is the Lassie of movie sleds. If Lassie had been a sled, she would have been this sled, if you take my meaning.' Youselli was not sure O'Dowd did. 'This is *the* sled in movie history. Steven Spielberg has one.'

'The same sled?' O'Dowd asked, confused.

'The same sled.' Youselli thought about getting the waitress's number now that he was technically single.

O'Dowd nodded, then grinned like some big idea had crossed his mind, and he tugged Youselli's sleeve. 'Yeah, but what's he going to do with it?'

Youselli sighed. 'The fuck do I know. Sled on it.'

McMahon made Youselli a present of the girl on his arm. She looked about seventeen. 'Take her, she's yours,' he said. 'This one's mine.' His choice was the prettier, which was the way it went with these people, thought Youselli.

McMahon was making the best of appearing elegantly wasted, swigging a bottle of Jack Daniels from the neck, his eyes bulging and glittery with near obscene excitement, and looking several galaxies away. Youselli had to hand it to him, he knew how to put on a party. There had been fire-eaters, a tightrope walker, and a snake that had got loose in the garden, subsequently recovered, and now, unless he was very much mistaken, hookers, hired for the occasion to be handed out as a demonstration of the hosts' largesse. Youselli handled McMahon's offer badly, sounding uptight as he muttered about having to work.

'Aren't you a reckless man?' asked McMahon with a sneer. 'I bet you're real straight.'

McMahon went on, his voice growing more whiny and insinuating, and Youselli was left with the impression that he was only there as a butt for the man's jokes. McMahon turned to the girl on his left. 'Ask him nicely and he'll show you his pistol.'

Unlike McMahon, the girl wasn't high. She looked bored. McMahon announced to the other one, 'We're going upstairs now. I don't have a pistol, like this big hard policeman here, but we're going to have a good old rummage round and see what we can find. *Parlez-vous français?*'

The girl looked panicked and said nothing.

'*Et toi?*' he asked Youselli who felt even more like he was there for the man's amusement. There were hangers-on in the background, grinning expectantly. Youselli wondered how the atmosphere had turned predatory so fast. McMahon sensed it too.

'I know what you are thinking,' he said while

Youselli held his eye. 'Do I ever exercise my *droit de seigneur*? Isn't that what you're wondering?'

'I might if I spoke French.'

The onlookers waited for McMahon who had the grace to laugh and then they tittered appreciatively. He took a pull from his bottle, gestured broadly, pointed at the girl and said, 'Feel free.'

He lurched off with the other girl and the crowd moved away with him. Youselli could see O'Dowd grinning in the background. He looked at his girl. Sure he would like to exercise his fucking *droit de seigneur* sometimes, he thought. It wasn't as if he was getting it anywhere else.

'You want to explore around?' asked the girl.

'What's your name?' asked Youselli forgetting it as soon as he was told. 'Maybe later,' he said.

O'Dowd came over grinning even more and said, 'I got another sled question.'

'This is Paolo,' said Anjelica, the wife, introducing a pale young man who had not yet taken his coat off. Paolo looked twenty at most, and happy with it, except for eyes which read dead soul. Drug dealers got younger all the time, Youselli thought, like tennis and swimming champions. He had noticed Paolo in the course of the evening and figured him for being in charge of the back room, which meant the muscle on the door was his. Youselli disliked people who grinned all the time and grew goatee beards and wore overcoats at parties.

Paolo and the wife both looked pretty high and not from booze. Youselli wondered if the wife knew what hubby was up to. She looked like she didn't miss much however long a leash she ran him on.

He needed her prompt before he realized that this was *the* Paolo, referred to in the letter, all grown up now and gone to college.

He was still not sure where everybody fitted. Paolo was Mickey's son and Mickey was the band member who had died. And Mickey had been married to Astrid, who was from Sweden but was not Paolo's mother.

Youselli had to shout over the music. It was hard playing the straight man when everything around was degenerating into one big fuck. One couple seemed like they were about to do it on the stairs. Youselli thought she looked semi-famous. Paolo noticed them too. Nothing seemed to faze him. He came across as the world's best adjusted drug dealer, smiling from ear to ear and happy to share tales of weirdness in France.

'Of course I was very young. I only remember what I was told.'

'And what was that?'

'That Leah and I must have been playing when it happened and I had gone and put myself to bed afterwards on my own.'

'You remember nothing?'

Even shaking his head Paolo kept grinning and Youselli wondered if it was a nervous disorder.

'Tough for a kid,' said Youselli. 'But you look like you got over it okay.'

Paolo replied that his unconventional upbringing had equipped him well for survival. 'I was serving the drinks at Mickey's sex parties when I was eight.'

'Sounds like model parenting,' said Youselli, feeling that Paolo was trying to rile him.

'Unusual, and it did no harm in my case.'

Youselli asked what he remembered of Leah and got the vague reply that so many different people had looked after him that they were all a blur. He then asked Leah's age.

'Oh, she was sixteen, something like that.'

'Isn't that young for a full-time babysitter?'

'She was a friend of Astrid. I think she was taking French lessons as well.'

'Astrid took her to France?'

'I suppose. They were pretty close.'

'Is Astrid here tonight?'

Paolo shook his head and grinned like he had some big secret. Asshole, Youselli thought. Maybe the kid had been grinning when the girl fell and it had stuck, like pulling faces when the wind changed.

There was a commotion at the top of the stairs and Youselli saw the girl whose name he had forgotten clambering over the couple. She saw him and gestured frantically for him to come up. It was trouble.

The girl McMahon had been with lay flat out on the floor of the master bedroom, her works by her side. There was no sign of McMahon. The bed looked recently used. Youselli wondered if the junk had come from Paolo.

The girl looked dead and he could not find a pulse. Maybe her heart was not working, he thought, but his was beating faster. He did not want any dead bodies on his first job for the client.

Under the eyelid her eye was glassy and unsighted. She looked like marble. The other girl was standing watching and scratching her arm, being useless. He wondered where McMahon was. His hands were shaking he noticed.

'Get a rug and make sure no one comes in.'

He clamped his mouth to the unconscious girl's, pinched her nose and breathed in and out, till he felt her heart flutter and she gradually revived, surfacing from a long way down. She came to with a fit of coughing then her body convulsed and she retched, throwing up, partly over him. Youselli didn't know whether to be relieved or annoyed. There was a bruise on her cheek and he wondered if McMahon was a hitter. The girl looked round with panicked eyes.

'Come on, sweetheart, you're not in heaven yet.'

He had to slap her to keep her conscious, and fired questions at her to stop her from nodding out. Her name was Charley, and her friend was Holly, which he was sure was not the name he had been told. He made Holly go downstairs for a jug of coffee, while he walked Charley round the room, which she did not want to do.

Twenty minutes later he left them lurching round like a couple of drunks. He found McMahon by the pool with a crowd of hangers-on. Youselli drew him aside, to his visible annoyance, and told him what had happened. With the music he was having to shout.

'Oh that's terrible,' said McMahon, with no sign that he knew who they were talking about. His faraway look announced he was still flying. Youselli gripped his arm.

'Take your hand off,' McMahon protested. Youselli refused. He was determined to make him own up.

'The kid you were with, remember?'

McMahon looked at him with glassy eyes and giggled. 'That wasn't me, that was my twin. Now get your hand off me.'

McMahon's nose wrinkled in distaste and Youselli was aware of the smell of vomit still on him in spite of his efforts to sponge it off. McMahon's expression also said that he would recall the insult of being touched long after he had forgotten what it had referred to. Youselli backed off, realizing, if he was being honest, he did not care overmuch about the kid either. The real cause of his irritation was having to act as dogsbody.

'Is she all right now?' McMahon asked, apparently unconcerned.

'She will be,' shouted Youselli over the throb of cranked-up bass.

'That's okay then.' Sensing Youselli's resentment, he added, 'It's a fact of life, I'm surrounded by people who bite off more than they can chew. They do it by themselves. It's not me who tells them to.' He turned to survey the party. 'See that man over there, with the silver hair and the cane. Go ask him why he's fucking my wife.'

Youselli was tired of McMahon's games. 'Ask him yourself.'

He expected McMahon to get annoyed, not raise an eyebrow the way he did and say that at least Youselli was no yes-man like all of the rest.

The silver-haired man was in discussion with a foreign-looking woman in a purple dress. He was handsome and older than McMahon, maybe even over sixty but well preserved. Sensing perhaps that he was being talked about, he turned and met their gaze with pale, unblinking blue eyes and a chilly smile, which Youselli took to mean that the two men went back a long way.

'He's a cunt,' said McMahon airily, still having to shout. 'And shouldn't be here because I asked specifically for him not to be. You should throw Mr Black-ledge out.'

Youselli decided McMahon was joking and asked how long they had known each other.

'Alex and I go back years. I first met him in the Philippines. He was the man in the white suit. He fixed things for Imelda Marcos. Blackledge turns up everywhere. He was in France.'

'When the girl died?'

McMahon nodded. 'You should talk to him. It's got to be him or Astrid or Aaron behind the letter.' He looked at Youselli and giggled. 'I can tell you, I was spooked for a moment back there. A letter from beyond the grave.'

'Who's Aaron?'

'My manager, ex-manager. Aaron doesn't go out since he got fatter, and balder.' The remark amused McMahon and Youselli realized they had both forgot-ten about the kid upstairs. Blackledge was looking at them again. He and the woman in purple seemed to be arguing about something. 'Are you losing your hair?' McMahon asked suddenly and Youselli experienced a moment of panic. 'The public figure's nightmare. And those hair weave jobs never look real.'

Because of the noise sustained conversation was impossible, but McMahon seemed in the mood to confide. 'They're all shitting themselves over what I'm going to write in my book, show them up for a bunch of leeches with revolting personal habits.'

With that he vanished, and Youselli decided to tell O'Dowd to take the kid out the back way then he would talk to Blackledge. It was bizarre, he thought, how McMahon's air of immunity seemed to brush off on him. He didn't like it and wondered why he enjoyed being in McMahon's orbit, and figured it had to be the fame.

When he got back Blackledge was gone. A woman in a backless yellow dress gave a bray of laughter showing pink gums. The next time he saw her she was carrying a shoe with a broken heel, causing her to limp, and her mascara had run from crying. The horseplay around the pool was getting out of hand. Several people had already been pushed in by a mean-looking man with a skull for a head. He wore a Stetson and braids in his hair and looked like a bounty hunter in a Western movie. He saw McMahon who kept fiddling with his nose. The helpers could not keep up with the accumulating debris. He wondered about Blackledge and McMahon's wife but could not bring himself to feel sorry for a man who could walk away from a dying girl in the certainty that someone else would tidy away. Youselli thought of something he had not realized before: crimes got solved because people didn't tidy up afterwards. Watching the party lurch into incoherence reminded him of his daughter's last birthday: high spirits turning to hysteria and over-excitement, ending in fights and tears.

CHAPTER TWO

Edith Weber was studying a copy of the letter Youselli had faxed when her phone went. It was after midnight but Edith had arranged for her daughter to call, regardless of how late, as she suffered from insomnia.

Edith was a sturdy, handsome woman in her sixties, with the finest white hair, who after all these years was still surprised to find herself living in New York. She retained a trace of German accent but had hardly spoken her native language in five decades and never returned to the country of her birth. Her survival when the rest of her family had perished still made it hard for her to form attachments and her life's main companions had been her own fierce intelligence and her daughter, Susan, the result of a brief liaison with a producer from the early days of television.

Edith regarded Susan as the only real success of her life. She had missed her dreadfully in the two months Susan had been gone. They lived only a short walk from each other and since the death of Susan's husband, five years earlier in a senseless traffic accident, they had grown closer. Their one shared regret was there had been no children.

Susan had gone to Los Angeles to work as an

accountant for a New York movie being made on location. Edith had been surprised when Susan had told her that it was necessary to go away. From the one or two hints dropped, Edith had gathered that there might be a romantic attachment involved. As it was, with Susan's work schedule and different time zones they did not speak as regularly as Edith would have wished. She very much enjoyed Susan's production gossip, a mini-soap opera that sounded far more interesting than the film being made. Susan knew who was sleeping with who almost before they did, who was throwing tantrums, which star had a chronic alarm-call problem, and what drugs were being taken.

Edith suspected the real reason Susan called was because she was nervous about her mother being alone, more so since Tom's death had shown how cruel life could be. Edith knew Susan fretted. Thirty years ago there had been no crime in the area. Now there were bus-stop shootings less than two miles away. Edith wondered about her reluctance to move. The house was in a nondescript suburb, a modest, single-storey building she had never particularly liked. But she had slowly grown to accept that her memories had stamped themselves on the place, and had become a part of its fabric and this made it impossible to leave.

Edith told Susan about the letter Youselli had passed on. She remembered Susan meeting him once and saying, if they were talking men as real estate, Youselli was unreconstituted outer suburbs and overdue for renovation.

Edith was about to say that she thought the letter showed signs of obsession when Susan was interrupted by a call waiting. Edith held and thought of the obsessives she had treated, including a bright young man with a good career who had found himself repeatedly calling a woman and hanging up. 'This is not rational behaviour,' he had said to her with tears of incomprehension.

Susan came back saying she had to go, a producer was suffering a late-night panic. 'I'll try and get back one of these weekends,' she said.

Edith knew it was unlikely. The film's production schedule had eaten into Susan's free time. She told Susan she missed her.

In the silence after replacing the receiver Edith looked around the hall. So much brown and too little brightness, she thought as she walked back to her desk, wondering what was troubling her.

For all her ability to rationalize and to err on the side of caution, Edith, even at her age, was still prey to childish superstition. She feared the bogeyman. She avoided cracks in the sidewalk. She feared an irruption of the violence that had taken away her family. She suffered the guilt of the survivor. She lived in the expectation of punishment and, for all her exercise of choice and control, part of her acknowledged an atavistic, pre-psychological state, somewhere in that dark fastness where templates were laid down for all time. She feared the irrational and was drawn to it. Sometimes she felt her whole life was a delay spent waiting for that moment of true horror when she would understand the fear and bewilderment, the rage and final naked terror her relatives had lived through at the end of their long, last journey, as they realized they were the victims of the most massive and cruellest deception.

CHAPTER THREE

—A man once told me I was malfated. Imagine being told that. I was very young at the time. He said I would never avoid my destiny to be malfated. Make a left instead of a right and it is there waiting. Our lives hang by the slenderest of threads, every minute of every day. You should remember that for when I come. It all ends in death, as you will know.

Sometimes on these sharp cold days I stand on the edge of my own particular canyon and look into the dark below which is as black as the blue above is bright. I have this recurring dream. It is now and I am standing on the street waiting for the lights. You are in a car, in the back, and you look up and at that moment you look so far away, so different from how I remember. Oh, yes, you are eating ice cream, which struck me as a detail. A sign really. A sign for us. That things will work out. Most of the time I think of us as waiting to be happy, you waiting for me. I only want to make everything better for you but sometimes I cannot help it, knowing it's hopeless. The biggest struggle is always on the inside. Malfated. It's not a nice thing to be. Love to love, Leah

CHAPTER FOUR

'Obsessive love focuses on the idealized lover, what Forward calls the One Magic Person,' said Edith Weber. 'This person is then invested with expectations they are unable to live up to.'

Youselli looked tired and preoccupied, she thought. When he lit a cigarette she was about to object, then decided there was something reassuring about the smell. She tried to remember if her father had smoked as she pliantly fetched a saucer for an ashtray.

Youselli's strong physical presence made her feel superfluous. Whatever dictated his tunnel vision – his sex drive probably – she fell outside its range. Her obvious lack of need for men seemed to puzzle him and with her he adopted a fidgety, sceptical manner. She could still see in him the boy who sat at the back of the class.

'Whether they know it or not,' she went on, 'these people are re-enacting feelings of loss, hurt and rejection experienced at the hands of their parents.'

He gave her an oh-is-it-that-easy look.

'Did you ever do a school play in first grade?' she asked, thinking their unspoken contest might be more interesting for being made personal.

24

'I guess,' said Youselli, not seeing the point.

'What was it about?'

He shrugged again. 'There were songs in it. I do not recall what I was, not a big part. I remember standing at the back of the stage and in front of me was a girl in a pink ballet dress.' He rolled his eyes, remembering he was talking to a psychiatrist. 'I was what you call precocious.'

'Did this play have a happy end?'

'It was a kids' play, what do you expect? We all sang a song.'

'Let's say that your adult relationships are re-enactments of this play.'

'I do not remember anything about it.'

'No matter. But let's say you're still playing the same part.'

'My life ain't exactly song and dance.' She seemed to have him on the defensive.

'There was dancing too?'

'I said.'

'No, you just said. That was the first time you mentioned dancing, if you discount the girl in the ballet skirt.'

'She was not about dancing.'

She ignored his smirk. 'What happens with obsessives is they find themselves acting out forgotten or suppressed childhood dramas.'

Youselli grinned. 'Same old production, new cast.'

She acknowledged the neatness of the conceit and wondered why playing the stooge amused him.

'Sexual obsession, like the sexual impulse, repeats.

We are all fetishists to an extent. Any sexual behaviour is a form of theatre.'

Youselli shook his head. 'I don't think you can tie sex down like that.'

'Even masturbation is a theatrical fantasy involving the need for a scenario.' He started to look uncomfortable and she wondered if he used visual stimulation. 'We are dealing with cycles of frustration here. And a deep-rooted need to repeat the patterns of hurt and rejection. It's a point made by Forward and worth quoting: "The re-enactment of childhood rejection in adult relationships is the basic need for all obsessive lovers."'

'And it escalates?'

'And ends in rejection.'

'Then what?' He was humouring her again.

'Things usually get dramatic,' she said. 'She will bombard him in the hope of making him see sense and accept what to her is inevitable and obvious.'

'Yeah, but say they did get together in some crazy scheme of things and she got her dream come true?'

'She will still find ways of rejecting him.'

He looked thoughtful. 'Sounds like my wife.'

That old double-hander, Edith thought, humour and hostility. She was surprised by the reference to the wife.

'Well,' she said neutrally. 'We all behave obsessively at times.'

'I get all the obsessive behaviour I need at work.' She felt the shutters go down. He gestured at the letter. 'The stuff she says about him, it's clear she knows him?'

'She writes like she does.'

'Except she is supposed to be dead.'

She did not appear as astonished as he had expected, and she said quietly, 'The letters are very close to death, they are suffused with the idea of death.'

He told her about McMahon's suspicion that someone who had been in France was responsible for the letters. Edith frowned.

'Maybe I am wasting your time,' said Youselli, 'if it is some game being played by one of McMahon's friends.'

'You haven't been wasting my time at all, and I think you're wrong.'

'About the letters being faked?'

'I would say they are the real thing.'

'But the person writing them is supposed to be—'

'I know. What I am saying is that the person writing these letters writes with a very clear voice and displays a degree of personal obsession that argues against your theory.'

Youselli shrugged. 'Beats me.'

'What was the relationship between Leah and McMahon?'

'None according to him. She was just some baby-sitter. Why are you looking so doubtful?'

'On the basis of what I have read I would say there was a significant relationship, even if it was unrequited.'

'Even if he was unaware she was nuts about him.'

'To the point of obsession.'

'But if she has been dead fifteen years how does someone duplicate that obsession?'

'I don't know but there is a deliberate element of surprise in that the sender is the last person you would expect to hear from.'

'And the intent is malicious?'

'Oh yes, I am sure. Once you get down to basics. See what she writes: "When I remember what you did, you should suffer too." The point is she believes there was a relationship and she was wronged. Of course it's possible there really was one and he is covering up. Have you considered that?'

Youselli inclined his head. 'He has a certain evasiveness, so maybe. Go on, what else?'

'I would say initially that the writer is a woman, around thirty. There is an intelligence to the writing that only comes from experience, but we're talking first impressions. She has a deep anxiety about patterns repeating themselves. The anguish of rejection is countered by the hope it will be different next time, and the fear it will not. There is also the moment of erotic binding, the look granted by one to the other. We should not discount the ejaculatory force of the eye as a source of obsession. I would also say the ice cream is significant too. It signals childhood and via that memories of the father.'

'So it's about fucking daddy.'

'Succinctly put.'

'And what's her interpretation of the malfate?'

'She sees it as their destiny. She wants to protect him from it but she also sees herself as its agent—'

'Why bother if she knows she is going to get fucked over – excuse me – in the end?'

'Delusion. I suffer from it myself.' She caught his

look of interest. 'Take this neighbourhood, I know it is becoming dangerous for an elderly woman on her own but I do nothing about it. I tell myself it's still safe.'

For all his swagger Edith suspected Youselli was frightened by loneliness.

'On a scale of one to ten, how do you rate her?'

'Based on content – she is dangerous, persistent, obsessive and almost certainly trouble.'

'My kind of gal.' Youselli's laugh went unreturned. 'McMahon thinks it is someone playing a game.'

'If so it is a very sophisticated game. I can only tell you what I think based on what is written down. Let me put it another way. You have not heard the last of her. I would liken her to one of those storms you see building in the Midwest. You are going to be watching those clouds for quite a while, but she will come, Lieutenant. She will come.'

CHAPTER FIVE

—Sometimes I have to write these letters over and over till I get them right. Today is one of those days. What you must understand is everything that got undone in France can be mended, if you want it. I have come back to show you the way. Everything taken from you in France will be given back.

I saw you had your party – I thought of coming and giving you a big surprise – and now you are writing your book. Does that mean you have to tell about us? And little Paolo, lost in the wood, and Mickey and Queen Astrid, and Alex with his aristocratic, British accent. You had long hair then. I can still see myself sitting outside with Paolo, helping with his drawings. Every time he wanted it to be the perfect picture – telling me just how it was going to look – and we would make the first lines and it would start to grow, then he would falter, like even at that age he realized his hand was not good enough to put down what he saw in his head. But I made him carry on till the picture was nearly finished. Then the same thing always happened. The rage took over and he scribbled and scribbled till nothing was left except a lot of angry scratchings.

I have scribbled out people that way too, many times. Love to love, Leah

CHAPTER SIX

The sight of McMahon freaking out made Youselli realize something he had not seen before, how cool and hysteria were the flipside of each other. He wondered if McMahon suffered stagefright.

Anjelica was sitting behind a desk, studying her nails, waiting for McMahon to be done pacing the room. She and Youselli seemed to be in silent agreement that this was a performance to be indulged.

'I was living thirty miles away! Mickey used to come to me. I saw the girl three or four times all summer!' McMahon snatched the letter and waved it at Youselli. 'She knows about the fucking party. And the book. I tell you someone is feeding her.'

'The psychiatrist—' began Youselli.

'Fuck the psychiatrist! What do they know? Look at the fucking letters. She knows about France. She knows what happened. Now she knows about the party. This is being done to jerk me around, and I want to know who it is and I want it to stop!'

Youselli wanted to tell the little prick to fuck off. Instead he gave the wife his best smile and asked if he could get some coffee. The request left them looking at each other like he had made the most outrageous demand.

'Cream and sugar?' asked Anjelica tersely.

'Two sugars.'

'Sugar's bad for you,' said McMahon.

'Not if you don't mind being fat.'

Youselli wondered if it was drugs that kept McMahon thin. Anjelica picked up the phone. Youselli was disappointed. He had been hoping the domestic staff had the day off – because McMahon had answered the door himself – which meant she would have to make the coffee herself. From what he could tell, she was calling a neighbour to borrow a houseboy to fetch coffee in.

Youselli was cheesed off. He had stopped by the Dakota apartment at McMahon's insistence. McMahon had called personally, sounding strained. Youselli had told him he had no time, which was true, but it had cut no ice. McMahon announced that it was too urgent to wait. There had been another letter and he needed Youselli immediately.

On the way into the Dakota Youselli had passed the usual gaggle of tourists hanging round the courtyard entrance, shooting each other with their handicams. As always he was struck by the Dakota's ugliness and wondered why anyone rich would want to live there. It was like something out of a horror movie. Plus McMahon buying into the Dakota was a bad security move, in Youselli's estimation, given the building's history. It could be seen as tempting fate.

He had arranged to come by during his midday break, hoping they would give him something to eat. Too many evenings these days he was forgetting to. But until he had asked they had not even offered coffee, just enough frost to leave him in no doubt that he had incurred their displeasure, presumably for having dared to suggest he was too busy to drop everything for them.

Together they made a formidable team, barely looking at each other but carrying between them a sense of secrets shared that excluded anyone else.

'What are your thoughts on all this?' asked Anjelica, folding her hands neatly, and addressing Youselli like he was an interviewee for a job.

He decided to bullshit the smug bitch. 'Well, she's not one of the "if onlys".'

' "If onlys"?'

' "If only we could meet." They're harmless. No, there is a complicated agenda behind these letters. They display privileged information, but they cannot be from who they say they are because that person is dead. So the information would have to come from a third party, it seems, and yet – this is the psychiatrist's point – the letters don't read like they're fake. I discussed with Miss Weber the possibility of Paolo writing the letters, like he's tapping into some memory block.'

Anjelica leaned forward. Youselli had her attention. He was sure she was one of those people who could not bear not knowing. Her husband being so secretive would drive her crazy.

'I'll talk to Paolo again, you give me his address. What about Blackledge?'

McMahon shot his wife a look and said with considered menace, 'Do we know where he is?'

She met his look deadpan. 'He's staying at the Gramercy Park but he's out of town.'

'Did he say where?' asked McMahon archly.

'California, but he wasn't specific.'

McMahon snorted. 'California! Where the letters come from! Come on, Mr Detective! I tell you, they're all in it together, like that dumb story about the murder on the train. The kid writes them and Blackledge mails them in Los Angeles.'

'Be sensible,' snapped the wife. Youselli watched them simmering on the brink of a major argument.

'And Aaron? Where's he?' Youselli asked.

This time he caught Anjelica looking at McMahon, who mumbled, 'Talk to the others first. I'll think about Aaron.'

Anjelica raised an ironic eyebrow. To Youselli she seemed the kind of woman who adopted la-di-da mannerisms from Europe.

McMahon looked petulant. 'I tell you, someone's trying to fuck me around.'

Youselli asked if there were any pictures from the time in France. McMahon looked surprised, and Youselli caught another exchange of glances between him and his wife.

'I don't have many private pictures,' McMahon said with a shrug. 'You get photographed to death as it is.' He turned to Anjelica. 'If there are any would they be here?'

'I don't see what use they could be.'

Youselli said, 'I'm pretty much in the dark so far.'

He watched each of them waiting for the other. Eventually Anjelica stood up abruptly, saying she would see what she could find.

Her exit was followed by an awkward pause.

Youselli was no good at silences and said, 'Nice place,' feeling foolish but McMahon apparently had not heard. Bickering with his wife seemed to have left him indolent and preoccupied. Youselli counted his way through the next silence and had reached sixty-something before McMahon spoke.

'My wife and I,' he said, 'inhabit households where a raised eyebrow says more than the spoken word. I am reminded sometimes of childhood games – rummaging in the dressing-up box – supervised by an adult cruelty that comes from being too long indoors.'

'What's that a quote from?' Youselli meant it as a joke. In fact they turned out to be lines from a script McMahon had been sent. He told Youselli he was considering a career in movies. People with a music background often did, he said, usually without much success, he added glumly.

'I don't think I should do it, do you?' he said, leaning forward as though he really cared what Youselli thought.

'Why should you care what I think?'

'I don't.' McMahon laughed good-naturedly, and for the first time there was a relaxation in the tension Youselli had sensed running through their encounters. Youselli laughed too, feeling it was expected of him, and was immediately annoyed at himself for sucking up to the man. With that McMahon appeared to lose interest and got up and walked across to the desk where copies of the letters lay. He picked one up and spent several moments reading it, a picture of studious contemplation, artfully framed by the high window. Youselli figured his positioning was calculated to the inch, as a result of knowing all the room's good angles and where the light was best.

'"A man once told me I was malfated",' he read, quoting what Youselli recognized was the first line of the second letter. 'It was me who told her about the malfate. I was that man.'

'Excuse me?' said Youselli, not sure of what he was hearing.

'What it says in the letter.'

Youselli let the man hear the disbelief in his voice. 'I thought she was just some kid hanging around, that you did not know her.'

'Sure.' McMahon was unfazed. 'But we were talking in the kitchen one time. About fate and destiny.'

'As one does,' said Youselli. It was his turn to raise an eyebrow.

'As one does,' conceded McMahon.

'This conversation took place in France?'

'At Mickey's place. She was feeding the kid while I fetched a drink.'

'And malfate, what is the meaning of that? It's not a term I am familiar with. Is it French?' He hoped he was getting a dig back at McMahon for putting him down at the party, but McMahon was too humourlessly preoccupied to notice.

'It means bad or ill-fate, like when you're on a collision course with something that's waiting to happen.'

Youselli pulled a face thinking of his bust marriage. 'But isn't the notion a little deep to be discussing with the child's nanny when she's feeding the kid?'

McMahon smirked. 'There was a lot of strange stuff

in the air that summer, a lot of I-Ching and Tarot cards and star-gazing.'

McMahon appeared lost in the past when his expression crumpled and Youselli, unless he was much mistaken, found himself witnessing a look of utter fear.

'What?' he asked.

'The girl's dead,' McMahon whispered, 'and some-one else is pretending to be her, but how could they know about a conversation that was just between us?'

Youselli decided McMahon was faking again. It was plain to him that the girl had reported the conversation on, though he didn't say so, and asked instead if McMahon was superstitious. McMahon looked puzzled until Youselli added, 'Are you uncomfortable with the notion of the malfate?'

'It was just a phrase. I don't think anyone took it seriously.'

'So what exactly did you say to the girl?'

'That maybe her life was some kind of bad trip, I don't know. I was bored. It probably amused me to spook her.'

'You were right, weren't you?'

'Right how?'

'Her life turned out a pretty bad trip, considering.'

'I didn't attribute her death to the malfate, that was just an accident.' McMahon said it without a trace of irony. He shrugged as though he had had enough of the subject. They fell silent.

Youselli looked around the room and eventually asked McMahon why he had bought the place. 'You mean considering the building's history,' he answered sharply, his apparent fear of a moment earlier forgotten.

'It was cheap and my wife likes a bargain, and in answer to your next question, no, I am not superstitious.'

The doorbell rang and Youselli listened to the clack of high heels on wooden floor and a few moments later the wife came in with his coffee and a couple of photographs.

'These were all I could find.' She sounded indifferent as she handed them to McMahon who glanced at them before passing them to Youselli. They were two black and whites, eight by ten, taken at the same time, showing a group eating outside in an orchard, seated round a table on a hot summer day. Youselli recognized McMahon who looked the same except for his hair. The other man he figured was Mickey. He was darker and more saturnine. Youselli asked whether the woman next to Mickey was Astrid. McMahon nodded, distracted. Youselli figured his vanity was unhappy at confronting his younger self.

'Who's the woman next to you?'

'Donna.'

'Nobody mentioned her yet.'

'She left early. Not long after the photograph was taken.'

'Should I talk to her?'

McMahon looked sour. 'If you can find her. She never had anything to say anyway.'

Youselli was disappointed. Leah was in both pictures but, unlike everyone else, her head was turned away.

'You don't have any others with Leah in?' asked Youselli.

38

'Why the fuck should I?' McMahon snapped. 'She was the child's nanny.'

Youselli looked again at McMahon and Mickey hiding behind their sunglasses, both pale enough to suggest a life spent indoors. He asked McMahon where the two other band members were and was told they had not been in France as neither wrote songs and were not required until recording. McMahon's disdain made it plain that he regarded them as vastly inferior, and Youselli saw how McMahon would be capable of putting the big freeze on people. No wonder Donna looked uncomfortable in the photographs, he thought, like her time was used up and she was wasting space. Next to her was Astrid, the only cheerful one of the group, and the only adult eating. Snapped with a mouthful of food and grinning at the camera so that her face distorted, she looked like a hungry predator. Youselli remembered she was from Sweden and asked McMahon where she was now.

'She moves around. You would not recognize her from that photograph. Astrid blew up.' McMahon sounded like he could not care less.

'Got fat?'

McMahon sniggered. 'No rehab for Astrid from what I hear.'

Youselli took another look. It was not the most flattering picture but he could see that Astrid must have been a fine looking woman in her time. As for Leah, Youselli could not even detect the trace of a profile.

'Was she pretty?' he asked.

'The girl? From what I remember.'

Youselli wondered how deliberate McMahon's vagueness was and exactly what he was holding back.

In the photographs he saw that on the table in front of the child were crayons and a pad, and on the pad what looked like a child's drawing, like Leah's letter had said, but with the sun's glare on the paper he could not make it out.

CHAPTER SEVEN

Youselli had always been called Beau since he was
little, except by his father. He remembered his father
in his blue uniform, slate-grey eyes and a trap of a
mouth, shirt tight as a drum over a gut that reminded
him of the steel bath he used to bathe in as a boy. His
father had been a typical Mick cop, albeit with an
Italian name, and a hard boozer's face, a shut mind and
a mean turn of phrase (his parting words on leaving
the house every day, 'Shit has to get shovelled').

His father was sick in a home for retired officers
now, dying with as little grace as he had lived.

Youselli found him sitting in his usual place in a
conservatory that looked like it had been stuck on the
side of the building as an afterthought. He was sitting
by himself. In the inner room four men seated round a
table played a grim game of cards. Youselli wondered
why his father always contrived to be sitting alone
when he visited; probably because it spelled out his
own vision of himself as a man who had been shoved
aside by his family.

'How's the bad guy?' said his father with sour cheer.

Youselli told him about McMahon's party. His
father grunted.

'What happens when they find out you're doing ten other jobs aside from the one you are paid for?'

'I told you, the captain knows.'

His father grunted again. In his estimation celebrity security was a form of ass-kissing, not worthy of a cop. Youselli duly ran down McMahon for the old man's benefit. 'The way I see it, he is unable to figure out what the rest of us do automatically – go to a restaurant, get gas. He does not do any of these things. He does not even drive.'

'Are you telling me the guy's been driven all his life!' yelped his father. 'Jeez.'

'I'm betting he could not do what we do.' Youselli was careful to include his father. 'Which is handle things one on one. I'm thinking: could this guy face someone down?'

'Do you remember that Dirty Harry film?' His father pronounced it 'filum'.

'You liked that picture.'

'Remember the end where your cop actor has a bead on this whiny little faggot punk reaching for his gun and slithering all over the jetty, trying to squirm out of the way of the man's .44. Is this musician fellow a faggot too?'

'I expect.'

His father snorted. 'They always are. And would he know what to do when some junkie with bad wiring produces a gun and there is no way he is not going to use it?'

'He has people to take care of that, he's famous.'

'How many times have you had to use your gun, son?' his father asked, and Youselli sighed inwardly.

He knew the speech off by heart. It had started when his father had spoken with wintry melancholy of the men he had shot and Youselli realized he was supposed to answer in kind. The next time it happened again, and the time after until Youselli realized his father had little or no recollection of his previous visits. He wondered bleakly if there was any sense in him being there and whether he would be missed when he wasn't.

'I have used my gun maybe a dozen times in the course of duty. I have shot two men. Dead. The first in the head. It was what you would call a lucky shot because he was moving fast and I was off balance. I never lost any sleep over that.'

He wondered whether by telling these stories he was trying to prove he had turned out all right. When he was a kid, his father had constantly said, 'Patrick, you are the rotten apple in the barrel' and it had been his stated belief that in the course of his duty he would end up drawing his gun on his own son. Youselli saw now that this fantasy had been the old man's way of coping with his failures.

The second shooting had been in a liquor store hold-up because he happened to be in there. 'I put six rounds in him and he kept coming,' he told his father. 'I give him the first three to the chest – all to the heart, I could see where they'd gone in – and in the normal run of things one of these shots is enough to stop a man in his tracks.' His father nodded. 'My fourth shot I start to get the feeling I am in a bad dream. The guy's got to go down, I am thinking, but he has this surprised expression like he just found out he was going to live for ever. So I nailed him again, but he keeps coming and I am starting to think, I carry on doing this I can take him home to Momma for a drainer.'

The story always made his father laugh – a terrible rusty sound, somewhere between a cough and an engine dying – and as usual he made Youselli repeat how after taking all six shots the perp was still stomping round like a deep-sea diver, arms jerking like he had been wound up, the adrenalin flooding his system, preventing shutdown. His father sat with tears of mirth running down his face, miming the shot man's clock-work arms. 'Then what happened?' he asked between attacks of agonized laughter.

His father was scared of dying, it did not take a genius to figure that. Another patient, of German extraction, had told him there was a German word meaning 'anxiety at the closing door'. 'That's what I got,' his father had announced more than once. 'They closed the door on Frank.' Frank had been his oldest friend in the force. 'Now they're closing it on me.'

Youselli supposed the reason he tried hard talking to his father was because in three, four months he would not be able to. As much as he detested his old man, part of him knew there was more of his father in him than he cared to admit. That was what he understood by heredity. One day he would be sitting where his father was now and his kids would hate him even more than he hated his father.

CHAPTER EIGHT

A man the size of a fridge answered the door and Youselli recognized him as Paolo's muscle from the party and guardian of the dope room. He waited on the step of the brownstone while his entry was cleared with Paolo, and was then shown up to a large second-floor sitting room at the front. The smart Manhattan address in the high eighties had taken Youselli by surprise, but on the inside it was less impressive. Once expensive decor had been neglected and gave the house a dated air. The place smelled of cat and was creepy with the drapes all drawn, as though its inhabitants didn't have any need for daylight. The framed photographs all over the walls were presumably of Mickey in his glory days, but Youselli did not get the chance to check because Paolo steered him to a seat in the middle of the room. Paolo was notably less affable, but still grinning, and polite enough to offer herbal tea which Youselli accepted without knowing why, as he hated the stuff. Paolo wore expensive looking black silk and was barefoot. The wet tips of his hair said he had just showered. Paolo's fastidiousness seemed at odds with the general smell.

'Nice house,' said Youselli insincerely.

'Belonged to my father.'

They made small talk while the fridge brought tea in dinky cups.

'What kind of work do you do, Paolo?' asked Youselli, watching the fridge freeze in the act of putting down the tea.

'I'm a dealer,' said Paolo. He stared at Youselli and after a beat added, 'In antiques.'

'Is it the kind of work that calls for a lot of personal protection?'

'You mean Boris? It calls for a lot of lifting. Furniture, you know. Say hello to the policeman, Boris.'

'Hello, policeman,' repeated Boris obediently as he let himself out, his eyes conveying that he would cheerfully kill Youselli.

Youselli was in no doubt that Paolo was a slippery kid. He showed him a copy of the latest letter, hoping it would knock the shine off him, but Paolo read it with detached amusement and asked what Youselli was going to do.

'I don't know. One theory is that the person writing these letters might not even know they are doing it.'

'But they would have to know about France.'

Youselli nodded and asked, 'What was she like?'

'You already asked.' Paolo's manner suggested something beyond indifference.

Youselli persisted. 'Was she quiet, was she noisy? You must have been the person closest to her.'

Paolo's head snapped up, and the voice behind the grin turned cold. 'I didn't want her around. I didn't want to be looked after by anyone except my mother, and she was dead.'

Youselli forsook the condolences. 'What do you think of McMahon?'

'I don't.'

'Don't think about him?'

'He's nothing to do with my life.'

'Doesn't he buy stuff off you, then?'

Paolo gave Youselli a hard look. 'I deal with his wife. She's the one interested in furniture. Take a look at the bureau in their apartment next time you're there. That was mine.'

'What I heard, McMahon and your father were very close. You must have some opinion.'

Paolo's smile broadened. 'Yes, I have an opinion. He was the uninteresting one. Mickey was the giver, McMahon was the taker. Mickey was the one who took the risks. He was the one with the record for assault, the drug busts, the pregnant heiress – my mother – and the bad politics. You know he took tea with Leni Riefenstahl in her Munich apartment. He was a fan.'

Paolo expected him to ask who Riefenstahl was, he could see, so he said, 'I hear Mickey was prone to errors of judgement.'

'Mickey didn't give a shit. What you have got to understand is Mickey liked mischief.'

'Like playing alongside those bluesmen and cosying up to the Ku-Klux-Klan.'

Paolo snapped his fingers like Youselli had just hit a clever shot. 'You got it. It amused him and he was quite open about it, unlike McMahon.'

'Who is more secretive.'

'Right. Mickey kicked down the front door.

McMahon sneaked round the back. He preferred closed doors, while Mickey worked the room. Once at a party he climbed stark naked out of a hotel window fifteen floors up.'

'Any reason?'

'A twenty-dollar bet. It was his way of handling the boredom of being on the road. He once told me his life was dedicated to proving there was more than one way of throwing the TV set out the window.'

Youselli laughed obligingly and asked what he thought of McMahon writing about his father. For the first time the smile disappeared off Paolo's face.

'I already said, in so many words, the man's opinion is of no interest.'

'I hear a lot of people are nervous about his book.'

'Who says?'

'He does.'

'He would, and now he's putting it about that someone's writing letters to spook him. Come on.'

'You sound like you don't believe him.'

Paolo brushed the remark aside. The grin came back, craftier this time, as he said, 'You said this person writing the letters might not even know they're doing it.'

'That's possible.'

'And you're thinking, here's this kid all fucked up by what he saw, maybe he's writing this shit in a trance.' Paolo looked at him like he was a total idiot.

Youselli tried holding his eye and failed. 'At this stage we're looking at every possibility,' he said lamely.

Paolo stood up and looked down at Youselli. 'You think I got nothing better to do with my time?' He was starting to get angry, Youselli was happy to see. The kid was too cool for his own good. 'And when I sit down and write these letters what happens? They come out like someone else is writing them?'

Youselli had no idea. 'I'd have to ask the expert.'

'Ask him about spelling.'

'It's a her.'

'Ask her what would happen to the spelling.'

Youselli shook his head, not comprehending.

'I went to thirteen, maybe fourteen schools,' said Paolo, pointing a finger. It was the first time Youselli had seen him look urgent. 'All over the place and I speak four languages as a result and I'm not at home in any of them. I speak them but I don't spell and I don't think my subconscious can spell either.'

'Hey, you're pretty smart.'

'Because I grew up around grown-ups. You want to know what I think? McMahon's having someone post him letters.'

'What for?' Youselli tried not to sound incredulous.

'To make out he's more interesting, and so he can work the letters into his stupid book.'

'What would he achieve by that?'

'Some weird shit happened in France, don't ask what, I don't remember, but it was going on and afterwards I heard they all took one of Alex's oaths never to talk about it.'

'What kind of oath.'

'Knowing Alex it was some supermarket version of the voodoo shit he'd picked up. But it must have worked because no one did talk, and I grew up asking. So maybe McMahon wants to spice up his book, and is going to elaborate lengths to pretend he's not the source.'

Seeing Youselli's scepticism, Paolo added, 'McMahon does manipulations for breakfast.' He gave the letter back and asked, 'What do you get out of this?'

'Excuse me?'

'You seem very curious.'

'Not really. Rich clients you indulge.'

'I'll tell you one thing, the letter's wrong.'

'Wrong?' For the first time Youselli thought Paolo might really be about to tell him something.

'That stuff about the drawing and the frustration. One thing I do remember, it wasn't me did that.' He paused, letting the implication of what he was saying sink in.

'The scribbling part happened?' Youselli asked slowly. Paolo nodded and watched Youselli working it out. 'Then you are saying it was her that did it?'

Paolo nodded again. 'I was reminded reading the letter.'

'What did she do, exactly?'

'We'd do my drawing and when I thought it was done she'd carry on and scribble it out till the whole thing was crossed out.'

'And do you remember how you felt about that?'

'I do. I felt she was pretty fucked up. And knowing Mickey's influence, those were probably the exact words I used.'

Youselli pressed him for more, but the door opened and Youselli saw a look of anger cross Paolo's face as he snapped to whoever was on the other side, 'Go back upstairs, I'm nearly finished.'

'What's going on?' a woman's voice said, but from the way the door was angled Youselli was unable to see her.

'Go back upstairs,' said Paolo sounding angrier.

A large mirror hung over the mantelpiece and in its reflection Youselli caught a glimpse of the woman as the door closed. She looked dirty and bloated and ugly and middle-aged. Youselli wondered who she was. She didn't fit with Paolo's world.

'Who was that?' asked Youselli but Paolo didn't answer and he was no longer smiling.

Someone was watching his house. Youselli was sure of it. A nondescript saloon stood across the street and someone was inside. But as it was away from the streetlamp he could not see who. He looked through the blinds again, trying to see if more than one person was in the car. Maybe he had been seen leaving Paolo's house and followed. The biggest nightmare would be Internal Affairs wanting to know whether he was dealing on the side, as well as moonlighting.

He went for another beer and found he had run out. The fridge's empty shelves were a mocking reminder of his solitary life. He was spending too much time alone, letting things run down. One night he had taken all the bullets except one out of a .38 and spun the chamber and clicked the gun several times, only aiming at the wall, but even so, it was not what he ought to be doing.

He thought of Paolo in his fancy townhouse with its big sofas and McMahon's accumulated real estate.

His own furniture amounted to little more than a couple of garden chairs, a TV and a mattress. He hadn't even got round to buying bed linen. Prison had a better standard of living. At least there you ate regularly, which was more than he was managing. He realized he was turning into a lonely man, which was not something he had ever expected to be.

His garage was reached through the house. Whoever was in the stationary car ducked down before Youselli drove past. He was pretty sure there was just one person, which meant it wasn't cops. The car didn't follow.

He drove to Manhattan and parked down the street from Paolo's house, eating a sandwich he had picked up along the way. The woman behind the door, he was certain, had been Astrid. Her accent hadn't sounded American.

It was impossible to tell if anyone was in because of the permanently drawn drapes, but he was prepared to bet Paolo was out. Staring at his own empty icebox, Youselli had figured that Paolo was the type to eat out and eat out smart. And if it was Astrid he had seen, based on the glimpse he'd had she wasn't the type you took along. Astrid would be left to binge alone at home.

Paolo needed taking down a peg in his opinion. Maybe he'd put in a call to Bremner. Bremner had a nice little sting going, busting dope dealers and confiscating their supply before selling it back to them in exchange for dropping charges. Maybe it was time Paolo got an education in the ways of the world. Youselli grinned mirthlessly to himself and bared his gums. He was depressed at the idea of being lonely. Maybe he had been lonely all along. He had never really thought about it. Maybe it was sneaking up on him unawares and there was still time to pull out of it, make a home for himself, start searching around for a sensible date. A half hour passed with Youselli trying to build positive thoughts that inevitably crashed as he tried to conjure up an image of patio bliss with a barbecue and a woman he loved.

He had decided to give it another twenty minutes when a white Mercedes drew up outside the house and Paolo and a female companion, not Astrid, got out. The fridge was driving and went off to park.

Youselli drew a bead on Paolo with his finger, then fired the engine and drove past, half hoping Paolo would turn and see him.

CHAPTER NINE

The next night Youselli was in position by 8.30 p.m., figuring Paolo for a nine o'clock reservation. Sure enough, at twenty-to the fridge drove up in the Mercedes and Paolo emerged from the house minus his companion of the night before. Youselli no longer felt so sure of his previous night's hunch. There was no guarantee it was Astrid indoors, or that she would let him in, but if she didn't he'd sick Bremner on Paolo and get the house turned over.

He waited ten minutes then leaned his hand on the bell a long time. Eventually the door cracked open. It was on a heavy chain. To go by the number of locks Paolo liked his security. Youselli said who he was. There was no answer.

'Can I come in?' he asked, showing his badge. Again he was met by silence.

'Hey, Astrid? This will only take a few minutes.' He said he was conducting a private inquiry for McMahon. There was no reason she should let him in, he thought.

'McMahon?' She said it like the name was some distant memory.

'Hey, listen. I got money. I will pay to talk. Just let me in a minute.'

That got her attention. A junkie would do anything for money, everybody knew that. With negotiation it cost him forty and she made him give her the notes as soon as he was inside. His eyes took a while to adjust to the gloom of the hall, which was as well because Astrid was a big shock. She was a mess. Her face was bruised and she looked like she spent most of her time falling down. Her skin was puffy and blotched and Youselli could smell the booze on her as soon as he stepped through the door. She wore a kaftan to try and hide her ballooned weight and she smelled like she was a week away from washing. She was also way taller than him.

She blinked at Youselli like she had no recollection of letting him in. Whatever else she was on besides drink, he figured she was coming down.

He followed her up the stairs, trying to avoid looking at her bloated ass. She took a step at a time, using the handrail for support, and once they were in the living room she immediately excused herself, saying bleakly, 'I need to fix my face.'

7 'It's fine as it is,' he said, but she was gone.

The room smelled more than before and the heating was on full in spite of the mild weather. He checked the photographs on the walls while she was gone. Most were of Mickey, as he had thought, but one unframed picture curling on the mantelpiece, with everyone but Mickey, was obviously of his funeral. There was Anjelica looking aloof and elegant and next to her McMahon in dark glasses, and two other pencils in suits Youselli recognized as the makeweight members of the band. A leather-coated Paolo floated near the edge of frame, next to an enormous unjolly giant in a black tent of a suit and a T-shirt bearing the partly obscured legend Mean Motherfucker. This bearded hulk was as gross as the three musicians were thin, as though he was carrying their excess weight for them. From the way he was backing out of the picture Youselli guessed he had made a career of avoiding being in them. He supposed he was looking at Aaron, former manager, conspicuous by his absence from the party, as was Blackledge from the photograph. As for Astrid, the weeping widow centre stage, she looked ravaged and well on track for obesity.

Fat or not, Astrid was light on her feet because Youselli never heard her coming, though he was ready for her because he had heard her toilet flush.

'Don't look at that stupid photograph,' she said, her voice husky and accented. She pointed to another on the wall. 'See how beautiful I was.'

Youselli thought she had to be kidding. No way was she the creature in the photograph, a modelling shot of a goddess of lofty beauty, in feathers and boas, and pants so tight she must have been poured into them, and eyes so confident and aloof they nailed the camera dead. Incredibly, it was her, though it took Youselli an almost wilful act of imagination to detect the resemblance.

'Do you know what they called me?' Bitch, he would have guessed. 'The Queen of the Night. They said my strength came from sucking people's souls. They said I sucked Mickey's soul.' She looked eager and projected all of a sudden.

'Did you?' he asked, trying to keep his voice straight, but she noticed.

'You should have watched me do it,' she hissed, 'and seen the husks. I was magnificent.'

And look at you now, he thought, but said, 'Tell me.'

From the way she told it Youselli figured that her story was one she had rehashed so many times she could no longer tell what was fact. She was vague about her background which seemed to have involved impoverished German aristocracy, relocated to Sweden. Youselli was willing to bet that in her day few would have dared push her on the point and any that did she would have looked down her nose at and silenced with her height.

Youselli was haunted by her vanished beauty, but most of the time she struck him as repellent. She smelled extra bad too and as she took him through the pictures on the walls he puzzled over what exactly she smelled of. It was like you found in woods, a combination of dark earth and fungus. He was jolted when he realized that it was sex, the definite odour of unwashed sex. He wondered who on earth would want to. Then he wasn't so sure. For all his revulsion he was aware of her allure. She still had the voice, like old Ingrid Bergman movies from when he was a kid, one of those cool Nordic voices that sounded like they were only waiting for you to fuck them.

'I got to use your toilet,' he blurted. He found it on the landing and after splashing water on his face felt better. The careless leftovers of Astrid's last hit lay on the cistern. Youselli dabbed his finger and rubbed the powder round his gums, flushed the toilet and went back downstairs, determined to take control.

In his absence she had lit an incense burner that gave off a heady, cloying perfume making the atmosphere even more oppressive. As she droned on about her conquests and life with Mickey Youselli tried to recall how the cold water had felt on his skin. If anything the room had grown even hotter. His mouth tingled but instead of making him more alert he was aware only of a dull panic. He stared dumbly at his hands. They looked like someone else's, not his at all, and he couldn't think what to do with them. Her ugliness excited and scared him. Her eyes gleamed with feverish excitement. For a moment he thought he was in a wet dream about to come. He tried to imagine how she would feel inside – as dry as a desert, he supposed. 'Tell me about Leah,' he said, clinging to the sentence like it was a lifeline out of a dark space.

Astrid's eyes narrowed. 'She was a stupid girl who made a lot of trouble for everyone.'

'Because she died?'

Astrid turned away with a look of dismissal. He went on, louder, angry that everyone was so indifferent to the girl's death. 'I hear you all swore never to talk about it.'

Astrid snorted. 'Who told you?'

'Paolo.'

'Then you're more stupid than you look. Paolo glamorizes everything.'

Since he was a kid Youselli had been vulnerable to

accusations of a lack of intelligence. Seeing the smug look on her face something snapped. He pushed her roughly into one of the soft chairs, leaned down boxing her in, and said, 'Either answer my questions now and I go away and leave you to your works, or I have you busted and we can talk in the box, see how you like that.'

She nodded, but she wasn't afraid. He grabbed her wrist hard and said, 'I'll have that creepy stepson of yours run in too.'

The fierceness of her reaction, like one of animal protection, triggered in him a bright moment of understanding. He realized what had been nagging at him since his arrival.

'How long have you been fucking the boy?'

'Stop it, you're hurting!'

'How long?' He was yelling now.

'Since he was eleven,' she shouted back.

'What about McMahon, did you fuck him too?'

She answered of course she had, in a way that told him he was stupid for asking.

'And McMahon was fucking Leah.' He didn't ask it as a question.

'After a fashion,' said Astrid tartly.

'So everybody fucked everybody,' Youselli said in wonder, like he had finally seen the light. 'And how did Leah get in the picture?'

'I spotted her around the clubs. She used to hang out with her mother.'

'Her mother!'

'Young mother, darling, both in hot pants, both great legs. She used the girl as a lure.'

'And you introduced Leah to McMahon.'

Astrid stuck out her lip. 'McMahon didn't have the guts to approach her on his own.'

'And she and McMahon had a relationship.'

Astrid raised her eyes. 'So formal – "introduced", "relationship".'

'Answer the question.'

'Big hard cop.' She threw him a look of contempt. 'They fucked a few times. Satisfied, darling?'

He had to fight to keep his temper. 'How come Leah ended up babysitting in France, was that to do with McMahon?'

'McMahon, McMahon, McMahon. Are you in love with him?'

He made to hit her and laughed when she recoiled.

'No,' she said. 'Sorry to disappoint. She pestered me to come, to get away from her mother and Mickey hadn't organized anyone to take care of Paolo. Leah was a lonely rich kid.' She went on, 'Her father was a stuffed-shirt lawyer with a fancy Manhattan practice.'

Youselli wondered why she was suddenly being so forthcoming. 'And?'

'She was a disaster! She moaned the whole time about being homesick, about the food and the language, and she was hopeless with Paolo.'

'You could have sent her home.'

'Then there would have been no one to look after Paolo.'

Sensing his disapproval she muttered as she reached for a cigarette, 'Come on, you must have been in love with someone enough not to care about anything else.'

Youselli realized his expression must have given him

away because Astrid immediately pounced. 'You don't know what I'm talking about. Do you?'

He grabbed her arm again, squeezing till he made her flinch. 'What are you covering up?'

Astrid protested that he was hurting her. He let go and straightened up. When he next looked she was crying. He was surprised. He had thought her too hard-hearted. Wiping her eye with the heel of her palm she told him he was a pathetic thug.

He decided he was enjoying himself after all. 'So is it you writing McMahon letters?'

'I wouldn't waste my time, sweetheart. Talk to Blackledge. It sounds more his style.'

'Who is Blackledge, exactly?'

Astrid made a dismissive gesture. 'One of those English upper-class faggots who makes a big thing of screwing girls.'

'And how does he fit with McMahon?'

Astrid gave a cracked laugh and made a fucking sign with her finger.

'Is McMahon that way?' Youselli was unable to keep the surprise out of his voice in spite of his agreement with his father about McMahon.

'Is McMahon that way?' Astrid repeated, mocking. 'This way, that way. These ridiculous little distinctions only exist in the minds of people like you.'

'And what kind of people is that?' he said carefully. He didn't want her getting to him again.

'People who live by the rules.'

'And look at you now,' said Youselli witheringly.

'And look at you,' she retorted. 'I know which I'd rather be.'

Youselli bunched his fists in his pockets. He felt he had been locked in the room with her for ever, but also saw that they were both liking it in a curious way. She seemed to need his audience, and her way of riding his questions and throwing them back at him excited him, he realized.

Astrid was staring off into space and eventually she said, 'Sometimes Mickey used to go blue in his sleep.'

'I want to know about Blackledge and McMahon,' he said.

Astrid looked at him wearily and said, 'Mickey and McMahon were kids, not much education, too much money and suddenly they were hanging round smarter people, who had the right taste and didn't care if they put you down. Mickey saw through them, and made it clear they took him on his terms, but McMahon wanted to be like them and swan around auction rooms and show off his good taste and make out he was some big connoisseur. Blackledge taught him how.'

'In exchange for what?'

'Influence, I suppose, or McMahon's body, or money to finance his movies.'

'What movies?' It was the first he had heard.

She was not listening. She had turned towards the door. It was the second time that night Youselli had failed to hear someone coming.

The fridge was eyeing him like he was the canary, and Youselli realized the fridge had known he would be there, which meant that Astrid had called the restaurant while she was out of the room. No wonder she had kept him talking.

'Thank God you're here,' she said faking sudden shock, 'this man has been terrorizing me.'

'You been hitting on a helpless woman?' asked the fridge.

Youselli was still thinking about his gun when he found himself flat on his back and the side of his head felt like it had been hit with a brick. He hadn't even seen the blow coming.

'Hurt him, Leon,' he heard Astrid say from a long way away.

He painfully levered himself on to all fours like a dog waiting for its beating. Paolo had called the fridge Boris, he was sure. He wondered stupidly if he was dealing with twins and tried in a desperate way to see the humorous side of the situation because he was very afraid he was about to be badly hurt or perhaps even die. This, he was certain, was not something he would do well, and the last thing he wanted was Astrid getting off on his funk.

He found himself taken by the scruff of the neck and shortly after took flight to end up flat on his back at the bottom of the stairs, arms outstretched like he was crucified, and praying nothing was broken. His wrist hurt especially and when he turned his head and opened his eyes he saw a shiny black shoe pressing down. Two shiny black shoes, in fact, because he was seeing double.

Paolo's voice sounded like a radio that was losing its signal. Youselli couldn't make out what was being said to him. He was dimly aware of another man next to Paolo and gathered he was Paolo's lawyer. Youselli tried to shake his head but it hurt too much. Paolo was leaning down, with a crazy look in his eye, saying, 'I'm going to have your ass in a sling for this.'

Youselli saw Astrid beside Paolo. He had no recollection of her arriving there. Her arm was linked through Paolo's, and Youselli could see she was high on excitement. He saw too how she and Paolo fed off each other's sick fantasies. He wanted to know what Edith Weber would make of that.

He was aware of her still grinning with full malevolence as he was pushed out of the building.

The car was parked in the street again outside his house. It hadn't been there when Youselli got home, but it was now, and he felt scared again.

He had forgotten about the car till he saw it parked in the same position as before. He felt like shooting out all the tires. Then his anger flipped back to panic. What if it was Internal Affairs after all?

In between checking the car was still there he drank too many beers and too much Jack Daniels and watched TV with no idea of what he was watching except for the canned laughter telling him it was funny. His vision was still blurred but it had more or less settled and was not unpleasant, he decided, like it was someone else's world. He thought of calling Bremner and have him bust Paolo, then decided the Sicilians were right; revenge was best taken cold. He called the local force instead.

Twenty minutes later he watched a patrol car pull alongside the saloon. Two officers got out and spent several minutes talking to the driver. A couple of times

Youselli saw one of them turn towards the house. Then the car drove away.

When they came to the door they were acting like they had some big joke between them. Youselli knew the sidekick by sight.

'Something funny?' he asked.

That set them off. Youselli saw himself sitting stony faced through the comedy show and wondered if it was his fault things were not funnier.

'You didn't recognize the car?' spluttered the sidekick.

'It was the same car that was parked there before.'

'Ha ha ha,' went the main officer like Youselli had said the funniest thing.

'What's so funny?

'It was your wife,' managed the sidekick between wheezes of laughter.

'What's she got to do with it?'

'It was your wife in the car.'

Suddenly nobody was laughing and the cops were giving him looks that said, cop or no cop, he was a waste of their time.

Now he felt a real jerk. She had made a complete fool of him. He should have known the car, except it was a model and colour like millions of others.

'You should learn to recognize your own wife, save us the time, huh?' said the main officer, aggressive now the joke was done. His sidekick shifted feet, looking embarrassed on account of their acquaintance.

Youselli shrugged in an attempt to play down the situation and thanked them for their time. His wife, he thought; fuck.

CHAPTER TEN

—I can feel you big and hard inside me filling me to overflowing, feel the hot wire of your love, the love I have for you consumes me, has no limits, come in my mouth, baby, I love you with all my heart, teach me to love you with my soul. I know I cannot live without you, I need to be with you all the time. My pussy is empty without you. Hey, bet you did not know I still felt this way. Love to love, Leah

CHAPTER ELEVEN

First meeting, Youselli fucked Leah's mother and felt bad taking advantage of the lonely rich. Most times he felt he was using women when he had them but normally that did not leave him feeling guilty. Mrs Mitchell Geffen was a lonely middle-of-the-afternoon boozer, loaded in both senses, and as soon as he saw her Youselli thought, what's wrong with fucking a cliché?

He had found her on the upper east side, not far from Paolo, as it turned out, in an apartment block near the park with a marble lobby that looked like a florist's and an elevator that was the quietest he had ever been in.

Meeting mother Youselli got the picture straight away. Leah had been the spoiled brat of wealthy, neglectful parents, socially sophisticated and emotionally immature. He was starting to feel sorry for her, but maybe he was being romantic. If mother was anything to go by, and Leah had been a chip off the old block, she would have been a bitch in waiting.

The mother had worked hard to keep herself together but she was starting to go puffy at the top of the thighs and kept her top on because she didn't want him to see her tits. While Youselli ground away he wondered why he was bothering because she fucked like she was having buttons pushed. He could have been anyone to her, which annoyed him, quite irrationally as he was treating her in the same way. He found she was just as mean and disagreeable in bed as she was out of it, and also demanded he do all the work, which was typical of a broad of her class.

'Thank you, that's all for today,' she had imperiously told the maid after tea had been served in fancy china, plus a Martini for her. At first she had been vague about her daughter's death – 'It was so long ago and it's so painful to be reminded' – but once the photograph album was out there were sniffles and boozy tears. While she dabbed her eyes, Youselli had looked away and studied the expensive Chinese rug. The woman had an Oriental pooch to go with it, a yappy thing like a big rat in a wool housecoat. Youselli supposed the lighter areas on the carpet were where the dog had peed. Mother – that's what she called herself to the pooch – fed it tidbits from her plate, making the creature stand on his hind legs and beg, which was probably nothing compared with what she made men do.

Her pictures revealed Leah to be a stunner. It saddened Youselli to think that had she lived she would be thirty now, maybe with a husband and kids, out in Scarsdale, married to a lawyer, a fate worse than death.

Mother was coming to life beneath him, clasping and clutching at him and hissing 'Go on!' when Youselli heard a scratching at the door. It was the damn pooch. He wondered if she had trained the thing to snuffle around under her nightgown and put the thought from his head and concentrated on the daughter in the full bloom of youth. In her pictures she had a fuck-me look and in her latest letter she was talking dirty. He was puzzled by the change of tone, the sex angle, and wondered what McMahon made of it. Next thing Youselli knew, the dog was on the bed, and with the woman groaning beneath him and the dog yapping next to him, he was pushed not to come laughing.

Afterwards they sat up in bed looking like an out-take from an old Dick Van Dyke show until Youselli excused himself, gathered his clothes and retreated to the veined marble en suite bathroom where he took a shower, enjoying its powerful jet compared with the trickle he got at his place, and wondered what was driving him. Curiosity, he supposed. Besides, he had found something he had wanted in the woman and her apartment. The flaccid boredom of these people's lives turned him on. Even the predictability of her responses had thrilled him. She had asked to look at his gun when he took his jacket off and he had watched her melt as he told her how many people he had killed with it. She wants me to be a cartoon – he thought with a suppressed snigger – that's what I'll give her, graphic sex.

'Your daughter had a pretty liberal upbringing,' he said as he came out of the bathroom, dressed. She had put on a silk robe and was watching a relationships programme. She shrugged to say it was no business of his, so he asked where her second daughter was. In some of the photographs there was a little sister, maybe five years younger and an ugly duckling.

'Last I heard she was working in a shop.' The woman sounded scornful. 'Daria went off to be an actress.'

'In Los Angeles?' he asked, knowing the answer and feeling something click into place.

'Yes.'

'And how old is Daria now?'

Twenty-five next birthday was the answer. His gut told him he was standing close to an answer. Maybe this was one of those cases that broke open like a sweet peach.

The way the mother talked about Daria they were not close, which struck him as sad. Having lost one daughter, Youselli thought she could at least make an effort to hang on to the other. He already had her down as one of the ungrateful fucks. He almost preferred them. At least they didn't cling afterwards. Youselli put his hands in his pockets and strolled round the room, happier now he was talking business. He wondered if they'd fuck again. He asked if Daria had been especially cut up over her sister's death.

'We were all devastated.' This was said with the rank insincerity of a third-rate actress.

As he left he thought, a mother not knowing the address of her own daughter, the kind of world we live in. These were the rich people, who were supposed to know better.

On his home answer-phone Youselli found a message from McMahon who sounded irritated that Youselli was not there to take his call. Youselli had been trying to reach him for days but, since he had learned about McMahon and Leah, McMahon had not returned his calls, which struck him as more than coincidence. He was angry at McMahon for being so evasive. McMahon was an asshole. Youselli thought of leaving a message back telling him.

He rang the house, got the answer service and hung up, dialled the apartment and found it engaged. He pressed callback. It took thirty minutes before Anjelica picked up. She sounded in a hurry and said she was on her way out. From the coolness of her tone he had the feeling she was uncomfortable talking to him. He said he was returning McMahon's call but she was vague, saying he was busy and she could pass any message on.

'It can wait. I need to talk to him,' he said, knowing that would crank up her curiosity.

Something in the way she spoke made him sure McMahon was with her. Youselli could picture him watching his wife as she took the call, sitting cocooned in a pool of light in an otherwise dark room, doing nothing, sniffing the airwaves like he was sensitive to everyone's moves. Youselli knew these kind of people dangled you for as long as it amused, then dropped you, and you were a fool to care.

Late next morning Youselli drove to the only contact address Mrs Mitchell Geffen had for her ex-husband. It was the law firm of Geffen, Muehl and Seaman. Youselli was surprised to find his thoughts dwelling on Mrs Mitchell Geffen. He had been pretty sure it was going to be a case of out-of-sight, but he found himself wanting her badly. It was not her so much as what she owned that he wanted to penetrate again. He wanted to fuck her apartment, her marble bathroom, the expensive Chinese rug she did not care about enough to stop the dog pissing on it. He also wanted to fuck the spirit of her dead daughter. Maybe he had taken the mother as a way of possessing a flake of the dead girl. At the time of Leah's death the mother would have been what, maybe not even forty – still tight, good looking, a snooty fuck, starting to worry about losing it. One day he'd go back, take a shit on her rug.

He found Geffen, Muehl and Seaman at a smart address on the middle east side with another marble lobby. Geffen turned out to be a WASP with perfect white hair, older than his ex-wife, with fixed teeth and a senior partner's corner office with mahogany panelling. He reluctantly granted Youselli five minutes before his lunchtime appointment and immediately pointed out that he had not had contact with Daria for several years. He added frostily that he did not know her whereabouts beyond thinking she was probably still in Hollywood, then, as though the inconvenience were his, asked if she was in trouble.

Youselli said he needed to contact Daria for a client. He made it sound mysterious and tacked on that it had to do with Leah. At mention of Leah, Geffen looked surprised to be reminded. Youselli knew he had gone to France because the mother had been declared too distraught to travel. He said he would appreciate anything Geffen could tell him about France. Geffen frowned and looked totally pompous. His version of his trip was brief, guarded and lawyer-like. He did, however, suggest that the circumstances of Leah's death had never been adequately explained, then pursed his lips, as though he had already said too much.

'You think there was more to the case?'

Geffen let his hand fall away. 'Nothing could be proved.'

'You weren't tempted to open a private inquiry?'

'I thought about it, but in the end what was there to reveal, that my daughter's death might turn out to be an even more tragic affair than it already was? No inquiry would bring her back to life.'

Geffen did his stuffed-shirt act for a couple more minutes then announced he had to go for his luncheon appointment. Youselli tried not to goggle. The man had actually said luncheon. Geffen sighed audibly when Youselli said he had one last query and asked what had happened to his daughter's belongings.

Geffen seemed surprised by the question. 'Daria made me keep them. I wasn't going to, but she insisted. I am not a sentimental man.' Realizing he risked sounding callous he added, with little conviction, 'I loved my daughter, you understand.'

When Youselli asked about the content of his daughter's belongings he showed emotion for the first time. 'I couldn't bring myself to go through them. They were already packed up when I collected them.'

'Did you meet any of the people she had been staying with in France, or talk to them?'

'I don't talk to degenerate scum,' Geffen said with hitherto unsuspected vehemence, which left Youselli wondering if, beneath the layers of formidable reserve, Geffen had cared for his daughter after all. It did not make him like the man any more. These WASPs would fuck you dead every time, and dig up the corpse to do it if they had to.

'Do you still have your daughter's belongings?' Youselli asked.

Geffen looked blank, then added uncertainly, 'I think Daria took them. Now, you will have to excuse me.'

In spite of his appointment Geffen showed no sign of leaving. When he got to the door Geffen was fiddling with his briefcase waiting for him to be gone.

'By the way, what kind of person is your daughter?'

'Leah?' he asked distractedly.

'Daria.'

Geffen looked up at him tersely. 'A major disappointment.'

Hey, little sister, Youselli thought, I am going to have to talk to you.

CHAPTER TWELVE

The big precinct room where Youselli and a dozen others worked was empty for lunch apart from O'Dowd who had brought in a sandwich. Youselli was on the phone long distance, chasing the Geffen girl in between a list of duty calls. O'Dowd was a couple of desks away, with his feet up, picking his nose.

Youselli asked, 'How's the weather out there?' In so far as the rules of correct professional behaviour permitted, he decided to flirt shamelessly with Linda Gomez on the strength of her smoky voice with a trace of Spanish. Gomez worked for the Threat Assessment Unit in Los Angeles and Youselli had cut through a lot of tape to get to her, using contacts to recommend someone with a reputation for being fast, efficient and flexible. And she was a looker, he had been told, which had alerted his interest further.

He had faxed her the Leah correspondence with Edith Weber's assessment and a polite note saying he needed someone to run some local checks on Daria.

'I'm asking a big favour here,' he said after explaining that he wanted to avoid going through the usual channels.

'Any reason?' asked Linda Gomez. He could hear the caution in her voice.

'It's on the side, for a friend.'

He was leaning forward, cupping the phone because he did not want O'Dowd to hear. O'Dowd asked questions about everything, down to why shops were called a particular name. It used to drive Youselli crazy when they worked together.

Youselli couldn't read Gomez's silence or guess which way she would go. O'Dowd got up and walked off towards the toilets, pausing to break wind and laugh at himself. What was it specifically about O'Dowd, Youselli wondered. It was not as though he wanted to kill all the other people he hated, but O'Dowd could do it every time.

'What's in it for me?' Linda Gomez eventually asked.

'You name it,' he said and she laughed and he knew it would be okay.

A week went by and there was nothing on Daria and no more letters either. McMahon avoided his calls. Youselli had plenty of other stuff to get on with and it was only after several days that he realized he missed the letters. He spoke to Linda Gomez a couple of times in the evening from home. With the time difference she was still at work. There was no boyfriend. He had asked. Gomez was between relationships. He in turn passed on the story of his wife sitting outside his house, as a way of saying that he too was between relationships. He thought he detected a rise in interest and it left him wondering why he felt the need to score with a woman he had not even met.

Youselli had heard his wife had moved her sister in, which was why she was out at night and not looking after the kids. 'She's the queen of anti-depressants,' he told Gomez, and a little later teased her about being a health freak. 'What's the point? Just living in Los Angeles is enough to kill you.'

'What I hear, you New York cops eat so many donuts you can't even waddle.'

Youselli laughed, hoping his discomfort didn't show. Weight was getting to be a problem, yet he was hardly eating.

Gomez had not been able to make Youselli out. He did not sound the type of man to waste time on the phone, yet the times they had talked he was the one who had kept the conversation going. When he told her about his wife it started to make sense. Gomez pictured him in some apology for a sitting room, in his vest, popping cans of beer, and hanging on to any call like it was a lifeline. He was the same as a lot of cops, she suspected – hated family life, lost without it.

She told him they had come up with a cold trace on Daria Geffen. More than a year before Daria had been on the books of a lowish-rung actors' agency for a period of around six months under the name of Daria Gallant. She had gone up for some minor television roles and got none. Minor roles Linda Gomez understood to mean three or four lines, little more than extras. She would rather be a dog than an actress, she told Youselli. One agent, on viewing the out-of-date picture of Daria that Gomez had faxed him, recommended Daria get her nose fixed for a start.

'Nobody at the agency knows where she is?' asked Youselli. 'Her mother said she was working in a shop.'

'Did she say which kind?'

'I can ask.'

'It might help. We have a lot of different kinds of shops here,' she said dryly and Youselli was late seeing the joke. 'Then again Daria could have got lucky,' Gomez went on, 'changed her name and gone to Arizona, or she could be turning tricks down the road. Is it your belief that Daria is writing these letters?'

'Edith Weber says the writer has a sense of personal belief. But I don't know.'

Youselli knew what he wanted it to be. He wanted Leah to be Leah, regardless of explanation, and not Astrid or Blackledge or any of the others.

Gomez told him she was cancelling a date to work late on his behalf, so he had better be grateful.

'Oh,' said Youselli. 'Don't do it for me.'

She did not add that she was only doing it because the date was a problem, being not as unmarried as he pretended.

'Are you and Edith Weber an item?' she asked and thought she heard him splutter on his beer.

'Are you crazy?'

'It's just the way you said her name.'

'She's, uh, a mature woman.'

'Excuse me. I thought I detected a certain *je ne sais quoi*.'

Youselli could not tell if she was teasing. 'I appreciate your help on this,' he concluded weakly.

'Thank you for the thought, but it's my trainee you should thank, he's the one putting in the hours.'

The capable Dwight trawled uncomplaining through anything she gave him. He seemed to have done just about every interpersonal relations and people management course going. Dwight was so polite Gomez wanted to shake him.

At 9.00 p.m. she and Dwight were still going through the escort agencies and the madams of the department's acquaintance. After countless useless calls, Linda Gomez phoned Capital Escorts at 9.32 p.m. Capital Escorts was run by Murray Kaye – 'Like the deejay without the "the",' he said. Murray the schmuck sounded like an ex-agent of the old school, querulous, a mouth, an exaggerated Jew, keeping close watch on his many ailments. He sounded like one of those men who couldn't go home – Gomez knew the symptoms well. She could see him surrounded by good-looking escorts, with nothing to go back to except a moaning wife.

Murray remembered Daria with a sigh that sounded like a cross between exasperation and fondness. 'Don't remind me, it's been a good day till now. Good day, bad day, what's the difference? What can I do for you, Linda?'

Murray was a relentless first-namer and over-insister. With all his embellishments, and a running list of his physical ailments, it took Gomez a long fifteen minutes to discover Daria no longer worked there. 'My girls are good girls,' he said. 'Many of them are regular churchgoers.' She resisted asking what his cut was if his girls' after-dinner arrangements extended beyond a regular date. Murray had fired Daria six months earlier, for spending too long in the restaurant toilets on clients' time.

'I don't need to spell out the problem to an intelligent woman like you,' Murray said, and Gomez added patronizing to the list of what she already disliked about him.

She asked about Daria's payments, hoping they might offer a trail. Murray huffed and puffed about confidentiality before opening his accounts, only, he insisted, because he kept them regular and had nothing to hide. Daria's pay had gone to a bank in Manhattan, he told her. She had probably had it since childhood, thought Gomez.

'You have a great voice, Linda,' Murray said. 'You ever make a career change, come see me.'

'It's been a pleasure,' Gomez replied with insincere cheerfulness.

Youselli wondered if Linda Gomez went to the beach weekends. He rather hoped she didn't as sunshine depressed him. He supposed there was a clinical term for his aversion. What he really wanted to know was if she had become Americanized and shaved under her arms. He would ask her when he felt sure she wouldn't take it as a race thing. One of the big turn-ons in his life dated back to when he was a kid, seeing armpit hair on a Puerto Rican woman.

He was drunker than he meant to be. His wife's car was outside again and he made it a point of honour to ignore her. He turned the music up, hoping she would think he was having a party.

After the clutter of his marital life, Youselli kept his bedroom samurai stark, but the tidiness was an illusion. His life was a mess. He knew it and what made it worse was he didn't mind. He liked the feeling of being on the slide. A life of boozing and solo sex seemed all right to him, certainly better than what he had left. Maybe he ought to talk to the shrink, rattle her cage some. Edith Weber, she would have been a good-looking woman, still was in her way. But she had spent too much of her life unfucked and ended up in some kind of denial. He was sure she could still be turned on, could still achieve what he thought of as full fuck potential. Dwelling like that on Edith Weber, he shocked himself, which did not happen often. He checked the tissues were on the table, next to the beer and handcuffs, and his gun.

The phone rang. Youselli cursed and checked his watch. It was way after one. Then he saw it was the fax. His first worry was that it was some legal shit from Paolo. He was still expecting the worst. With the threat of Paolo and the car outside again it seemed like he was under siege. As he lurched over to the machine he realized he was even drunker than he thought. He twisted his head to see the message coming out of the machine. It took him several attempts to focus, then his throat went tight as he read.

—I'm thinking of you right now, remembering how your hands feel on my body and the way you

like me to feel the pulse of your cock when you
come. I get so carried away by these fantasies,
which sneak up unawares . . .

'Jesus,' thought Youselli. 'She can read my fucking
mind.'

There was an intruder in the house. Edith Weber was
sure of it. She lay, fearful and alert, sure something had
woken her, but, as her ears strained in vain for some
further rustle or creak, she decided it was the dark
playing tricks. Outside a car went by. The illuminated
panel of the digital clock clicked to 1:46. Then, as she
persuaded herself everything was all right, she heard a
tiny but distinct noise. It took her several heart-racing
moments to identify it as metal on enamel, perhaps
something as mundane as tweezers falling off the bathroom shelf over the basin.

She lay there, images of her dead relatives' final
helplessness swimming before her eyes. Part of her own
guilt at surviving was, she knew, to do with avoiding
any testing of her own resistance. In an attempt to quell
her panic she told herself she could either ignore whatever it was, in the hope that it would go away, or she
could dial 911, except the phone was in the hall past the
bathroom, or she could go and look.

She reluctantly gathered her resolve, got up, neither
hurrying nor taking special care not to make a noise.
As she opened the bathroom door and her hand
reached for the light switch she didn't know what to
expect.

She froze at the sight in front of her. In spite of her astonishment, part of her continued to function rationally. She had not been altogether honest, she told herself pedantically. She had been expecting a black male youth, she was aware of the prejudice. But the apparition before her was not black but white, not dark but blond, like some Aryan messenger from the darkest reaches of her psyche, a tiny, undernourished child, perhaps not even nine years old. She noted the open quarter-light, too small for any adult, through which he had crawled. Edith experienced the same involuntary fright and loathing she felt when surprised by a cockroach or a rat.

He stood calmly surveying her. The eyes displayed no shred of anything except profound contempt, perhaps not even that – only a terrible indifference. Then suddenly he was gone, scurrying past, pushing her aside.

She listened to him banging around like a trapped animal. She realized the bolt on the front door would be too high for him and they were locked in together. It was only a child, she told herself, as she hurried through to find the boy with a raised chair he was about to pitch through the window.

'Put that down,' she said with more authority than she felt.

The boy held the chair defensively, like she was the aggressor. Edith turned away to undo the double locks and bolts, hoping he would not brain her while her back was turned.

'Now get out,' she said when she was done.

The boy threw the chair aside and walked slowly

towards her, with a cocky strut, leaving Edith with the strongest desire to wipe the grin off his face with a hefty slap. He paused by the door and laughed, revealing a row of corroded stumps for teeth.

'Next time you're dead, bitch,' he said, making a pistol with his finger.

Youselli read the faxed letter again. He had thought at first in his drunken logic it was her writing to him, that she knew about him and had found his number. When he saw the letter had been sent via McMahon he experienced a terrible disappointment, but now he was more familiar with its contents he decided that knowing about her and her most intimate thoughts when she did not know about him was even more thrilling and illicit.

—I really surprised myself doing it right there in
the kitchen, without going to the bathroom, which
I prefer to bed. Bed is a kind of sleepy thing, lying
there touching yourself, pretending it is you. I used
to sleep on my arm so it was dead when I woke
up, then it really felt like another person's hand!
I like the bathroom for giving myself what I call
a shiny fuck. The thing about just now in the
kitchen is – God, am I really telling you this? I
have never ever swear on my life told anyone any
of this before – the vibration of the juicer! My
hand is on the juicer and the shudder is going up
up my arm and the rotating cone feels like your
tongue (or something else!) reaming me. Okay,

just now was not the first time in the kitchen. I do
it all the time. I fantasize you are with me. It's
not like me doing it to me, you are there too,
and what really turns me on is looking down
and knowing that's what you see, white panties
stretched tight round my ankles. I want to get my
feet wider but the panties are stopping me, my
heels are straining at crazy angels, I am in danger
of falling over and when I feel the first flash of
coming I think: this is us. And it gets pretty wild I
can tell you! You like it when I moan your name,
it turns you on even more. And when I orgasm I
make sure you can't not come any longer and
wow! Meltdown! Does it shock you when I say
I am writing this with trembly legs because I had
to break off to see if that's how I remembered it?

I think all of us have a part they show to
nobody. I think I am very privileged being able to
talk to you like this but you would not want to see
me in the mood I have been in today! Remind me
to tell you about the bad people. Love to love,
forever Leah

The third or fourth time he read it he noticed how she
had written 'crazy angels' instead of 'crazy angles'. He
saluted her slip of the pen with his beer and said,
'That's us, baby, crazy angels.' Feeling stupid he tried
laughing it off. But it felt good talking out loud as
though she was in the room. He checked the window.

'At least the car's gone. Remind me to tell you
about her one day, she's one of the bad people. How
do two people get it so wrong?'

CHAPTER THIRTEEN

—Nights I lie awake trying to imagine how it feels to have no feeling left, like Lazarus or Jesus in the tomb. I lie like the dead with my arms crossed and these are the times I am Lazarus. And I know how it feels to be dead.

People who know me, they would say, no way is she like that, she is always so positive and on top of things, pardon the pun (a sense of humour is very important). The stuff I wrote in the last letter, I blush to think of it, but sometimes I feel so needy. All those times we went together I could not tell if I was the fuck or the fuck was me. I mean this in a kind of religious way. People who know me would be surprised to hear me talking of Jesus and what is sacred, or Lazarus who they wouldn't even have heard of.

You know how easily I break, how there are days when my secret self can't cope, and I have to go away and become out of reach. Then I become Lazarus till Jesus comes. There is no record of what Lazarus said on being raised from the dead or how he viewed dying a second time. Once is enough! I get Jesus and Lazarus muddled sometimes.

Maybe you know the Lazarus story. He was the

brother of Martha and Mary. Martha did the housework and grew jealous of Mary listening to Jesus's
stories. Mary anointed Jesus's feet with oil and dried
them with her hair, which must have been a sexy thing
to have someone do, Son of God or not.

You will see I have my reasons. This is a hard letter
to write today, there are too many forces interfering
with the flow. Do you think hurting bad people is
wrong? If someone has wronged you, really wronged
you – like you did, I want to say, but I'm biting my
tongue – are you right to hurt back? For too long I
was too scared but now I believe that hurting bad
people is cool and I intend to do something about it!
Play the Lazarus game with them and then let's see
their total fear and let's really get to stretch their reality
a little!

This stuff I'm telling you is only a teeny part of me.
I don't want to think of you as one of the bad people.
I know forgiveness is love and I'm working on it. I
am basically a nice person as you know! Remember
when you once said the gift I made of my body was a
sacred thing.

CHAPTER FOURTEEN

When Youselli phoned to say he was faxing another letter, Edith was alarmed to find herself linking it in her mind with the child intruder, like the letters were an extension of his threat. To her they both represented the intention to harm. What had shocked her most about the boy was how seriously she had taken his parting words – parting shot she had been about to say, then remembered the soft 'Pyow!' he'd made. She believed in her bones he would be back.

Youselli came by at the end of the day. Edith had not realized how overwrought she was until he found her weeping in the kitchen while making them tea. Susan had been unreachable all day, which had made everything worse.

Edith wiped her eyes with the back of her hand. She thought he was embarrassed. Cops always were by displays of emotion. She waved him away and was surprised when he took her shoulders.

'What happened?'

She thought he would think her feeble, but he said an intruder was an intruder regardless of age. Any stranger in the home was frightening.

'Time I was most scared was when a pigeon got

trapped in my apartment. It was nothing, but the fear of the bird communicated itself and afterwards I was shaking so bad I had to sit down.'

Edith said, 'But this was only a child.'

She wanted her tears not to be seen. Instead she found herself being held by him as she told him how terrified and alone she had felt, and how the feeling of aloneness had frightened her most of all. It was the first time she had felt such an acute isolation, to the core of her being, and she knew now it would be her constant companion – near or far it didn't really matter – there as a growing reminder of her own mortality.

'Thank you,' she said afterwards, blowing her nose, embarrassed. She had not expected his sympathy.

'Give me a description of the kid,' said Youselli. 'I'll tell the local patrols to keep an eye out and you call me any time.' He wrote down his number. 'Any time, day or night.'

Edith busied herself making the tea and half-apologized again, saying her reaction was out of all proportion.

'Hey, it's okay,' said Youselli. 'Cry on my shoulder, who's to tell?'

They moved next door and Youselli watched Edith sipping her tea while studying the latest letter. He had found himself aroused by all the bible stuff mixed up with the sex. It reminded him of early memories provoked by women at Mass in the gloomy churches of his childhood. He had preferred fantasizing about the less obvious and attractive ones, to demonstrate that his desire was random and indiscriminate – all embracing, hah hah, in keeping with the Church's teaching that love is without condition.

'Well,' said Edith, more composed now, 'the addressee continues to be identified as the obsessive object, and the obsession is now specified as erotic.' She looked at him. 'Wouldn't you say?'

'You bet.' Addressee; he was impressed.

'There is a pronounced degree of secrecy, plus a continuing emphasis on the connection between sex and death. The religious thread is harder to decipher. She identifies with Mary from the bible, not the Virgin Mary but—'

'—Mary Magdalene. She was a hooker.'

'No, I checked. She means Mary sister of Martha who anointed Christ's feet with oil and dried them with her hair.'

'Yeah, Mary Magdalene.'

'I don't think so.'

'I tell you,' Youselli insisted. 'Mary Magdalene cleaned the Lord's feet with her tears then anointed them with oil and dried them with her hair. It's one of the few things I remember from bible classes because she was a hooker.'

'No, that was Mary the sister of Martha. I looked it up.'

When they looked again they were both right. The two different Marys had performed the task at different times. Youselli made a sound that came out as a cross between a snort and a laugh, as though he wasn't sure if this was a satisfactory end to the argument.

'Then they are easily confused,' he said.

'Perhaps they are in Leah's mind too. She says she

sometimes gets Jesus muddled up with Lazarus who was also raised from the dead.'

'By Jesus,' said Youselli flippantly. 'And Lazarus was the brother of the other Mary, and it was Mary Magdalene who was the first to discover Jesus wasn't dead. So we got two Marys and two anointings and two raisings from the dead. Where does that get us?'

Edith knew he was fooling around to cheer her up but she felt belittled. 'I don't know!' she said with a sudden vehemence, clenching her fists as a bolt of anger passed through her. She could not understand where it had come from or why it left her feeling so drained and inattentive.

She stared at the letter, trying to collect her thoughts. 'Martha grew jealous of Mary—' she repeated mechanically, and stopped, struck by the overwhelming barrenness of her life, and by her own store of resentments, which she so carefully shielded from herself. A wrenching sensation in her chest made her even more acutely aware of her isolation from everything around her – the man in her room, the letters on the table, and the lack of everyday meaning in relation to the survival of those people's story from so long ago. She wept swiftly and bitterly, for the sisters she no longer had.

This time Youselli stood there uncertainly. Even as she wept Edith wondered if it was because she had gone too far and he was embarrassed, or if he understood that part of her was inconsolable.

'I don't know why I am making such heavy weather of this,' she said briskly, relieved when the tears disappeared as quickly as they had come. She directed

Youselli's attention to the reference to hurting bad people. It concerned her.

'Are you saying she might have other targets?'

'Maybe the hostility she feels towards McMahon, which she hasn't allowed herself to express yet, is being channelled elsewhere. Maybe our Leah is already being a bad girl, Lieutenant.'

'Beau. Call me Beau.'

She would have preferred more space between them after what had just happened. She found him as baffling as the letter, and suspected she was reading both of them wrong.

'It bothers me,' she went on. 'This Lazarus game she talks about, it may just be in her mind, but what if it isn't?'

'But what would the game involve?'

'Trying to raise people from the dead, I suppose,'

'But to be raised from the dead, first you've got to be what?'

'Dead.'

'Are you saying she might start killing people?' he asked carefully because it added a whole other dimension.

But Edith didn't answer, putting her hand to her mouth in shock instead and saying, 'Oh my God! Of course. There could be another explanation entirely.'

Youselli could not tell if what he was seeing was inspired by awe or apprehension, or fear even.

'Look what she writes,' said Edith in a voice barely above a whisper. '"I am Lazarus."'

Youselli laughed in disbelief. 'You are not trying to tell me what I think you are?'

Edith gave a bewildered shrug. 'I know, it defies rational explanation.'

'You bet. We know she's dead. Rationally.'

'I know, but all along there has been this recurring note in her letters. The idea of returning.'

Youselli looked sceptical. 'From the dead?!'

'Not literally. What I mean—'

He jumped ahead of her. 'You mean this *is* Leah?'

She could see the idea excited him. 'I suppose what I have been thinking at the back of my mind from the very beginning is that this person does not write like she's a fake, and in a way what makes the most emotional sense – as opposed to rational sense – is if this person is, somehow, the person she says she is. I can't argue the logic of it, but what if we ask ourselves: did she really die?'

Youselli shook his head. 'She died. Too many people have said.'

'But what if she didn't *actually* die.'

'Then everyone would know. She has to be dead. Someone would have identified the body, there'd be records.'

'Are you sure?'

Youselli sighed. 'It's a neat idea, but we're walking the plank here. The father was over there. No, she's dead, or we're talking miracles.' He laughed with more conviction than he felt.

'Who saw the body?' asked Edith. Youselli had to admit he didn't know.

'I think you should check,' she said.

CHAPTER FIFTEEN

Los Angeles

I'm normal. I lead a normal life, I do the right things. I take a left outside the house, a second right and I'm on the freeway that takes me to work. I shop at Safeway. I like the smell, that combination of fresh produce and air conditioning. I work. I support myself. I keep a tidy house and wash the car every two weeks. I think of myself as self-sufficient. I line up my clothes and shoes in the closet. For someone with such a troubled past I am doing very well, thank you very much. When I say, 'Have a nice day,' I mean it.

Driving to work and back I have plenty of time to think, and what do I think about? Like the old Frank Sinatra record says, I think about you. I like driving, chasing stations on the radio. I like that feeling of being between two points and out of reach. At work Daddy wants to give me a portable phone so he can deliver one of his little homilies whenever he feels moved to do so, but I keep saying no. It's not like he doesn't get most of my time as it is and for a slave's wage, while he pretends we are the beneficiaries of his major philanthropy.

When I am driving life seems at its best. I am doing something but my mind can wander free at the same time, like a sleek cat racing across desert after gazelle. I saw such a scene once on a nature channel and could not understand why I was so excited. Only lying in bed did I realize, and it took the form of a shiver of excitement at the feeling that I could think anything. Think anything I wanted and there wasn't a damn thing anyone could do about it.

Driving is a movie inside my head. The stuff around the house is fine most of the time. But sometimes I look at something and think: this is not me. Or the distance between the sink and the garbage suddenly becomes huge, and some automatic act, like throwing out the trash, becomes as big an effort as climbing a mountain. 'You would not think to look at me,' I say to myself as I push the trolley down the aisles of the supermarket. Nearly all the time I am happy to be like everybody else, happy to stand in line to see the same movie and have the same thoughts as the rest of you nice people out there. We're all dunkin' donuts, that's what I say.

At other times it feels like such a cruel world, so cut off. Then nothing helps, not your friends or anything. Times such as these I hardly dare move. Flesh and blood feels such a fragile vessel, and any foreign body becomes a threat. See the red car coming, what's to stop it losing control and jumping the sidewalk and killing me? At these times I find myself staring at the electric sockets and have to resist sticking a knife in them. I saw a dead dog on the highway today.

All the squishy babies. I don't know what I mean by that. Sometimes words form in my mind, I don't know why they should, or why they are in that particular order. Then much later I understand. At the moment I'm trying to figure the connection between the dog and the babies, which is the wrong thing to be doing because maybe there is none. The mind is such a complex thing.

Another thing that puzzles me is why we remember this tiny tiny stuff when a lot of the bigger things get put in the basement and forgotten. Why from a particular day do I remember the exact way the pizza packet lay on the check-out belt? It was a single item purchase. The bar-code cheep I can still hear. I'm curious to know why this stays when the rest of the day has been erased. That frightens me sometimes. This kind of samey feeling. One day after another. If you look at a clock go round time is pretty boring and on the black days I feel the same about life. I'm trying to describe what waiting for you feels like. I want to let you inside my head, feel what I feel, see the way I see. I have got so many channels inside my head now. Satellite, cable, local, weather, shopping. Got them all click click click, see the world so many different ways.

These are the kind of things I think about when I think about you. Like I said, most of the time I feel like everybody else, better maybe because I lead a fulfilled life. I want to show you and share it with you. I know you would like my place. Even the boring old housework I enjoy because I do it in the expectation – no, certainty – that one day you will be here. I do that contented humming when I do the dusting because I am thinking about you and no one can stop me from doing that. Actually, I am pretty fine all the time. I try not to make up stuff because I get nervous you might think I am too ordinary for you.

My belief is that you have been cut off from normal experience. I am sure you have had an adventurous life but there are so many things you must have missed, those everyday kind of things. I bet you have not been in a supermarket in years. I suppose what I'm saying is that it's in the middle of the most ordinary things that the feeling of love is strongest. Pushing the trolley, unlocking the cap to the gas tank, that's when it hits you: I love this person so much. Clear blue sky, kind breeze, Texaco station and it's like the experience believers must get in church. This feeling that everything is exactly the way it should be always and because of the love you feel, you would be happy for the moment to go on for ever and ever. I love gas stations. I love the curve of the gas nozzles and the way they hang in their holsters. There has never been a time when filling up a tank with gas has not been a time of hope. Now each gas station reminds me of the journey I will one day make to be with you.

Sometimes I shop for two, picking out things I know you will like, things that will keep till you come. It is my hope I will write all or some of these things in my next letter to you. But the fact I am addressing *you* makes me feel I have got to make everything more dramatic. You have led such an exciting life, I feel obliged to give some kind of edge to what I tell you, like only describing the mountain peaks. In fact a lot of my thoughts are of us doing nothing together, just being. There is a way you lean on your elbow when you lie on the floor reading and look up from your book and it just melts me every time. You see, I am trying so hard to explain that this is not some crazy fantasy on my part. It is also a matter of explaining to someone that you know you are right. That you see things they can't, that you see in a way they can't. Maybe I should write you now while I still have these thoughts in my head.

CHAPTER SIXTEEN

Surprise number one, Youselli thought. No record of Leah's death in France, not according to Interpol who had contacted the local prefecture. Surprise two was McMahon saying, without batting an eyelid, 'Of course, there wouldn't be.'

He was seated on a giant leather sofa in the Dakota apartment, looking languid.

'Are you playing me for a fool again?' Youselli asked.

McMahon looked taken aback. 'No, sir,' he said with apparent sincerity.

'What do you mean, "Of course, there wouldn't be"?'

McMahon made a money gesture.

'Because the French cops were paid off?' ventured Youselli.

McMahon gave a cynical smile. 'Good work, detective.'

Youselli sighed. 'Isn't it about time you told me the truth?'

'Ah, the truth,' murmured McMahon. 'When do we ever know the truth?'

Youselli had expected him to be angry or upset by

99

his news but none of it was even getting close to him. 'Stop looking like you want to punch me,' McMahon added, standing up. 'Relax.'

He gave him an affectionate pat on the shoulder. The gesture threw Youselli.

'Okay,' said McMahon. 'There may well be no record. For a whole host of reasons Aaron entered into delicate negotiations with the French authorities.'

'Aaron? Nobody said anything about Aaron being there.'

'He wasn't. We sent for him.'

'It must be nice always having someone tidy up,' said Youselli. It did not come out sounding as unpleasant as he intended. He wanted to break McMahon, crack his façade, make him care.

'Don't look so shocked.' McMahon appeared rueful as he lit a cigarette. It was the first time Youselli had seen him smoke. He offered Youselli one as an afterthought.

'I figured you for a smoker,' McMahon said when he declined then came over and laid his hand briefly on Youselli's shoulder. 'Please, it is not easy for me to talk about these things.'

Youselli could not tell if this was just another performance. He felt vaguely discomforted by McMahon's touch.

'When we first made it,' McMahon went on, moving away, 'we were treated like gods. People laying down for us all over the place, you could take your pick. Inside I was still just some kid from a village. No one tells you how to handle this stuff, or someone like Astrid. She was supposed to have fucked Salvador Dali.

Way out of my league. One time I even saw her give a monkey a hand job.'

'Come on, you expect me to believe that!'

'I swear!'

They sniggered like dirty schoolboys. McMahon was the least self-conscious Youselli had seen him.

'Compared to her I was a tourist,' he went on, shaking his head. 'A few times I ended up watching her and some kid get it on in a hotel room while totally out of my gourd. Astrid was a great one for hotels.'

'And she didn't give a fuck.'

McMahon nodded appreciatively. 'Exactly. I hadn't thought of it like that. Sex for Astrid was an everyday thing, like shitting or eating. She would take some guy down an alley if she felt the urge. I don't know about you, but, much as I like it, I don't feel I have to organize my life around fucking. She did and maybe that's why she could be so casual about it. Like you say, she did not give a fuck.'

'But Leah was different.'

McMahon paused, letting Youselli see that he knew he was being led. 'Sure. She was a brat but she had something.'

'How old was she when you started banging her?'

McMahon said archly, 'There we get to the heart of the matter.'

'Straight answer me for once.'

'Hey, tough cop questions.' He gave Youselli a hooded look. 'Fifteen. She was fifteen.' He smiled cruelly. 'Ever fuck a fifteen-year-old?'

Youselli felt the tug of the man's power. 'You recommend it?'

'There's a law against it,' McMahon retorted lightly.

'But she looked old enough to go to the party.'

'My,' said McMahon, 'are we a tad jealous?'

Youselli held up his hand. 'Stick to the subject.'

McMahon gave a look that said Youselli was spoiling his fun. 'There's another reason it stopped. Aaron.'

'Aaron?'

'Aaron was scared the DEA was about to move in. Aaron had informants in the FBI who told him there was a case being put together against me because of the girl, but I don't know whether I believed him.'

'Why not?'

'Aaron freaking us out with his talk of the DEA and the FBI was, I figured, a way of keeping us in line, and it worked because it got so we hardly dared smoke a joint.'

'Why should he care if you were seeing some under-age girl?'

'Because he worried himself sick that we were going to get caught doing something that would take away his cash cow. We were making him a raft of money.'

'But you fired him in the end.'

'He'd been ripping us off for years.'

'I'm going to ask you a question,' said Youselli slowly. 'What would you say if I told you Leah wasn't dead?'

Youselli was amazed at the way the man fell to pieces in front of his eyes. He sat for a long time with his head in his hands and when he looked up Youselli was rewarded with a brief glimpse into the pit of terror McMahon carried inside himself. He gave himself a mental pat on the head. He had rolled the man over.

McMahon finally managed to say, 'She's dead. She's got to be. She can't not be.'

'Did you see her body?'

McMahon began nodding, then shook his head.

'Tell me what happened, exactly.'

'We came back in the morning, from my place.'

'Who did?'

'Me and Mickey and Astrid. Blackledge was waiting when we arrived. He had driven down from Paris and was outside drinking coffee. He said the others were still asleep.'

'What time was this?'

'Eleven, maybe. I stayed outside with him while Mickey and Astrid went in the house and Mickey came back and said there was a problem.'

'How did he seem?'

'How do you think?'

'Then what?'

McMahon looked at him with a flash of anger. 'Hey, I'm not your suspect.'

Youselli held up his hands in conciliation and McMahon went on. 'We called Aaron in New York and he arrived sometime the following night.'

'What did you do in the meantime?'

'Went back to my place to wait for Aaron.'

'Leaving the body?'

McMahon looked at him quizzically. 'We could hardly move it.'

'What about the kid?'

McMahon went blank for a moment. 'Oh, Paolo. Astrid must have taken him with us.'

'And he never said anything about what happened?'

'Nope.'

'And you never saw the body?'

There were tears in McMahon's eyes. 'I couldn't face it. It wasn't till after she was gone I saw how much I cared.'

'Who saw the body besides Mickey?'

'I remember Blackledge going to take a look.' He looked at Youselli pleadingly. 'She's got to be dead.'

'So we don't believe in ghosts?' Youselli asked sarcastically, thinking at least he had managed to wipe the smile off the man's face. 'These letters,' he went on. 'Do they read how you remember her?'

'I don't know. It was a long time ago.'

'But you do believe she could have written them?'

'Yes.'

'So they feel authentic?'

McMahon nodded, then added, 'But people don't come back from that.'

'I think it's time we talked to Aaron.'

'My God, this is awful,' said McMahon and Youselli felt almost sorry for him. He lit another cigarette and this time Youselli took one too without knowing why. It was his first in six years and it tasted as good as he could have wanted. He watched McMahon regathering his energy until he stabbed out his cigarette decisively and stood up.

'The spooky thing is, a couple of times I have caught myself thinking it is like she has come back and is alive. But it is not a realistic option. Where was she all that time? In a coma in some private clinic?'

'Aaron took care of the business, we need to talk to

Aaron,' said Youselli feeling pleasantly light-headed from the cigarette.

McMahon was reluctant. For some reason Aaron appeared to be the last person McMahon wanted to see. Youselli had to push McMahon to promise to fix a meeting.

'Sure,' said McMahon vaguely, lighting up another cigarette. Youselli had never seen him so nervous.

CHAPTER SEVENTEEN

—I want to tell you about when I was a kid and used to make up friends. I think even then I knew it was something I would have to grow out of, and there would come the day when I would have to say: okay, guys.

Did you guess already? They never really went away. Except now they have become angels.

When things get rough they talk to me, tell me what to do. I keep them in the closet mostly, which I guess is the right place for them! I don't know what brings them to me. I guess it must be that old fugue state people keep talking about!

I never told anyone before, and it's kind of muddly to say. When I was a girl there was a best, best friend I hid in a drawer. One day when she did something really bad I left her there, and when I went to forgive her she was not in the drawer anymore. I cried and cried because I could not find her, and I knew I could not say to the grown-ups, I have been so bad, I have lost my best friend. In the night I got up to look for her, thinking I had misremembered putting her in the drawer. That night I understood what grown-ups meant by despair.

Then IT happened.

The angel came, with a message to say my friend was safe. The angel said she was there to look after me now. And she still is my angel.

The despair and the angel came together. Somehow that was very, very important. I had to know despair before I could see the angel. There's that old song, 'For you and I have a guardian angel'. It is true. Walking and driving around I can see everyone's guardian angel. In crowds I make sure people don't brush too close, so there's room for the angels. A lot of the time I can convince myself that the angels will protect me from the malfate. But there is always this chink of doubt, like a light under a door. I'm aware that the door could crash open any moment and all the doubt come flooding in. It is because you are famous I'm writing you.

CHAPTER EIGHTEEN

Leah's father made it difficult for Youselli. According to his secretary he was in conference whenever Youselli called and not to be disturbed. In the end Youselli drove over and waited in the street till Geffen emerged just before one. When he saw Youselli he quickened his pace. By the time Youselli caught up and grabbed his sleeve they were half running. Geffen turned to face Youselli, white with anger.

'Don't you touch me.'

'Then don't give me the brush off.' Youselli took his hand away and breathed in the man's face, wishing he had been eating garlic. 'This'll take a minute, then you can toddle off to your luncheon appointment. When you went to France did you see your daughter's body?'

'What is the meaning of this impertinence?'

'Did you see her dead?'

Geffen looked around wildly, hoping someone would rescue him. 'I got to France late. I was away in Japan, a very tricky set of government contracts.'

'Did you go to the funeral?'

Geffen dithered. Youselli felt real loathing for the man's protected affluence and took cheap pleasure in stepping on his nice clean shoe.

'Are you telling me as a father you did not even have the respect to attend your daughter's funeral?'

'I was surprised. I was expecting the funeral to be after I arrived, but they told me it had taken place.'

A man interrupted them, a colleague of Geffen's, Youselli supposed, asking if he was all right.

'Mind your own business,' said Youselli, sharply enough for the man to step back. Geffen mumbled that everything was fine and the man went away uncertainly.

'You spoke to a policeman in France?' asked Youselli.

'Yes.'

'At the police station?'

'He came to the hotel. I was under a lot of pressure, with paperwork.'

'You sure he was a policeman?'

Geffen seemed impatient with the wildness of Youselli's questions.

'You are sure he was?' repeated Youselli.

'I had no reason to believe he wasn't,' he replied stiffly.

'And you had just the one visit and this man gave you back your daughter's possessions.'

'Listen,' said Geffen starting to rally. 'I don't see what all this is about.'

'We're looking into the possibility your daughter is still alive.'

Youselli enjoyed watching the changes in Geffen's face, from incredulity to hope then anger. 'You're crazy,' he spluttered. 'Do you realize what you are saying?'

'I know what I'm saying. Tell me I'm wrong.'

'Of course you're wrong!' Geffen was shaking. Youselli was feeling good because it wasn't every day you got to bully a lawyer.

'Tell me about the grave,' he said.

'I, uh—' Geffen cast around wildly.

Youselli shook his head in astonishment. 'You flew out without going to your daughter's grave.' As he said it he felt the anger drain out of him and a terrible sadness take its place.

Geffen shook his head, eager to make his excuse. 'I looked for it on the way to the airport, but I couldn't find it. There was no headstone and no one to ask and the taxi was waiting, and I was going to miss my plane.'

'Asshole.' Saying it made Youselli feel good. He turned on his heel and walked away.

CHAPTER NINETEEN

Linda Gomez decided to trawl through the X-rated industry for any sign of Daria, though there was no guarantee that she had gone that route. From the few leads she had managed to pick up Linda knew Daria was on a downward spiral, and was hoping her guess that Daria had moved down into porno would pay off. She had run a check through vice and eliminated several Darias in their records. Daria had also been reported as a heavy narcotics user.

She gave Dwight a list of production companies specializing in X-rated movies and told him to call them. Dwight was surprised how much they mimicked their industry counterpart, screening producers behind an array of receptionists and PAs. In three hours he managed to get through to only one producer and had been expertly stalled by a series of friendly but firm voices who had been programmed to take evasive action when confronted by any official-sounding voice.

He changed tack, figuring these desk women probably knew more than the producers anyway. Instead of being truthful and negative – we're looking for this woman who might have passed through on her way to skid row – he became positive and fanciful, saying his business was a matter of a financial inheritance willed to Daria. His story must have boosted several idle mornings because soon he was faxing copies of Daria's picture to curious offices, and received several time-wasting calls as a result, until his phone rang and, before he could say anything, a voice boomed, 'What's all this bullshit?'

'What bullshit, sir?' Dwight asked in his best polite voice.

'What's Sky done so you're looking for her?'

'Sky?'

Sky, it turned out came with an 'e' on the end. Daria Gallant née Geffen had metamorphosed into Skye Blu, sometime actress in X-rated movies, notably Larry Lustbader's trilogy, *Screw*, *Horn of Plenty* and *Wet Heat*, produced by Acme Films with a front office on Pico.

Linda Gomez managed to squeeze in an appointment at Acme between two others, one with a Hollywood wife being stalked by her estranged husband, the other a woman's dog which had been receiving threatening tapes from another dog – twenty solid minutes of growling and barking – until that morning. The latest tape sounded like a small animal being ripped to pieces by a much larger one. The imagination of some people was a constant source of surprise to her.

Acme was a single-storey cube like a sugar lump, with a reception area that reminded Gomez of a car rental office – chocolate-brown carpet, orange settee, rubber plant, and an undusted air. Behind a counter sat a receptionist with a name-plate that said: Hi, I'm

Kaydee. This was repeated verbatim for Linda's benefit, with a smile out of proportion to the occasion.

'I'm here to see Mr Grant. He's expecting me.'

Kaydee announced Gomez by phone then said, 'Daddy will see you in a minute,' adding for her benefit, 'Everyone calls him Daddy, Daddy Duggie. We're just one big happy family here.'

Daddy Duggie was a big, grinning bear of a man, with a wild beard and thick reddish hair that looked inherited from a Forties movie star. He stood as Gomez entered and reached across his desk and shook her warmly by the hand. If Acme Films had a hallmark, Gomez thought, it was relentless cheer. Daddy Duggie had crinkly eyes like he had spent too much of his life laughing. His office, a cheap Scandinavian wood affair, was decorated with *bon mots*. *You Don't Have To Be Mad To Work Here But It Helps* and *One Day I'll Get Organorganised* were two Gomez groaned inwardly at. Nothing in the room indicated Grant produced pornographic films. The only sign of company business had been in the long corridor on the way to his office. Several rooms off contained editing equipment and in one or two Gomez had noted people working.

'These are our editing suites,' Kaydee had said with breathless pride as they walked past. 'Most of them are hired out. They are very popular. Maybe you know people in the industry? I'll give you our card.'

Daddy Duggie was either in his late thirties pretending to be older or early fifties pretending to be younger, Gomez could not decide. He looked like he liked a lot of leeway. His clothes announced him as a serious man who did not take himself seriously: dark double-breasted suit, with a Disney T-shirt and flip-flops.

He beamed and said, 'I hope you aren't here to give me a hard time. My horoscope promised me a good day.'

She said nothing, waiting for him.

'Well,' he finally said, 'I sure hope Skye has done nothing wrong. We all loved her here.'

'When did you see her last?'

'I would have to check. Not for a while.'

'How did she end up here?'

She realized how careless the question had sounded when Grant immediately held up his hand. 'Hold it right there. I take it you have a judgement problem with Skye coming here.'

'I'm only interested in her movements, Mr Grant,' she replied, thinking how prissy she sounded.

'Daddy, please,' said Grant. 'Everyone calls me Daddy.'

He proceeded to lecture her on common misapprehensions about the X-rated business. 'Do you think CAA or Disney or Fox give a damn for the people they hire, underneath the fancy wrapping? Ask around and you'll find more respect in the X-rated business than anywhere. Ask the girls.'

She endured Grant's bluster, nodding politely, while Grant gazed at a point somewhere over her shoulder. 'I know it's hard you being a police officer and all for me to convince you that I am evangelical about my girls. I lose one it's a splinter in my heart. Girls here treat us as family. We are not pharisees, Ms Gomez, not like the straights up in the hills. We do not judge. Our girls are aspirational. They often come from damaged backgrounds, you understand. If a girl has problems she comes to Daddy and we sort it out together.'

'But not in the case of Skye.'

'Truly a thorn in my heart, as I said.'

'Was drugs the trouble?'

Grant switched his gaze to her. 'I paid for her rehab out of my own pocket. Such an unusual girl. She came from a good East Coast family.'

'Was Skye the name you gave to her?'

'We chose it between us,' said Grant with a terse smile and Gomez decided he was as bogus as a hellfire preacher. He also proved a shrewd stonewaller, for all his apparent frankness, and left Gomez none the wiser about Daria. As she was preparing to leave the door opened and a vision with flame-orange hair, wearing white hot pants, thigh boots and a feather boa walked in.

'Honey-pie,' Grant said, 'how many times have I told you to knock during business hours?'

The vision looked at Gomez and asked her if she was testing. Grant explained she was a police officer.

'*Pardonnez-moi*,' the woman said with a splutter of laughter. She lowered her voice and said in a stage-whisper to Gomez, 'He's always terrified I'm going to find him sampling the goods.'

'Ms Gomez is here about Skye.'

The vision put her hand to her open mouth, in a

parody of distress, and the words tumbled out in a comically insincere rush: 'Oh-poor-Skye-baby-what's-happened-to-her?'

Gomez caught Grant's glower prior to introducing the woman as his wife. 'Why don't you and Lallah get acquainted while I attend to business. A pleasure to meet you, Ms Gomez.'

Gomez delayed the appointment with the threatened dog and she and Lallah went a few doors down to an empty coffee house, an unintentionally preserved relic from the Formica era. Lallah had no information on Skye's whereabouts but plenty to say about herself. Before marrying Grant, Lallah Bonaventure had been one of his girls.

'I looked the ingénue so I got to play Little Miss Innocent,' she said, batting her eyelashes.

Linda Gomez calculated she was around thirty, perhaps. Reading her thoughts, Lallah said, 'In movies a man can go the distance. Look at Warren Beatty still playing Romeo at sixty. It's disgusting, he's like a lizard. But for a woman it's a short race and in my particular part of the business even shorter. I used the job to get ahead. No way was I going to be working on camera past twenty-eight. And, honey, I was good. I got a Suck award from an Erotic Film Festival in Europe. Maybe you heard of that. And now I got a husband and two lovely children and my own Mercedes and a nice house with a desirable address, which is not bad for a girl from a dirt-poor background who was abused by her father and brothers practically from the day she could stand.'

She gave a frank smile and Gomez realized that for all her fluttery act Lallah was as tough and unyielding as her husband.

'What can you tell me about Skye?'

Lallah took a gulp of coffee and snorted. 'Daddy was soft on her for a start. Broken Wing he called her. Broken Wing, can you believe that! I said right away she was a bad influence but would he listen? Skye was up to her eyes on drugs, as plain as the fingers on my hand. I tell you, there was many a fight Daddy and I had over Skye. Things she did ought to have disqualified her ages ago except Daddy had such a crush. She was stealing, however much she denied it. There was never any problem with theft before she arrived. We shoot out at a warehouse near the airport – means the sound's shit and all with the planes, but we dub on the track later, including different actors' voices a lot of the time, so that doesn't matter – but you could leave your clothes lying around, go off, do your thing and they would be where you left them when you got back. With stuff disappearing I had to install regular lockers, at some cost too, and because most everyone was stark naked I ended up having to look after the keys. It's maybe a small thing but it spoiled the camaraderie.' Lallah gave a little hiccup Gomez realized was a laugh. 'Couple of times Big Johnny couldn't get it up worrying about his possessions. We joke about it now but it wasn't funny at the time. We lost half a day and we operate on a very tight margin.'

'You think Daddy knows where Skye is?'

'Crosses my mind from time to time he's got her stashed somewhere, but I'm not a jealous woman. Daddy can handle the goods all he wants, far as I am concerned, so long as he doesn't get emotionally involved.'

'Which he did with her?'

'With a bitch who'd already fallen out the airplane. Are men stupid or just plain dumb? I was the one had to get rid of her, Daddy was too soft. She was doing crack and missing her calls and looking like shit and poisoning the atmosphere. Daddy, I said, she's got to go, and Daddy hung his head and cried real big tears because he knew I was right.'

That was two months before.

'And you haven't heard from her since?'

'Not for about four weeks. She came by the office and sat in the lobby trying to see Daddy or me and plead for her job back, so we hired a security man for a week and that got rid of her. Then I had to change the number at home because someone kept phoning and hanging up over and over, no guesses who. And after that it stopped. I guessed she found someone else to pester. Sometimes I wonder if we didn't get rid of her too easy.'

'How do you mean?'

'You hear of people who don't let go. I figured her for one of those. Clingy and not understanding the meaning of the word "no". I wouldn't have given Daria her job back anyway, even if she had cleaned up.'

'Why not?'

'You know what the glint is?' Gomez shook her head. 'Believe me, honey, when I tell you I had the glint. It's a little something in your eye the camera picks up and communicates to the audience. It's the glint that says, Fuck me.' Lallah gave a whoop of laughter that briefly attracted the attention of the only two other customers, an ancient couple around ninety, then leaned forward and whispered, 'I could make myself come just by crossing my legs. Being ready and wanting it helped give you the glint, but it wasn't just a physical thing, it had to do with mental preparation too. Try telling that to the girls these days. For all the feeling most put into it they might as well be at the dentist. "Open wide."'

'Skye didn't have the glint?'

Lallah shook her head slowly. 'No, sir. Tried to teach her, even though I didn't like her. I tried. Thanks to me she mastered the techniques of an adequate blow job, six-and-a-half out of ten no more. She'd never remember to raise her eyes for the camera on the up-stroke. These girls, they refuse to understand it's a technical job and not just getting fucked for money. But she never got the glint, not once. Getting fucked, *pardonnez* my French, she had the eyes of a fish.'

How sad, Gomez thought, to wind up in porno movies and still get a reputation for being a bad actress.

Back at the office, Linda phoned Youselli and reported her findings and said Lallah was sending her a tape of a movie featuring Skye Blu.

'What's it called?' asked Youselli.

'I think it's one you've seen already. *Wet Heat*.'

'I didn't see that one yet.'

She wondered why she humoured him. 'I'll Fed-ex it soon as I get it.'

She hung up. She could picture Youselli punching the air after he had put down the receiver.

This was not the case. Despite the banter of their phone call, Youselli was close to crumbling, having received notice from Paolo's lawyer of his client's intention to sue for illegal entry, harassment and bodily harm. He was being charged as a private individual but how long, he wondered, his palms sweating, before the department found out?

He called Sidney Betesch, his lawyer, who immediately said, 'I was about to call you. I got some bad news. Do you want it now or wait till you come in?'

The roof of Youselli's mouth went dry. 'Give it to me now.'

'I just heard from your wife's lawyers on the question of your access to the children.'

'They want to restrict it?' interrupted Youselli.

'In total. No access.'

'Hey, wait a minute, they can't do that. The bitch can't cut me out of her life like that, they're my kids.'

'She's saying you hit them.'

'No way!' Youselli felt himself getting mad. He would have to be careful. 'On my mother's head, no way did I hit my children.'

'She's saying you hit her too, in front of the children.'

'She's fucking insane! Do I strike you as a violent man?'

Betesch persuaded him to calm down, and said that these were routine preliminary moves. 'If you can assure me that none of your wife's allegations are true, then I can draft a reply. Have you ever hit your wife or children?'

No, he started to say, then he said, once, and repeated it with emphasis. 'Once I had to slap her but she was hysterical and upsetting the children.'

'Was this in the course of a domestic dispute?' asked Betesch neutrally.

'No. She had burned their supper and she just flipped, screaming, saying she couldn't carry on. The kids started wailing and the only way I could bring her to her senses was slap her.'

'And that was the only time.' It was said as a statement rather than a question.

'My honour.'

'It says in their letter "repeatedly".'

'My wife is a depressive. She takes pills without regard for their prescription. What she believes happened and the reality of it are two disconnected things. That is the sad truth. I don't hit women and I don't hit children, my own or anyone else's.'

Talking to Betesch was like he was in confession. He felt dirty, even in denial. He finished up by telling him that his wife had taken to sitting outside his house at night. 'No way does she get unrestricted access to those children when she is incapable of looking after them properly. Do what you have to.'

'Would you consider bringing up the children yourself without allowing their mother access?'

'On my own? I don't see how that's feasible, the hours I work.'

'You'd have to pay for care of course.'

'I still don't see how, unless I got married again except I'm not about to.'

Youselli listened to Betesch thinking. He had taken him on to spite his father. It was one of the rare times he had seen the old man speechless, at the thought of him hiring a Jew. Betesch eventually said, 'What you want then is reasonable access to your children to ensure they are being raised to a proper standard.'

'I don't know what I want.'

'Most people don't,' said Betesch kindly. 'That's why lawyers get rich. I'll draft a letter and send you a copy. Don't worry. We can fight dirty too.'

Betesh was one of the few human beings Youselli ever felt reassured by. Sometimes he wished he were his father, this wizened little old man with leathery skin and a look of quiet amusement.

Only after he had hung up did Youselli remember they had not talked about the reason for his call. He knew he should call Betesch back to tell him about Paolo's move, but after this latest news he didn't have the energy. He called McMahon instead but McMahon had his answer service fielding calls so Youselli left a message for him to call even though he knew it would not be returned.

For the rest of the day the pressure built inside his head, like someone had stuck a bicycle pump in his ear. His wife's accusation had left him on the edge of a permanently violent state. Even he could see the irony in that and spent several hours trying to wind down. The idea of not seeing his children left him feeling turned inside out.

He went to bed at one and spent an hour staring at the ceiling. At this rate, he thought, he would not get to sleep before it was time to get up. Though he was not aware of it, he must have drifted off because the telephone woke him. He fumbled for the receiver, cursing, his first thought being that he had overslept, but then he saw the clock showing not quite two.

His caller was McMahon – Youselli had already guessed – sounding way off in a cave of his own. Youselli told him it was too late to talk.

'Don't hang up!' McMahon sounded hysterical. After that there was the longest silence. Youselli called his name a few times and got no reply. Thinking McMahon had nodded out he announced he was going to hang up.

'Don't,' came back McMahon's spooky whisper. Again he said nothing for a long time and Youselli got the impression McMahon was crying. Finally he confessed he was feeling bad because Anjelica had flown to Switzerland and he was certain Blackledge was with her. Youselli shut his eyes till he saw stars to cut out the slow drip of the other man's paranoia.

'Did you fix to see Aaron yet?' he asked.

'I didn't reach him.' Youselli could tell he had not even tried. 'You got to help me, man. I'm in a bad way,' McMahon continued.

McMahon's whining self-pity acted like a switch on Youselli. Suddenly he was sitting on the side of the bed, clenching the phone and pouring into it his accumulated venom. He called McMahon a little fucker and after that was just a red mist. He was amazed at the bile spewing out of him. At one point he asked if McMahon had someone wipe his ass for him. Like the rest of his tirade, this was met with silence.

'My, my,' McMahon eventually said when Youselli was done. 'I didn't realize your feelings ran so deep.' He sounded fortified by Youselli's outburst, his gloom quite vanished.

'I don't need these games,' said Youselli more evenly though anger still chased him. 'I'm having my ass sued in every direction, my kids are being taken away, I don't sleep, so the last thing I need is some cocksucker phone call in the middle of the night. Are you going to phone Aaron? If the answer's no don't call back. Get someone else to handle your business.'

It was long past Edith's bedtime and she was still puzzling over Leah's latest letter. She sighed and took off her glasses. It was two in the morning. Ridiculous, she thought, going to the kitchen where she poured herself a rare Scotch, in fact not so unusual since that child had broken in. Her sleeplessness had got worse since then too. She was regularly drinking a quarter a day, not excessive except she usually drank nothing.

It was the further change of tone in the letter that disturbed, the switch to the past. The apparent blanks − 'must be that old fugue state they talk about' − were the clearest indication yet that the confusion between fantasy and actuality was deeply embedded. Whoever had written this letter was very capable of confusing the two. This newly emerging Leah was both more revealing and more distant and altogether colder. None of the previous letters had made any mention of a life before France.

This could almost have been written by someone else, she thought, not for the first time. She rubbed her eyes which were gritty with tiredness and promised herself she would go to bed after a final reading. Her eyes skipped forward to the last line which had troubled her since first reading it – 'It's because you are famous I'm writing you.' All the other letters had been written on the basis that sender and addressee knew each other. Now it was almost like they did not. Edith wondered if this distancing was a prelude to a more vengeful phase. She sighed and went back to the beginning of the letter hoping that what had been previously opaque would, through sheer repetition, become clear.

Before going to bed Edith tried Susan's office in Los Angeles. It was quite usual to find Susan or someone else still there until twelve their time. The woman who answered sounded tired and disgruntled and told Edith that Susan had left. For the day, Edith assumed, but when she asked what time in the morning Susan would be in she was told, 'She no longer works here.'

Edith could not think of a single sensible question. She was aware of the floor looking a long way off and thought she was about to faint. The woman answering the phone made it clear she didn't have time to talk and hung up. Edith replaced the receiver shakily and sat down in a state of shock. She had no way of contacting Susan. She had no private number for her. Susan had not given her one, saying she was always at the office anyway.

CHAPTER TWENTY

McMahon said little on the drive, claiming a headache, stretched out in the back. Neither made any reference to their previous conversation. The night after the call Youselli had got home to find a message saying they were to meet Aaron in a bar north of Hudson. The news hadn't pleased him. The meeting was fixed for Sunday, which was when he was supposed to visit his kids, plus he had intended to spend the morning catching up on regular work. He was feeling the pressure and starting to cut corners.

Later on, he looked back at the drive as a turning point, where, in theory, it was still possible to walk away.

The parkway was busy with weekend traffic. At one point McMahon woke up and asked Youselli to put the radio on. Listeners were voting for their top 100 dance records. Youselli asked if any of McMahon's songs would feature.

'We didn't do dance music,' he said tersely.

From the sounds of intense concentration coming from the back Youselli guessed McMahon was doing drugs. He glanced over his shoulder and wondered whether to complain.

'You want some?' McMahon asked casually.

Youselli shook his head. McMahon did his lines. He asked Youselli to turn the radio off and showed signs of wanting to talk but Youselli killed the conversation. Their relationship had changed since the phone call. McMahon treated Youselli like the chauffeur, but now Youselli felt he was in the driving seat. The image made him smile. They were rivals now, Youselli thought, more like equals. Sitting in the back of his car seemed to deprive McMahon of his aura. Seen in the rearview he was just a little guy with a big head. Youselli smiled again.

'What's so funny?' asked McMahon, sounding petulant.

'Nothing.'

Skeet's bar stood in its own empty stretch of blacktop. Given its remoteness, the large asphalt parking lot with painted lines looked out of place. Only a couple of pick-ups stood parked. A flight of outdoor steps led up to the bar which was built proud of the road, allowing any arrival to be seen. The pine-fresh air smelled sharp after the city.

There was no sign of Aaron. Youselli was half-expecting him to play them for suckers. McMahon seemed ill-at-ease in public space.

There were three men, besides the bartender. Two big, tattooed youths, upstate rednecks with long hair, wearing heavy metal T-shirts, played pool. The third man was older and on a solo drinking jag, drifting off and waking with a start when the cigarette clamped in his fist burned down to his fingers, or with the start of every new game when the pool balls crashed around.

McMahon made for the corner furthest from the players, by a window overlooking the parking area. He sat drumming his fingers.

'Do you think he's going to show?' he asked.

'I don't know, I didn't speak to him.'

'He sounded okay on the phone, almost like he was expecting my call.'

McMahon was twitchy. Youselli could see how the day-to-day stuff was beyond him. He was willing to bet he didn't have any beer money either.

'Maybe the guy behind the bar knows Aaron,' ventured McMahon.

'You want a drink?'

'Sure, beer and a Jack Daniels. You got money?'

'Don't you?'

'We can settle up later.'

Youselli thought it unlikely. The bartender didn't look like he stretched to waiting so he fetched the drinks.

McMahon was certain Aaron was not going to show. 'I fired him, man. He won't even cross the street for me now.'

'Can you stop drumming your fingers? It makes me nervous.'

'Oh.' McMahon looked down at his hand, unaware of what he was doing.

Twenty minutes crawled by and nothing changed except one of the boys played an old Johnny Cash number on the jukebox. McMahon had a couple more fast drinks and went to the toilet leaving Youselli to nurse his beer. The boys looked like they were playing pool for the rest of their lives. The bartender read his newspaper without turning the page, and the drunk shifted in and out of focus. A pick-up drew into the lot and a man in a cowboy hat got out. Youselli had seen him somewhere before but could not remember where.

The man was at the top of the stairs before Youselli recognized him as the asshole from McMahon's party who had been throwing people in the swimming pool. Close up by daylight he looked even meaner, his expression only too easy to read. It spelled trouble.

McMahon was coming out of the toilet when he saw who it was and paled visibly. The man grinned an evil little grin, finger pistolling McMahon, who, to his credit, recovered quickly and raised his hands to acknowledge that the other man had the drop on him. Then they were embracing like the oldest friends, backslapping and kissing cheeks to the sneery amusement of the pool players. For the first time that day Youselli had a bad feeling about how things were turning out.

The man's name was Royal. When McMahon introduced Youselli, saying what he did, Royal did a sneaky double take and feinted a recoil, and gave a sideways look of hostile amusement.

'You wearing your cop hat today?'

'He's my driver,' said McMahon with a giggle. 'What are you drinking?'

'Same as you.'

'Get us more drinks,' McMahon said to Youselli

who was about to refuse when Royal summoned the bartender. He appeared to be a regular.

After several quick drinks and whatever he had done in the toilet McMahon was looking wired, and Royal seemed pretty loaded too. It did not take a great detective to figure him for a speed freak. His manner was malevolent and his appearance unprepossessing, ratty denim and fingersful of chunky gold rings, one with a death's head. Long greasy hair poked out from under his hat. A couple of locks were braided and plaited with bright beads. Youselli wondered if the long duster coat hid a knife or gun, or both. His own gun was at the back of his waist, which was better than being stuck in a shoulder holster.

'Where's Aaron?' asked Youselli.

'Patience, cowboy, patience. Get your thumb out your ass and enjoy your drink.'

McMahon's response to Royal was to continue getting high. They were seated at a table for four which was bolted to the floor, as were the benches, probably to stop the furniture from getting thrown around. Skeet's looked like it had a history of brawls. McMahon sat by the window next to Royal who was opposite Youselli whose mood had not been improved by McMahon's instinctive siding with Royal.

McMahon explained that Royal had travelled everywhere with the band, first as one of the rigging crew, then as Mickey's assistant, which Youselli took to mean he brokered with local dealers.

McMahon had adopted an uncharacteristic bonhomie that seemed to be taking him to the edge of a reckless high. He and Royal were drinking at several times Youselli's rate. McMahon leaned forward with the air of a man about to up the stakes.

'Royal was known as Snake Eyes behind his back. He once thrashed a kid doing publicity for calling him that to his face.'

Royal's eyes narrowed. 'I ought to shoot you in the knees,' he hissed and McMahon looked anxious till Royal followed the threat with a long braying laugh.

'Royal's the only man I know who could match Mickey drink for drink and end up standing,' said McMahon, sounding relieved.

'Hey, man,' said Royal. 'We should drink to Mickey.'

They touched glasses and knocked back a long swallow before Royal turned on Youselli for not joining in. 'Show some respect for the dead.'

Youselli was aware of a dangerous calm inside as he decided whether to up the stakes. 'I didn't know him,' he said.

'That doesn't mean you can't drink to him,' said Royal, sticking his face in Youselli's.

'How did Mickey die?' asked Youselli.

'In a boating accident,' said McMahon.

The remark struck him as inapposite and funny. Drugs, liver failure, or suicide was what he expected, not getting hit by a power boat while skin diving. Whether from nervous tension or real amusement, he found himself laughing uncontrollably.

'What's so funny?' asked McMahon. Royal was bug-eyed and could not have looked more shocked if he had discovered Youselli had just crapped in the chalice. Youselli was still weak from laughing when he saw Royal reach inside his coat. His own reflexes were slow and he was only half way to his gun when he felt the barrel of Royal's press into his leg.

'Hands on the table, pig.'

Youselli cursed himself for letting McMahon choose where they sat. His own preference would have been the bar but it was too late, he was fenced in. Youselli looked at McMahon who was enjoying every second of Youselli's discomfort. Youselli reckoned this was his improvised revenge for what had been said to him on the telephone.

Royal said to Youselli, 'You're going to drink to Mickey now.'

Youselli contemplated his beer. It was going to be a long afternoon. He took a swallow and thought about bringing the glass down on Royal's head. Royal meanwhile was making his own move, reaching round the table leg to swap the gun to his left hand so he could slip in beside Youselli. Youselli felt the gun dig into him as he was forced along the bench till he was opposite McMahon who winked.

'Having fun?'

'How badly wired is your friend?' Youselli asked.

'He comes with a short fuse,' said McMahon with a grin which Royal capped with his irritating laugh. Royal then frisked Youselli for his gun and the same Johnny Cash song came back on the jukebox.

'Check he's carrying nothing on his leg, man,' Royal ordered McMahon. 'He could be one of those sneaky cops, packs an extra tool.'

Youselli felt McMahon's hands moving over his legs

and, unless he was mistaken, lingering. He was angry at the thought of the little fucker getting turned on by his humiliation. Youselli could not tell who he was more annoyed at, McMahon or himself for his lack of anticipation. Even if he did manage to smash Royal across the mouth with his elbow the gun would almost certainly go off in the process. The pool balls dropped but without enough of a crash to distract Royal. McMahon gave a hiccup, patted his mouth and said, 'Dearie me.'

They made Youselli drink endless toasts to Mickey. Youselli guessed that Royal's idea of a good time involved a seamless move into violence with none of the usual warnings. The gun continued to press into Youselli's side and every now and then Royal gave him a dig to remind him it was there. He used his free hand to smoke and drink.

'Hey compadre,' he said to McMahon, 'what happened to all the hellraisers? Sometimes I think there's only me left.'

McMahon seemed content to let Royal hold court, but Youselli sensed that Royal's bullshit had been boring him for years.

'Us pistoleros on the road, we were living out that old pioneer spirit, after all the squares had settled down. We were the outlaws, man, and in years to come they will be telling stories about us like they do the Greek gods.'

Youselli looked at McMahon. 'Was the road always this boring?'

McMahon flashed him a look of complicity. 'Pretty

much unless you learned to make your own entertainment.'

'As we are doing now,' Youselli replied as wryly as
he could manage.

'Pretty much,' said McMahon, indifferent again, and
Royal gave a twisted giggle. Youselli turned to him.

'Let me ask you something. Didn't you feel that he
and the rest of his faggot crew were just along for the
ride?'

'Faggot?' queried McMahon.

'You're a rock star, man,' Youselli sneered, 'grew
your hair and prettied yourself with make-up, isn't that
right?' He turned for confirmation to Royal who was
cackling and nodding.

'Yeah, they were right there on the cusp.'

'The cusp!' McMahon's lip curled.

'You bet,' said Royal. 'You all were, coming on
like cocksmen when you were taking it up the ass half
the time.'

Youselli felt Royal's attention shifting away from
him. He could not feel the gun any more.

'That's bullshit and you know it.' McMahon had
got louder and was red in the face.

Youselli decided to make his move.

'Don't even think about it, asshole,' said Royal,
jabbing hard enough to make him grunt. He sounded
whiny and dangerous as he turned back to McMahon.
'Let me tell you something. When all the little chickies
were hanging round the band I never had me any
trouble getting the ones who were at the front of the
line, if you take my meaning.'

'Do you remember anyone called Leah?' Youselli asked bluntly. He was rewarded with a look of alarm from McMahon who said that Royal hadn't been in France.

'Before France then,' said Youselli.

Royal scratched his head, intrigued. 'You mean the chick with the cute ass in the white jeans?'

'He doesn't know what he's talking about,' said McMahon. He started to stand. 'We should get going.'

'Sit down,' Youselli said. 'The man has a story to tell.'

Royal snapped his fingers, remembering. 'Hanging round backstage?'

'She wasn't on any tour,' retorted McMahon.

'I'm not talking about a tour, Mr Big Star. I'm talking about a benefit you played in New York. She was there to give Mickey's dick a tug but Mickey was more interested in talking to his pharmacist.'

'You're making this up,' protested McMahon. 'She never wore jeans in her life.'

Royal made kissing noises. 'Maybe not for you, sweetheart.'

The gun jabbed into Youselli's side again and Youselli said to McMahon, 'Let the man tell his fucking story.'

'Fucking story is right, man,' said Royal aggressively. 'She fucked me right across the room.'

McMahon made to stand up again. Royal told him to sit down or he would shoot him too.

'Don't mind him,' Youselli told Royal. 'He's jealous.'

'You know what pisses me off the most about these

people, even Mickey, God rest his soul?' said Royal. 'They never did the asking. I don't know what kind of nerve it takes to stick your ass out and wiggle it on stage, but you would think it would give you enough balls to go up to some chick and say, Fuck me, baby. But hell no. You never took the risk of being turned down.' He turned to McMahon. 'It was, "Hey, Royal, ask the chick over there if she wants to come upstairs," or "Hey, Royal, get some girls up for a party." Like I was your fucking pimp.' He looked at Youselli. 'Know what I mean?'

'I know what you mean,' said Youselli slowly. 'He's not even paying for his drinks.' He looked to McMahon. 'I thought you met Leah in a club with Astrid.'

'So?'

'And Astrid did the asking. What was she doing hanging round backstage for Mickey?'

'He's bullshitting,' said McMahon. 'I was there, I would remember.'

'Not the way you were that night,' interrupted Royal. 'I asked her if she wanted to meet Mickey and she goes, "Uh, okay", all cool like.' He did a grotesque parody of preening. 'So I tell her I got to escort her to the hotel where the party is or she won't get past security. When we get there I tell lill' ol' Lay-uh I got a message to call Mickey's room in fifteen minutes, so we have a drink, break the ice. I compliment her, but generally act like I'm hanging in there waiting for the man.'

'How old is she?' asked Youselli like they were making polite afternoon conversation.

'I would say she was, uh, still at an impressionable

age,' replied Royal with a titter. 'Then I phone again and come back and tell her Mickey's going to call my room when he's ready and I apologize for the delay and offer her a drink upstairs.

'And the funny thing is Mickey never calls,' volunteered Youselli and Royal laughed like it was the punchline to the best joke he had ever heard. But the gun stayed stuck in Youselli's side.

'The way I see it,' he went on, 'she was only there to get fucked. So I Lay-her, huh huh huh, and maybe she's thinking of Mickey or you when she is doing me but who cares? Nails sharper than a wildcat.'

'That's my girl,' said Youselli, pleased to note McMahon smouldering with rage. True or not, the story had got to him. Youselli thought it would need only one more shove to tip him over. He spoke to Royal, indicating McMahon. 'You didn't like him, did you?'

'Never signed a contract saying I had to. Vietnam.'

'Vietnam?' echoed Youselli obligingly.

'The military officers did not earn the respect of their men. Most road crews will tell you the same.'

McMahon threw his punch, but after so many beers it came in slow motion and Royal, who held his liquor better, was easily too quick. He caught McMahon's fist, twisting it sideways and down on to the table top. McMahon's squeal coincided with the rumble of pool balls at the start of a new game. Royal turned away for a second, and Youselli – praying the gun would not go off – drove sideways, pushing Royal off the bench. The gun stayed quiet and Youselli threw himself after Royal wanting to grab his ears and slam his head into the ground. But when he hit the floor Royal had already rolled away. Youselli could see the gun in his hand, not yet aimed at him but only seconds away. He had no idea where McMahon was and when his shoulder exploded with pain he thought it was McMahon kicking him. Then, out of the corner of his eye, he saw McMahon still at the table, nursing his hand and surveying the scene with a fearful excitement.

The blow saved Youselli from further harm. It had come from the stock of the bartender's shotgun, which was now trained on Royal. Youselli thought this was probably a fairly regular occurrence. It had a well-rehearsed air.

'Guns away, boys,' said the bartender. 'Now who's paying?'

'My amigo buddy's treat,' said Royal pointing at Youselli who was disappointed that the bartender showed no signs of calling the cops. The prospect of leaving with Royal was not one he relished. Standing at the bar, paying for the drinks, he realized how drunk he was, and Royal still had his gun. What a mess, he thought.

McMahon was still at the table, scared now they had to go. Royal held the door open and grinned at Youselli, saying in a low voice, 'I got all the guns.'

'Be seeing you, boss,' Royal said to the bartender as they filed out. The pool players acted like nothing had happened and the drunk was now oblivious to anything.

He followed them down the steps to Youselli's car, and said, 'Let's go see Aaron, good buddies, and have us a taste of the old days.'

He kicked Youselli's back tire. 'This yours?'

'Yes, but I drunk too much.'

'Hey, asshole, we haven't even started. You drive. Faggot here is next to you, and I'm in the back.'

CHAPTER TWENTY-ONE

Youselli drove with drunken deliberation but repeatedly found himself way over the speed limit. Part of him started not to care. Would it be so bad if everything was taken away? It was not as though his life was anything other than a semi-fuck-up. He could walk away from it all tomorrow, go into private security and fuck them all. His life might even be prolonged by several years for never seeing O'Dowd again.

It was coming on to rain, darkness falling. They were in the middle of nowhere, moving into an even deeper nowhere. Youselli hated the countryside, had always hated green ever since an early memory of his father decked out in shamrock on St Patrick's Day. His wife had worn green too, which he had failed to take for a warning. He glanced sideways at McMahon who was hunched down, hands between his knees. He didn't look so famous now. Royal was in the rearview, eyes wild with animal excitement. Everything was like in a dream. Details were correct but overall the order made no sense: how had they got to where they were? Most of the time Youselli had expectations of what might happen in any given situation, now he had none apart from an apprehension of the pain Royal might inflict given the chance.

A few miles down the road they came to a hamlet where everything looked shut. By then it was almost full night and raining, the macadam slick in the beam of the car lights. The sound of the wipers added another detail in Youselli's head.

'Take a left at the crossroads,' said Royal.

After the turn the road narrowed to a single lane with trees and a high bank with gaps through which Youselli could see a small valley nestling in the last of the daylight, with a low hill beyond. He tried to picture himself not in the car but standing alone over on the hill watching the lights of the car threading through the trees, and he suddenly felt like they were actors in an old black and white movie who were not the main players as they had been told, but bit parts in someone else's scenario. He tried to think of some plan, some trick to gain the upper hand but his brain could cope with nothing beyond driving. An air of fatalism seemed to cling to the interior of the car, sealing them off from the outside world.

The turning to Aaron's place was by an old barn and a track rose steeply through woods full of the smell of wild garlic whose pungent aroma suddenly invaded the enclosed space of the car. At the top of the hill the ground opened out to reveal the silhouette of a mansion. As the vehicle's lights splashed the façade Youselli saw the extent of its neglect. Whole areas of masonry were missing, brickwork showing beneath.

Royal ordered them out. The big oak door that was the main entrance to the house stood open and waiting. The air was much colder than when they had set out and Youselli suppressed a shiver. McMahon stepped a dainty path through the mud and Youselli wondered if the man realized how fortunate he was, because if Youselli had still had his gun he would have gladly used it on McMahon. They moved indoors where it was dark except for a dim bulb lighting a long passage that smelt of mildew, its floor tiles covered in polythene. Buckets had been positioned to catch the rain from roof leaks.

At the end of the passage they entered a cavernous room with furniture covered in dust sheets. Under one of the drapes Youselli noted the shape of a pool table. It was lit by an overhead canopy light, the room's only source of illumination apart from a huge blazing hearth. In his present frame of mind Youselli could believe these were the flames that would engulf them all. The place stank of something he could not identify. At first he thought the room empty. Then, sitting in the gloom beyond the fire, he saw the shadow of a giant of a man.

'Dear boy. Introduce me to your friend.' The voice was fruity and loud, and exaggeratedly British.

Youselli was curious to know how McMahon was going to play this. Demure, it seemed, as he crossed to Aaron and took his hand, helping Aaron to his feet. As Aaron unsteadily hauled himself up, Youselli was shocked to see how much he had aged since the photograph from Mickey's funeral. He still carried massive bulk, but a wasting illness had eaten away his face, turning it gaunt. His hair was thinning and scraped back in a ponytail and he wore a fuller beard than in the photograph. It had been allowed to grow unkempt but it failed to conceal the turkey wattle under his jowls. He wore a grubby white tuxedo jacket on top of several sweatshirts, piled on indiscriminately and all filthy, making it look like he had slept in them and added another each morning. His pants were especially foul, once suede, now bald and shiny black. McMahon had told him that this old hulk was a man of delicate sensibility, a collector of the most fragile porcelain.

As Aaron approached the fetid smell grew stronger and Youselli realized it was maximum body odour laced with a sickly eau de cologne, a mix that nearly made him gag. If McMahon was put off by the stench he showed no sign.

'My, a policeman!' said Aaron in mock delight, showing both palms in the campest of manners when McMahon introduced him. 'We will have to be careful.'

'He's off duty,' said McMahon flatly. Youselli had a nasty feeling from the way it was said that he was the patsy in all this.

'Fine, fine,' said Aaron, 'I'm sure it will all be fine. We are just going to have a little tea and a nice chat. You will be staying the night of course.'

'I think we will have to get back,' said McMahon, falling in with Aaron's way of speaking, with its hint of a lisp.

Aaron tutted his disappointment and looking at Youselli, continued to McMahon, 'I don't think your friend enjoys being with us. He disapproves. He thinks he is better than us, perhaps.'

'Don't mind him,' said McMahon. 'He's still got a lot to learn.'

'Manners for a start. He can't come round here with that look on his face, like there's a nasty smell under his nose.' Aaron spoke with booming good cheer, then dropped his voice to one of confidential sincerity. 'Depravity and good manners are what count in the end.'

'Sweetheart,' said McMahon sounding matter of fact. 'How can you talk about manners?' He turned to Youselli. 'At Helsinki airport I watched him flatten a photographer.'

'Because he was too much in your face, dear heart.'

Their banter made Youselli see the extent of McMahon's chameleon nature, always appearing to side with the person he was with by subtly adopting their manner, imitating but always on the right side of parody.

Aaron turned to Youselli. 'So good of you to come. Have a drink.'

'No thanks.'

'It's not an option.' He moved to a drinks table and poured two large tumblers of whisky, one for Youselli, the other for McMahon.

Youselli looked at the liquid in the glass and threw it on the fire which spat back a jet like a flamethrower, just missing Aaron. Youselli heard the click of Royal's gun. Aaron merely laughed and poured another and made Youselli down it in one. Tilting his head to drink, he was uncomfortably aware of Royal's gun nestling at the base of his neck.

'Good man,' Aaron said, watching. Youselli felt the liquor hum in his bloodstream.

'Now,' Aaron went on. 'Are you here on business or is this pleasure?'

'We're here to talk about France.'

'My, would that be Bourbon dynasty or the Albigensian heresy, perhaps? What a civilization!'

'I was thinking of something a little later,' said Youselli. 'Involving a girl.'

'Girls!' exclaimed Aaron, turning to McMahon. 'Do we allow the word in the house?'

McMahon smirked and Aaron leaned towards him with a stage whisper. 'Do you remember once you were with me in the back of a limousine in Chicago, and I told you I was the keeper of your secrets. And that is how it should stay. Our secrets are not to be shared with the likes of him.'

'The secret is already out,' Youselli said. When he told him about the letters he was sure Aaron knew already and was faking his surprise. 'So someone's telling, or the girl's still alive.'

'Alive?' echoed Aaron. The double take seemed real enough, though Youselli was finding it hard to read anything with the booze. 'Oh no, I don't think so at all.'

'Think?' asked Youselli. 'You don't know.'

'I saw her, and her blood all over the wall.'

Youselli caught McMahon's sharp look at Aaron.

'Wait a minute, she was supposed to have fallen.' Youselli frowned, trying to get things straight. 'How do you get blood all over the wall from a fall?'

McMahon appeared caught out for once.

'What have you been telling him?' asked Aaron.

'Only what was agreed.'

Aaron sighed. 'Don't jigger me about, boy.' He looked at Youselli wearily as one adult would to another when dealing with a difficult child. 'How I loved my boys, how I made people afraid on their behalf. Have you ever been the victim of unrequited love?'

Youselli shook his head, but Aaron was not interested. He pointed at McMahon. 'Such a vain, egotistical monster, Mickey was the same.'

McMahon didn't argue. Maybe humiliation was a necessary component in his relationship with Aaron, thought Youselli.

'I knew France would come back to haunt me,' Aaron said and Youselli saw his chance to ask how the girl had really died. 'She shot herself, I believe,' said Aaron like they were making casual conversation.

'Shot herself?' Youselli said in astonishment.

'Isn't that right?' Aaron asked McMahon, who appeared even more sheepish when Youselli asked Aaron if McMahon always lied.

McMahon mumbled, 'It's more complicated than that.'

Aaron clucked his tongue in disapproval. 'He doesn't see it as lying. The problem is our friend here is always centre stage, in the spotlight, and thinks the world revolves around him because the bright glare he lives in makes it impossible to see what is going on outside his immediate circle. So, what can he know of the drummer behind him, or the people watching in the wings, or the man standing at the back of the hall nursing some homicidal grievance, or the two women backstage vying over who's going to get him later, or Royal here banging some slut who'd rather be out front watching the show but agrees to let him shoot his wad in her, in exchange for introductions to the band?' Royal laughed his mulish laugh. Aaron ignored him. 'What can he know of all these things? Or my feelings?'

McMahon shrugged and said, 'You were on the payroll, you didn't have to get involved.'

'So heartless,' he said to Youselli. 'Of course I was involved. My boys, my creations. With this one especially,' he said, pointing at McMahon, 'I knew what he wanted better than he knew himself.'

Youselli tried to steer Aaron back to France but it was like a rowing boat trying to turn a tanker. Aaron stayed him with his hand and said, 'We'll get to France, but there's a lot more dirty water under the bridge. I looked after you well, didn't I?' he said to McMahon.

McMahon gave a churlish nod and Aaron turned to Youselli. 'I made these boys and did one of them thank me?'

Youselli shook his head slowly, like in the dream of being on stage in the wrong play with the wrong lines.

'Do you know what his problem was?' Aaron went on. Youselli drew comfort from the fact that the process involved the dismantling of McMahon. 'He was a sampler, a dabbler, a bit of this and a bit of that, sticking his nose in the gutter, then pretending he hadn't done it. Reading his fucking Cocteau and calling us Beauty and the Beast.'

Wait a minute, Youselli thought, did that mean

something had gone on between them? Aaron sensed his confusion and moved forward and laid his hand possessively on McMahon who stood, eyes downcast, as still as a Roman statue. Youselli felt he was witnessing something ageless and beyond his comprehension, like some play between the gods. Maybe Royal had been right. Youselli would not have been surprised to look out the window and see Vesuvius erupting.

Aaron took the back of McMahon's neck in his paw-like hand, his expression a mixture of affection and exasperation as he continued to address Youselli. 'Do you know what I overheard him say about me to Mickey one time. Quote: "He's in love with me, man. Suck his dick and make him happy. Why not? It doesn't mean anything. You know me, always ready to lend a hand." Snigger. Unquote.'

'I never sucked your dick.'

Aaron squeezed, making McMahon flinch. 'No, because you were too much of a cissy. Tell him about the times you wanked me off.'

McMahon burned crimson and started to shake.

'He toyed with affections, I knew that,' said Aaron. 'But I thought I had a place in his heart. More fool me because then what happened? The dear boy fired me, didn't you?'

McMahon smirked in spite of himself. 'For financial irregularities.'

Aaron laughed at that and Youselli saw how much they were enjoying themselves.

'Did you come to tell me you were sorry after all these years?' asked Aaron and McMahon shrugged and Aaron asked Youselli if he realized what he was witnessing. 'It is a condition of whatever contract he has made with whatever devil he serves that from time to time he needs to lay himself bare, expose everything, because it is the only way he knows how to come to terms with his own naked failure. There is the public performance, the showing off, then there is its shadow, the dark side that you are witnessing now, the humbling, the chastisement. It is what feeds the other. Think of the brightness of the light that he stands in. There has to be a shadow, and this is it. But he still has to be taught his lesson.'

'And what is that?' asked Youselli, feeling an unhealthy fascination creeping along the back of his scalp.

'That he can't let it all hang out.' Aaron guffawed.

'If he does?'

'He'll cause a lot of pain, which won't do.'

'What kind of pain?'

'The kind you get from digging up bodies.'

'Are we talking about Leah here?'

'We may be,' he said smoothly, with a knowing look. 'But let's start with the general before getting specific. We are talking about careless lives, gentlemen, careless lives. I know what happened in Manila, and Rio and Caracas and Auckland and anywhere else you care to mention. Did you know about Mickey and the Chief of Police in Manila and how they enjoyed nothing more than a night in the cells?'

'What are you talking about?' sneered McMahon.

'Watching, watching through a two-way mirror while prisoners got interrogated. Didn't Mickey show you the movies he shot?' Aaron mimed someone in electric shock: tssst-tssss. 'Mickey was even trying to attend an execution.'

'Bullshit.'

'My point is you know nothing.' Aaron spoke to Youselli. 'Rock and roll band, lot of girls hanging around, that's a given. Girl meets boy, boy fucks girl, it's like watching airplanes. They come in, they get refuelled, they fly away. Once in a while there's a crash, and then it was my business. Let's say it was our boy here's turn to fall out of the sky and there were plenty of nights when he ended up blind puking and passing out and having to be put to bed – and I did that with a tenderness I did not extend to the others, not even Mickey – and he woke up next day not remembering a thing. Someone could have driven a truck through the room and he would have had no recollection.'

'What are you saying?' McMahon asked. Youselli felt queasy at the idea of McMahon as unconscious participant in Aaron's necrophile fantasies.

'I am saying there are too many secrets for you to go overturning applecarts,' he said.

'Is that why you're getting her to write these letters?' asked McMahon with a sneer.

Aaron looked puzzled a moment. 'I don't need anyone write you letters. I'm talking to your face, boy.'

'Who called you from France, was it Mickey?' interrupted Youselli.

Aaron looked surprised, like he had forgotten Youselli was there. 'It was the middle of the night my time and I got the first flight and arrived late the following evening. Mickey had been in tears on the phone, saying he was going to have to go to prison and his kid would be taken away from him.'

'Go to prison?'

'It was his gun she shot herself with. Mickey didn't have a permit for France. I had tidied up some messes for these boys in my time but the babysitter shooting herself was a new one on me!' Aaron gave a bellow of laughter and slapped his thigh.

'Wait a minute,' said Youselli. 'First of all she fell downstairs, then she shot herself.' He looked meaning-fully at McMahon. 'What exactly did happen in this latest version?'

'We came back to find there had been an accident, except she had shot herself.'

'Shot herself? Next you'll be telling me that you and Mickey were using her for target practice.'

McMahon looked pleadingly at Aaron. 'Tell him.'

'I don't know what happened, I got there twelve hours late. To go by what I saw the kid shot herself and, as she wasn't the suicide type, from what I have been told, she and the kid must have been playing with the gun when it went off.'

'And killed her?'

'She was dead,' confirmed Aaron.

'What did you do?'

Aaron grunted. 'Our boy here had run back to where he was staying, leaving the rest to twiddle their thumbs till I arrived, which they did by getting so drunk that Mickey and Astrid passed out – like I said, careless lives. The kid was the only one conscious when I got there, but he wasn't saying anything.'

'What about Blackledge?'

'He had already left.'

'Any reason?' asked Youselli.

'Because Mr Blackledge doesn't like me and is afraid of me.'

'How did you feel tidying up after these people?'

'I did it because I loved them. I loved them however much they despised and laughed at me, and you willingly tidy up after the children you love.' He sounded sincere, a sad old man all of a sudden, until he caught Youselli's eye and moved on quickly. 'I did it for me too. It was my sport. Fucking with the bureaucracy, scaring people, paying them off, getting them to bend the rules. And the French are always a pleasure to deal with, they understand the business of compromise when it is spelt out correctly.'

'So the French cops were happy to buy the idea that she died from a fall?'

'And to provide the paperwork that said so, though I have no doubt it got mislaid along the way.'

'And have her in the ground before the father showed up?'

Aaron gave a worldly smile. 'The French can move faster than you think, given the incentive.'

'And all this to protect Mickey who laughed at you behind your back.'

Aaron looked rueful. 'Mickey was valuable too. He may have been a dimwit and a fuckhead, with the mind and heart of a nasty little fascist but he was money in the bank. I was merely protecting my assets.'

Youselli missed what happened next. He was aware of McMahon squealing. Then he saw that Aaron had grabbed a fistful of McMahon's precious hair and was looking at Youselli with a sly expression that said he knew how much Youselli would appreciate the sight of McMahon's pain.

Aaron whispered hotly into McMahon's ear. 'You and me understand each other, don't we, boy?'

McMahon squirmed like a kid in bad need of a pee and Youselli watched, knowing he did not want to see what happened next, did not want to know where it was going but was unable to tear himself away.

Aaron went on, his voice enticing. 'Think of us all as family again. We'll get ourselves a nice ass-tight situation going. Tell me what's on your mind, boy, and I'll tell you what's on mine. Sit on my knee and tell me.'

Royal gave a constipated laugh while Youselli goggled.

'Come sit on my knee and tell me, as a young nephew might his kind old uncle. Think of me as your kind old uncle.'

Youselli wanted out but Royal blocked his way, grinning, gun still raised. 'Show's just starting.'

Aaron went on, 'You know I carried a torch for you till you went and spoiled it all, and look how she treats you now.'

Again he ordered McMahon to sit on his knee. McMahon shook his head and Aaron said softly, 'It's no humiliation. Make an old man happy.'

'You're not old,' McMahon said, trying to sound placatory.

'Not in my bones, in my soul. In my soul I am Methuselah. Come here and tell me your heart's desires.' Aaron purred on. 'Your heart's desires, dear heart.'

McMahon sat on the guy's knee. Maybe he wanted to, Youselli thought. Maybe he needed the humiliation, like Aaron had said. What Youselli had not been prepared for was his own thrilling to the sight of McMahon seated on the fat man's knee like some ventriloquist's dummy, and wanting it to be the prelude to some terrible revenge by Aaron for years of shit-eating on McMahon's say-so.

Aaron cupped McMahon's cheek with his huge hand. 'In spite of everything that happened between us, I forgive you. I want you to call me Nuncle because you, dear boy, have always been the long-lost nephew I have been looking for. Say it, or Royal here will drop a brick on your balls.'

'Nuncle,' McMahon mumbled and Royal tee-heed.

'Louder,' said Aaron. He made McMahon repeat it over till McMahon was yelling like a marine in drill.

'Tell me something, nephew,' Aaron said, switching to sinister softness. 'Did you really want to fuck all those girls, or was it a way of covering up?'

McMahon hung his head. Youselli saw that his feet were dangling clear of the ground and he was pigeon-toed. 'I wanted to. I didn't care what I fucked.'

'But most of them were, I don't know, so boyish,' declared Aaron and they both giggled. 'What should we do about your friend?' murmured Aaron looking in Youselli's direction. 'He looks lonely all by himself. Shouldn't we accommodate him?'

'Oh no,' said McMahon. 'I don't think he's one for

joining in. He's scared of all those nasty old feelings banging around. He's Mr Macho. He probably stands to attention when he fucks.'

'We all stand to attention,' said Aaron with an arch look at Youselli who could feel his carotid artery jumping furiously.

'What you do is your business, don't make me part of it. I'm going now,' Youselli announced. 'Are you coming?'

Youselli failed to see the double entendre until the others laughed, and for the first time he understood something. Whether he liked it or not, and however much he pretended not to be, he was involved.

He spun round to face Royal. He knew he was drunk but his recklessness felt controlled. He no longer had to shut one eye to keep the room from swimming. The barrel of Royal's gun looked frighteningly clear. He recognized it as his own, which made him even madder.

'Shoot me, you little fuck, or get out of the way.'

As crazy as Royal was Youselli was betting he had never shot anyone. Royal huffed and puffed but his aim wavered and Youselli pushed the gun aside and brought his knee up to mash Royal's testicles, and heard his breath whistle out of him like an old singing kettle. As Royal jack-knifed Youselli adjusted to grab his ears and drive his knee up into his face, and felt justified satisfaction at the noise of breaking bone. Royal yelped and clamped one hand to his bloodied nose, the other cupping his bruised genitals. Youselli kicked him twice, hard across the knee, taking his feet out. Royal went down with a pleasing crash and

Youselli gave his elbow a sharp kick, knowing that the pain of that would hurt as much as the rest together.

'Not such a tough fucker now.'

Blood and snot were all over his face, but Royal wasn't broken. Dragging his good arm from between his legs he lifted his finger to his temple and made like Youselli was crazy. Before he was even aware, Youselli had drawn his foot back to kick Royal's head across the room. Seeing the fear in the man's eyes as he flinched in anticipation was enough. Youselli checked and leant down instead to retrieve his gun.

Seeing Royal's relief, Youselli jammed the barrel in his forehead and liked the way his eyes rolled back till the whites showed. He released the safety and pulled back the hammer. Royal's face was deathly pale and suddenly wet like someone had poured water over him. He was making little scrabbling noises in his throat between howls of pain.

Youselli was vaguely aware of McMahon shouting not to shoot and sounding scared. He started to squeeze the trigger and Royal slithered around trying to escape the gun. Youselli was glad to see he finally had Royal's full attention, along with everyone else's. He felt a loathing for all of them, for the humiliation they had made him endure, and pulled the trigger.

He put the shot in the floor about two inches from Royal's left ear and saw from his terror that he had truly believed his last moment had just been used up. McMahon was still on Aaron's knee, looking just as shocked.

Youselli said, 'You still want to play?'

Before McMahon could answer Aaron started

clapping, a slow ironic hand clap. 'Bravo, sir, what a show, what a round off to the evening!'

Youselli knew Aaron could see how close he had been.

'Come on,' Youselli said to McMahon. 'We're out of here.'

In spite of his shock, McMahon looked disappointed at the prospect of being deprived of his entertainment.

'Time for beddy-byes,' said Aaron shoving McMahon aside and standing. 'Well, delighted you could come. Poor Royal, reduced to such a sorry state for the sake of our amusement. I do believe the dear heart has pissed himself, but no doubt he'll be as right as rain in the morning.'

Royal gave a broken gurgle from the floor. Youselli congratulated himself. It would be a while before Royal heard anything properly again.

McMahon announced petulantly, 'I say when it's time to leave.'

'If you know what's good for you,' interrupted Aaron, 'you'll leave before your friend shoves your expensively capped teeth so far down your throat you'll have to stick a toothbrush up your ass to clean them. Your man's blood is up. It was probably the sight of you on my knee that did it. Now fuck off the two of you and leave me to tidy up, as usual. See,' he said, looking at Youselli, 'you're as bad as them with the mess you make.'

Youselli was aware of McMahon studying him as he drove. McMahon lounged in the front passenger seat, apparently unconcerned about the scene they had fled.

His casual indifference conveyed the impression that Youselli was the one who had behaved excessively, frog-marching him out of the house. In the car he had put on sunglasses and sat with a look of superior amusement until Youselli asked what the fuck he was looking at.

'You were very controlling back there,' McMahon offered. 'I think it was because you saw something you didn't like.'

Youselli tried to concentrate on the thrumming of the tires on macadam.

'I think,' went on McMahon, his voice needling, 'it was because you saw something about yourself. And you didn't like what you saw. So you beat the crap out of Mr Nasty instead, which was something he had coming for a long time, so congratulations.'

Youselli's knuckles were white from gripping the wheel. Stopping was the obvious thing to do but that did not strike him as an option. It seemed more important to put miles between him and Aaron. From the way the road kept bending when it should have been straight and the white lines kept jumping, he knew he was still way too drunk to drive, and would probably end up smashing them into a tree. His brain told him to stop, but his body refused and the speedometer kept rising. McMahon's drone was a further provocation, and in the split second before he turned the wheel he could not tell if it was the safe ending he wanted or the crash. Ten, fifteen seconds, they could both be dead. He wondered if anything specific made him turn the wheel. In his mind's eye he saw a deer standing petrified in his headlamps.

Outside blackness hurtled past, with a splash of fir trees lit by the car lights, and McMahon's voice rose to a scream.

The car slewed off the road and in what felt like an eternity Youselli tried to decide between flooring the brake and the gas. His reflexes chose for him and his foot clumsily stabbed the brake in time, he thought, to pull up short of the verge. He was wrong. They were still travelling fast when they hit it. McMahon pitched forward and his head cracked against the windscreen. The car banged around, threatened to roll then came to a halt short of the line of trees. Youselli sat behind the wheel calmly feeling that it was natural for them to have ended up there. McMahon was rubbing his head. He did not seem badly hurt because he was already starting to complain.

'Should have worn your belt,' mumbled Youselli.

He got out. His foot jarred on a rock as he hit the ground. He lurched a few feet and stuck his fingers down his throat, dry heaved a couple of times then vomited a splashy torrent of liquid that smelled sourly of alcohol. He was ashamed at the thought of being watched while he emptied himself by the roadside, but even that was not enough to dampen the mean streak of exhilaration he still felt at the pain inflicted on Royal after hours of humiliation. When he was done he stared up at the night. The bad weather had gone. Stars shone in a cold sky. He took them for a good sign, a change of fortune. He heard McMahon asking if he was all right. He wondered about Leah. It was the same sky for her. He hoped she was for real.

McMahon had got out and was inspecting the car like it was some piece of nocturnal art he had happened across.

'Is it okay?' he asked. 'We're not going to be stuck here or anything?'

He didn't sound unduly alarmed at the prospect.

'We'll be okay,' said Youselli, checking he hadn't ripped the tires. 'Is your head okay?'

McMahon nodded. Youselli could see a bruise already starting to form.

They got back in, their mood now one of wary intimacy. Youselli turned the ignition. He didn't remember turning the engine off and realized McMahon must have.

'I'm sorry,' said McMahon. 'I can't help with the driving.'

It was the first time Youselli could remember him volunteering anything. The thought touched him and McMahon asked why he was smiling. Youselli told him and McMahon seemed amused.

They drove in silence. Youselli's head felt clearer. He thought about the crash. Maybe it had been to do with his fear of the violence in himself, and the realization that the greatest threat to his safety was himself. Maybe he had always been the type to get drawn in deeper, unlike McMahon who knew when to walk away.

'What were you worried about back there?' asked McMahon, voicing his thoughts. 'That you would like what you saw?'

Youselli suddenly felt soiled by his association with McMahon.

'Did you think I was going to let Aaron stick his dick in me, or I was going to wank him off?'

'I have no opinion,' Youselli said awkwardly. 'I didn't like what was happening generally, and didn't like that asshole having my gun.'

'You didn't like being unmanned,' said McMahon archly. 'Hey, whatever picture you have in your head is wrong. Aaron's a broken old man. I would have sat on his knee a while, we would have reminisced about the good old days, he would have had a good cry, then got out his china.'

'Come on, you were sitting on the guy's knee.'

'I thought you didn't have an opinion about it,' McMahon replied coolly. 'I don't make a habit of it, but it's good sometimes to behave out of character, to experience some erasure, break down the old ego. Go with the flow. What's the worst you're going to feel after? Embarrassed, ashamed? What's wrong with a little shame every now and then? Plus it made an old man happy.'

'It's wrong.'

'Says who? You don't like it, you can always leave. But I didn't see you turn away, till the end. You were right in there, front row, eyes wide open.'

Youselli's jaw clenched and McMahon said, 'Hey, relax. This is between us.'

They drove in silence until McMahon said, 'Do you have any idea how bored I am in here?' He tapped his head.

'Why? You got everything.'

'Exactly.'

'I wish I was bored like that.'

'You want to be famous?'

'If it means going first class and having the *maître d'* kiss your ass.'

'You would soon grow bored of it, believe me. I'm going to impart the total of my wisdom to you. Fame is a condition, it gives you power up to a point, but show business doesn't give you real power — like politics. That's why entertainers create a retinue. So you get to tyrannize your hairdresser, big deal. What fame does is make you a blank slate for people to scribble their fantasies on. But I believe there is a condition in all this. I believe there will always be — in some shape or form — a trace of that person's fantasy already existing in me, so they maybe see something in me that I had not seen in myself. What would you do when confronted with this fantasy? Deny it or accept it?'

'I don't believe in being controlled by other people's fantasies.'

'Maybe it's only by obliterating the ego you find out who you are.'

'Yeah, but what if someone believed you to be their victim, or that you were meant to kill them?'

'Kismet. If it's going to happen it's going to happen. But if I am forewarned then I will take precautions to avoid it, that's only common sense. I have no real interest in getting shot in the head by some scruffy kid. Why do you think I hire you? To stop me going too far.'

Maybe he was serious, Youselli couldn't tell.

'You should have told me she shot herself.'

'You had to find out for yourself. You were the

detective. I could not tell you because we all made a promise never to talk about it.'

Youselli shook his head at what he had got himself into. 'Unbelievable.'

'It's true,' said McMahon defensively.

'Do you believe what Aaron said?'

'I never believe Aaron, that's why I hesitated to see him in the first place. There have been times when I could have sworn on my mother's grave he was telling the truth when he wasn't.'

'Do you really believe there is any way she is not dead?'

McMahon didn't answer and Youselli sensed a confusion rather than just another evasion.

'I don't know what's going on,' he said eventually. 'I wish I did. I lie awake nights turning the whole thing over in my mind, driving myself crazy wishing it was her.'

'So you can be young again?'

'There's that, and redemption maybe. Maybe she was the point where my life forked. Maybe I never laid her to rest and if there was some way of doing that it would be okay again.'

'What do you think happened with the others after you left?'

'I left partly because of the others. Maybe they performed one of Blackledge's ceremonies.'

'Ceremonies?' McMahon shrugged, leaving Youselli to say it for him. 'You mean some black magic shit?'

'Ridiculous, I know.'

Youselli sensed a whole other dimension sliding into

place, then he decided to laugh it off. 'You got to be kidding.'

'Blackledge took it seriously, still does for all I know.'

'What, you sat around the table holding hands?'

'I didn't say I did. Blackledge was on a big power trip. People like Astrid were happy to go along, whispering their secrets and making like they knew stuff you didn't.'

'Next you will be telling me they have been conjuring this whole thing up.' He felt good, still alive, driving through the night, teasing McMahon. 'Are we talking about the old resurrection shuffle here, that old black magic?' McMahon was not happy with his joking. 'You don't go along with any of that shit, do you?'

'Of course not, but that doesn't mean I'm not superstitious.'

'You said you weren't.'

'When?'

'About your apartment.'

'I was lying. I bought the place because I was superstitious.'

'Excuse me?'

'The old saying that lightning never strikes twice.' He gave an embarrassed laugh and Youselli was touched by his vulnerability. 'Anyway, we did all promise never to talk about what happened, so maybe I'm bringing bad luck mentioning it.'

'Bad luck happens, it's not fixed.'

'Remember I was talking about being a projection

of other people's fantasies. Well, the thing about her, it feels almost like it's the other way round. That she is a projection of separate and collective fantasies. And you're right.'

'About what?'

'I am powerless in too many ways. Other people fetch for me too much. This stuff with Leah I'm always left feeling there is nothing I can do to respond. I'm always waiting on somebody else's answer. And I'll tell you something else. Famous people are of little interest by themselves. What is interesting is the effect they have. Maybe I am nothing beyond how I am perceived by others. The same with her. The big attraction is I feel exactly that way about her. Maybe what she's doing to us is more interesting than who she is. It makes you wonder.'

Somewhere under the same sky, thought Youselli.

CHAPTER TWENTY-TWO

Los Angeles

—Often I see myself like I am someone else in a movie. Interior. Supermarket. Dusk. Leah guides her trolley down the aisles of Safeway, shopping for one, past the bright lit deep-freeze trenches. Packed in the lower ice is where they bury the bodies, she knows. Outside darkness falls on a movie-town sky. This image is always an evening one, after the heat of the day and before the night's promise is lost, when you can still see but start to switch on the lights.

My picture of you is always later, pure night, in another time zone, snow falling, you watching from an unlit window in a big house, while the security cameras scan the empty grounds of your mansion and your soul.

At the check-out Leah looks away from the candy racks, placed there for the temptation, and stares at the big store-front window, noting how the fluorescent reflections of the interior of the not-full supermarket bleed into the shadows of the palms outside and highway lights beyond.

You don't know it, you are waiting for me. I have this bad dream image of you turning – it is outside now, city outside, but I am not sure if you have come to me, or me to you. It is a winter city. The pool of blood on the sidewalk, a black halo, surrounds your head and slide-away eyes. One hand on your chest tries to feel the last flutterings of your heart. I don't know where I got the gun. I want to get in close, smell and touch you when it happens. This is the dream talking and it is still the dream when I say I guess bad Leah is writing this.

PART II

CHAPTER ONE

Everything looks far away – buildings, people, feelings. I don't remember when anything last touched me.

To look at me today, as I make my way through the terminal – sober suited, short hair – you would not guess what I do for a living, how once I made all the little girls squeal. These days I hide behind my irony, safe but insecure, knowing what lies behind stellar burn-out – the black hole of deep space. Once I believed I understood fame's bright power, that it was mine to command. Like the culture of which I was an image, I stood at the fateful crossroads where primitive mythology and technology meet, where paranoia makes connections beyond the normal. I no longer remember if my fame is real: the cabin crew shows no signs of recognition; I travel incognito, fly business. I entertain fantasies of disappearing (as I am doing now) and beyond that lurks a more powerful dream, barely acknowledged, of going past the vanishing to leave a permanent trace. Beyond celebrity. Beyond the vapour trail of ordinary fame. Beyond the cover of a magazine. Common fame is never enough. The dream is immortality. Perhaps by some collision of accident, talent and alchemy, carnal fame will translate into something mythical and immutable. I dream of projecting myself into the stratosphere, a rocket man on his lonely journey to becoming a fixed point. Like Elvis. Marlon Brando, Pocahontas and me. A Sun King. Dream on.

Now I know there is something even more fascinating than fame: the terror of dreams come true. Has she come back for me?

I arrived at LAX unmet, secure in the knowledge that not a soul knew where I was. I had my regular room booked and the hotel sent a car.

Till now I always had someone take care of the between spaces, getting from the hotel to the airport, negotiating from the terminal entrance to the departure gate. For the first time in as long as I can remember I did it myself – fixed my ticket, packed my bag, badly, and made the doorman flag a cab. I passed through as invisible as I had once been conspicuous, blending in where I had once stood out. There are rules for dealing with fans, told me by a veteran Hollywood actress: 'Walk fast. Don't stop and shake hands. You touch them, they don't touch you.' I am familiar with the rules. You do not stop. ('Hey, Mr Lennon!') One concert I got caught between the stage door and the waiting car, which was not where it should have been, and the crowd tore into me with what sounded like a single, high-pitched ululation as I went down under a wave of bodies, and chunks of hair were torn from my head and my clothes ripped. It was without question the most terrifying experience of my life, and yet the core of me exulted in it because I was its cause. I can still hear the exhilarating thwack of the cops' riot sticks on bone and for the first time I understood the obsession for going all the way.

'I used to think some behaviour – the seriously bad behaviour,' she wrote in her last letter, 'was outside the realm of normal experience, like the difference between jumping off the side of the pool (normal behaviour) and diving off a twelve-meter board (not normal). It is not. It is no more difficult than walking through a door. Night after night you sit watching some house. Part of you can explain why you are doing it. You don't have any choice. At the same time, part of you is saying this is not me.'

I have always felt I have been watching my own life in the same way.

'There is the excitement too,' she wrote, 'even when everything is going horribly wrong or you feel trapped in the vice of this obsession.'

Yes. It eliminates the emptiness. In fact, it doesn't. She will realize that in the end. It only creates another vacuum, but the thing about all of it – the sitting, the waiting – is the hope.

Before leaving for Europe Anjelica knew her marriage was in effect over. The ties were no longer emotional but the more complicated and binding ones of finance. What McMahon did not know – because she had not told him – was that the European trip was an act of dangerous extravagance on her part because there was nothing like the money there had been, owing to reversals on the Tokyo stock market, plus the failure of certain key crops. For the first time since she had turned his fortune around, Anjelica was seriously concerned she might not be able to repair the damage because their money had contracted the financial equivalent of cancer.

Her real problem was a lack of someone to talk to. McMahon, once her confidant, had been too long sealed in his own vacuum. Her consorts were nothing more than social and sexual decoration. Blackledge was more complicated but she was on her guard with him because he was a predator.

In Zurich she was hit by depression. Blackledge had disappeared to Munich, mysteriously and with as little warning as the arrival of the black mood that had left her incapable of getting out of bed. She began to rethink her trip in terms of an abdication of responsibility. Previously she had justified it as a way of putting distance between herself and McMahon, and her dalliance with Blackledge a reinforcement of that. The truth was she was letting things slide. The deals she had set up for him needed her supervision and she was neglecting them. The publishing contract had been a way of generating cash, but she suspected she had promised more than he would deliver. He would procrastinate, and she would not be tough enough to insist because of her unease about his past.

For her the past was something to keep firmly in the dark. The lesson had been absorbed early from her parents whose blanked-out background had dominated her childhood like some sub-terrain of uncharted space. They had settled in the United States from Germany shortly before her birth. Her mother only ever talked about the war in terms of it being too terrible to discuss. As to the question of what her father had done, her mother had snapped, 'The past is past and there's no point digging it up,' then added, more considerately, 'Your father has suffered terribly. The best you can do is be a good girl.'

She did not want to be a good girl. In adolescence she developed a complicated erotic fixation on her father. How innocuous war criminals looked, she had thought, and how easily her self-effacing father would slide into that gallery. She didn't even know what part of Germany he was from, East or West. All she knew was the family name had been Weiss and now it was White.

Towards the end of the second day of her depression she had got up and hired a car via the hotel desk and driven the short distance to Germany. She crossed the border and drove several miles before pulling to the side of the road. For the first time in her life she realized she wanted more and wondered about the child she had never had. She put the thought away, dismissing it as ridiculous, turned round and drove back. Dusk was falling and the headlights of the approaching cars splashed her face as she tried to concentrate on the road.

Edith was out of her depth, not something she let happen very often. Youselli had been passing, he had said, to check she had been okay since the break-in.

Edith had nodded uncertainly. It crossed her mind he was there to discuss something personal, but she was wrong.

'You're a good-looking woman,' he announced, leaving Edith dumbfounded. Unless she was mistaken he was flirting. It left her flattered in spite of herself. Her protest that she was old enough to be his mother sounded perfunctory.

'I thought that was the point,' he said, making a joke of it. 'You should get out more.'

He leaned forward, staring. 'We both do the same job. Which is to make people talk. With you, I'm thinking, here's this woman and I get the feeling she doesn't get too many sentences with question marks. You do all the asking, is what I am saying. Am I right?'

'Lieutenant, I constantly ask questions of myself.'

'Hey, I'm only asking.'

'Asking what, precisely?'

'That's a favourite word of yours, precisely.'

'Asking what?'

'About you.'

He stood up and roamed the room. Edith had to remind herself of her age.

'Like why you never married?'

'Marriage isn't the answer to everything.'

Youselli paused and cocked his head. 'True. How long is it since you, you know?'

'I would say it's none of your business.'

Youselli itched his nose. 'That's not what I was going to ask, but since you bring it up.'

'I would still say it's none of your business.'

'I was going to say how long since you went out for

an evening?' She didn't grace him with an answer. 'What are you doing Saturday?'

Edith looked blank. She tried to guess his age. Thirty-five, thirty-six. There was a weight about him, a gravity that made him seem older. She shrugged, bewildered. Saturday always was a difficult night.

'Escalope, profiteroles and a bottle of Chianti. Then I drive you home.'

'Why would you want to take me out to dinner?'

Youselli laughed. 'I didn't say I was paying. We go Dutch then you don't have to worry I'm expecting anything back.'

'I don't think—'

'You got something better to do?'

'I'm more than used to my own company.'

'I'm not. Saturdays I stay in and drink too much, watch some shit on the TV, or go out and eat by myself. All I'm asking is, you want to come along?'

Edith saw herself sitting alone with her Saturday dinner on a tray, pretending the slow hours of darkness were no different from the rest.

'Seven o'clock,' she said.

CHAPTER TWO

Exploiting the zeitgeist, Mickey called it when I had found him grinning in some dressing room, ramming his shameless dick into another bent-over crack. A lot of dick got sucked back then and none of us read the small print. We thought of ourselves as sex-charged conductors able to transform thousands of pulsating libidos into one mass that could be teased to the edge of erotic terror. Sure we got to take our pick: the roar of the crowd reduced afterwards to a single squirming body, that night's reward. In Bangkok we ate the local pussy. We let the genie out of the bottle.

A local publicist named Dore, pronounced Doray, fixed me with talk radio and daytime television hosted by young presenters with too-white smiles and eyes that danced to some higher control. One show I was put next to an actor with halitosis who had once died heroically in a Peckinpah Western. The rest of the time I took to drinking in a bar with a green door and steps down into a cool dark room where nobody bothered you.

'Line two, we got a Leah,' the producer in my headset said, and my throat went dry as the deejay asked, 'Hi there, is this Leah?'

'Yes,' she said. It wasn't. Nor were any of the others. I had said I was in Los Angeles, staying where I normally stayed, and looking for a Leah I once knew. Ricky Montello was the deejay and afterwards I remembered nothing about him except his name and a dumb sentence of his: 'And what can we do for you this sunny funny day, Leah?'

In between I waited in the room for her call, and counted the hours and the days. The greater the fame, the greater the insecurity. They never tell you that.

What I need is a ghost. I have no interest in telling my story. Life was little more than itineraries and tour-date T-shirts. We did not lead narrative lives. We led ones of tired old songs rehashed, with squabbles over what new ones to include, of suitcases packed and unpacked, excessive air miles, identical hotel rooms, wake-up calls, altercations with desk clerks, ticket trouble, sleeping the wrong hours, irregular meals, mislaid backstage passes, bad security, too much random sex too quickly forgotten, and a lot of waiting.

When she writes about Lazarus she writes about me. I like the idea of a relationship with a dead person. In her letters I can read her soul. The people I walk among are as good as dead, as am I. Maybe she can save me from myself. Maybe we can bring each other back. I like the idea of a second chance.

It seems so long since any of it was real, since the act took over. You get so used to being watched you end up watching yourself like you were someone else. The hardest sentence I can write is: I am no longer as famous as I used to be.

Which is worse, the paranoia of being recognized or the paranoia of not being recognized?

We crossed so many borders and moved through so many time zones it was easy to put space between you and anything you wanted. Waiting was always the hard part. We were always waiting.

In answer to a prayer, the phone rang.

Edith was in the middle of changing again when the phone went, and she swore, at her indecision rather than the interruption. She hoped it would be to cancel dinner and end her misery. But it was Susan calling for the first time since vanishing. Phoning at the wrong moment, thought Edith, unpleasantly. Now was not the time for catching up. Listening to Susan apologize for not having been in touch made Edith see how she had resented her silence, whatever the relief she felt at her being safe and well. Edith was hoping that Susan was phoning from the airport to say she was coming home, but she was still in Los Angeles.

Edith asked weakly why Susan had left her job.

'That asshole producer kept harassing me.' She spoke with a vehemence Edith had not heard before. The blunt language was a shock too. Susan rarely swore.

'Are you all right?'

'The guy made a pass, it was no big deal.'

Susan's apparent reason for staying in Los Angeles was the chance of another film. That in itself wasn't enough to keep her there, Edith thought. Susan, usually so scrupulous at keeping her informed, had to be hiding something.

Edith asked where she was staying and Susan answered she was living with a man she had met on the previous film. Edith was thrown by how casually Susan dropped this. It was clear she was talking about more than accommodation sharing, but she volunteered no further details and Edith was left feeling it would be prying to ask more.

'I have to go out,' Edith said, wishing she could start the call over.

'Oh, I'm sorry, it's not a good time,' said Susan in that sing-song way she used to cover any perceived slight. 'I hope it's something interesting.'

Edith could hardly tell her she was going for dinner with Youselli, and lying made her feel worse.

'I dare say I'm just an old grump,' she concluded, relenting. 'I miss you and I'm disappointed I won't see you.'

'Come and visit.'

'How long are you going to be there?' she asked carefully.

'Oh, Mom, don't make me feel bad.'

'What about the house?'

Edith was appalled by her determination to sabotage her daughter's cheerfulness.

'I don't want to think about that right now,' said Susan quickly. 'Don't you want to know who he is?'

As if that made any difference, thought Edith, at a loss to identify her bitterness. She had never begrudged her daughter's happiness before.

★

'Hi,' she said. 'I heard the show.'

Hers was a teasing voice, knowing even, not one I recognized at once, but from her tone I felt we had talked before.

'You sound so right,' I said, feeling she would understand.

'What an asshole that deejay was.'

'I hoped you weren't listening.'

'The radio was on scan.'

There was nothing difficult about it: it was like finding the perfect dancing partner. We talked, about that afternoon and the TV shows I had done and how bad it had been doing them.

'What are you doing in Los Angeles?' she asked and for the first time there was a tension in her voice.

'I came to find you.' She was silent. 'Did I say the wrong thing?'

She said nothing again. The noise of traffic at her end grew louder and I realized she had walked away without hanging up.

After what felt like half a lifetime she called back with no explanation for quitting the previous call. She sounded relaxed. Our conversation was a natural everyday thing until I said I wanted to see her.

'I'm not ready yet.' She sounded defensive.

'Are you close by?'

'Why did you come to Los Angeles?' she asked. 'Besides wanting to see me.'

'It seems crazy to come so far and not to meet.' There was another silence. 'I have been thinking a lot about someone I used to know. I think you might be that person.'

With her silence I thought she had walked away again.

'I want to come over,' she said finally.

'Wait,' I said, nervous she was dangerous after all, but she had gone already.

'I brought flowers.' Youselli held up an innocent-looking bunch with no romantic connotations, Edith was pleased to note. 'A long time since I seen flowers at your place.'

He was wearing a suit and a pressed shirt with no tie. Edith was distracted by Susan's call. She still hadn't decided what to wear and didn't have time to change again. She took the flowers through to the kitchen to put them in water. Realizing she had probably taken them gracelessly, she called out, 'They're nice. Thank you. I'll cut the stems later.'

She apologized for not being ready and retreated to apply a little make-up. The suit she had tried lay on the bed. She had phoned him twice to cancel but there had been no answer.

When she returned to the hall he asked, 'What's the duck for?'

'I beg your pardon?'

He was referring to a child's yellow rubber duck sitting on the hall table.

'Oh that! It's a testament to my lack of housekeeping skills. It belongs – belonged I should say – to my daughter and has been there so long that leaving it has become a superstition, I suppose. I think you're the first person to mention it.'

He helped her with her raincoat and opened the car door for her. She was struck by his solicitousness.

'I appreciate you coming out,' Youselli said.

She decided he probably wanted to use the evening to talk about his failed marriage. She was wrong. They talked about her. Maybe the wine and the aperitif, served at the patron's insistence, had loosened her tongue. She told him what she could remember about Berlin and the large apartment near a busy thoroughfare, close to her father's shop. The apartment had been so big it had a double front door. 'It was painted brown and we must have lived high up because I remember an elevator with a grille. There was a large tiled stove in one of the living rooms and from the window you could see the trams in the big street at the end of the road.'

She was describing a world so remote to him that it must have sounded like something out of a nineteenth-century novel. 'It was a long time ago,' she concluded lamely.

He sensed her embarrassment. 'My grandaddy used to sit me on his knee and tell me about Dublin.'

Edith was surprised. 'I always thought you were Italian.'

'Italian-Irish, can you believe. The story is my great-grandparents were supposed to go all the way to America but ended up in Dublin. Did you ever go there?' Edith shook her head. 'You do, ask if people remember Youselli's ice cream. There was a famous parlour by that name on O'Connell Street.'

The conversation fell into a lull, brought about by the arrival of a huge plate of food Edith could not possibly finish. They had a corner table away from other diners. Nobody stared so perhaps they didn't make such an odd couple; almost never going out had made her self-conscious. She commanded her own domestic space effortlessly but outside felt cut off and ill-at-ease.

'Is it good?' asked Youselli of her choice. Her approval seemed important for some reason. Edith tried to decipher the man opposite her and what he wanted of her. She had scrupulously avoided questioning her own motives. Youselli was obviously a man of hard physical appetites. She sensed they perplexed him. It probably shocked him to find her attractive. But that would interest him too. He was almost certainly drawn to the forbidden, and what could be more outrageous than wanting a woman society said was too old to desire.

'Thirteen years is the answer to your earlier question,' she said and waited for the laugh of disbelief that didn't come. He stopped eating and looked serious.

'I couldn't do that. I just couldn't. A week goes by, I get all wound up. I get no release I go crazy. Maybe it's the job. Too many dead people. I need something to—' He shrugged. 'You know what I mean.'

'You itch, you have to scratch.'

Youselli smiled. His face lit up. 'Precisely.'

They both laughed.

'Don't you itch sometimes?' he asked.

Edith considered this. They were grown up, after all.

'I masturbate.'

'It's not the same,' he said.

'You're young. You still have choices.'

He put down his knife and fork. 'You always got a choice.'

Edith shook her head and was silent a long time.

'My father wore pince-nez glasses and a stiff white collar and my mother wore a fur coat in the daytime. In the end they had no choice.' Youselli nodded. 'I was sent to stay with relatives in England being the youngest. I still don't understand how my father got me out. I suppose he was able to travel long after most Jews because so much of the diamond business was in Amsterdam. I remember being on a train with him and on a boat without him. I don't know who looked after me then and I still don't understand why I was sent when my sisters and brother were not. Maybe he could only afford to get me out. All I know is I believed I was the one being punished by being sent away. Perhaps I still feel that. Why did I deserve to survive?'

'So the family could carry on.'

'Maybe.' Edith stared at her unfinished plate. 'I think I'd like you to take me home now. It was very nice. I'm sorry I was such poor company. I had not intended to talk about these things.'

I have waited all my life. Waiting in hotels, waiting at airports, waiting to go on, waiting for a connection, waiting to get stoned, waiting to get laid.

Waiting for her I behaved like a kid on a date. I showered. I put on fresh clothes, decided it looked like I was trying too hard and settled on a clean shirt. I brushed my teeth and mouthwashed to get rid of the alcohol, and phoned the desk to say send her straight up. I wanted her to announce herself with a knock at the door not by phoning up. I wondered whether to shave. I had a beer to get rid of the mouthwash taste.

Time stretched and I started to feel I was waiting too long. Worry turned to impatience and it took the edge off the anticipation. Instead of nervously looking at the door I grew irritated, and started to feel she was making a fool of me.

She invited him in. If she had a choice, then she was making one now.

He put a record on while Edith made coffee. It was an old Sinatra album. From the kitchen she said, 'To me Sinatra was America more than anything else. After Germany and England there was an openness to his voice that was incredible.'

She came through with the coffee. Youselli was standing in the middle of the room. She put the tray down and as she straightened he was in front of her, hands out, palm up. She didn't see at first that he was inviting her to dance, and gave a small laugh of incredulity before accepting, more generously than she had taken his flowers.

He held her lightly, swaying to the music. She rested her head on his shoulder and felt young. There had been dances before America with clumsy English boys who'd pushed her round the floor trying both to disguise and reveal the stiffness in their trousers.

She didn't know if she should ask Youselli into the bedroom. Then he would see her earlier indecision in the suit she'd discarded on the bed.

'What are you thinking?' he said.

'That this is not right.'

'You're a good-looking woman, Edith. You've hidden yourself away too long.'

'I'm old.'

Youselli shrugged. 'The only question is, are you itching?'

Edith looked up at him. 'Yes.'

'Then I'm scratching.'

They laughed too much, and the moment was spoiled.

'I think you should go,' she said. 'I'm sorry.'

Youselli nodded in respect of her wish.

In the hall she said, 'I have something to say.'

'I know. You're going to tell me how much older you are and there's no point, and I'm going to say, So what? Let's do it anyway.'

There were no preliminaries. He kissed her standing, open mouthed, something Edith had not thought she would ever do again. She couldn't remember anyone kissing her like that, breathing so much desire into her, turning her giddy. Don't ask, she thought, do it. She dreaded the undressing and getting into bed. But again Youselli surprised her. Still kissing, he steered her in time to the music through to where she held her consultations and pushed her down on to her patients' couch. She lay there blinking uncertainly, aware only of him pulling at her skirt, then her underwear. She had a moment to register the night air cool on her skin then he was turning her on her front and she panicked, fearing what he might be about to do, until she realized with a shameful thrill that he was using his tongue and she moaned in spite of herself.

With the first shock of his touch she gripped the arm of the couch and asked herself: is this me? Gradually she relaxed and let herself float on his drift, making him do the work. She wanted him not to stop while wanting him to do more, which gave rise to the spoiling thought that he was using his tongue because he didn't physically desire her. He sensed her hesitation apparently because he drove deeper. His hand worked at her too and Edith gasped. When she came, with little warning, she was overtaken by the unfamiliarity of it and again cried out, knowing he was right. Feeling him make her come she didn't know how she had managed without.

She wanted to be left alone to enjoy the drowsiness settling over her, but he wasn't done. Turning her round, he kissed her mouth. Edith, who had almost forgotten the earlier sensation of their kissing, became aroused again. She was not a dried-up old woman after all; so shameless, she thought. It was like watching someone else as she unbuttoned his shirt, her hands roaming over his smooth, hairless chest, unzipping his pants. She glimpsed the flash of condom as he rolled it on, not sure she would have had the presence of mind to insist. Her excitement returned and she was surprised at her fluency as she grasped the shaft of his penis and guided him inside. In the past she had verged on the squeamish, perhaps because the few men she'd known had always been secretive about their bodies.

The phone went. Edith tensed. She felt a confusion of emotions listening to its shrill ring — guilt, then defiance as she determined to continue letting go.

'Leave it,' grunted Youselli.

The machine clicked on and there was Susan's voice. Youselli paused. 'Who's that?'

'My daughter.'

He levered himself on to his hands. He tilted his head listening to Susan apologize for earlier, smiling as he slid into Edith whose pleasure grew at the sight of him listening to Susan as he took her.

At some point I fell asleep waiting and woke up fumbling for the phone, heart jumping at the thought of her downstairs.

'I've been driving around,' she said. From the way she spoke it was evident she wasn't coming.

'You sound like you were asleep,' she said accusingly. Evening sun slanted through the window, bathing the room in a soft red glow.

'Peter did that,' she went on.

'Peter who?'

'Peter the Apostle.'

'Did what?'

'Fell asleep, in the garden of Gethsemane.'

'Am I meant to understand anything by that?'

'You can understand whatever you want.'

'I feel I am letting you down somehow.'

'I wasn't expecting you.'

'Are you saying I should not have come?'

When she spoke the hard edge that had been in her voice softened. 'Where are you now?'

'My room.'

'I know that!' She laughed. 'Where in your room, *caro*?'

'What did you call me?'

'*Caro*. It's Italian.'

'That's what she used to call me.'

'It's what *I* call you.'

'Wait a minute, do you realize what we are getting into here?'

'I know,' she said, sounding nonchalant.

'And if I said, you're supposed to be dead.'

She laughed a bright laugh. 'I would answer, I am definitely not.'

'And if I say, then you can't be who you say you are, what do you say?'

'I would say you are the one playing games. Trust me.'

'Tell me what you look like.'

She sighed. 'You know what I look like. Don't waste time.'

'This is hard for me, talking to someone I know is supposed to be—'

'I know. Tell me what happened.'

'You were there.'

'I want to hear it from you,' she said in a faraway voice.

'I don't want to talk about that now. It's incredible, you even sound like her.'

'This is not easy for me either. I want everything to

be right. I have laid my soul down on paper and that makes it hard to see you. I'm scared you will be disappointed.'

Because you will no longer be able to keep up the illusion, I thought. Then I saw there might be another reason.

'Are you scarred?'

'Scared of what?' She was very good.

'Scarred. You know, from the accident.'

She didn't even falter. 'Oh, you're worried I don't look the same. Well, I do.'

Please let it be her, I thought.

'I don't remember what happened,' she said, spacing each word for emphasis, making her frustration clear. I was learning that her mood could switch without warning, like in her letters. 'I have no recollection of what happened at the end.'

'You fell,' I said to test her reaction.

'Fell?' She sounded surprised. 'If you say so.'

'What is the last thing you do remember?'

'I don't know. My memory doesn't have any sense of time. I remember the orchard and sunny days, then it gets darker till I can't see any more, and there's a long blank.'

'Till when?'

'Till I started writing you I guess.'

'That's fifteen years! You must have some recollection of in between.'

'Maybe I was another person in that time, then something happened to – I don't know.' She searched around for what she was trying to say and gave a joyful whoop of laughter. 'To bring me back to my senses. And here I am. With you again.'

She was spookily good, really good, impossible to fault. The room seemed to get bigger like some invisible boundary was being crossed.

'How do you feel now?'

'I don't know.' She sounded surprisingly vehement. 'Tell me what happened,' she said, before quickly adding that maybe she did not really want to know.

'When do you leave?' She was sounding more composed.

'When I want. There's no hurry.'

I told her she had no reason to be afraid. I could hear only her near silent crying, then she said something I did not catch and hung up. It was not until a long time after, in the dead of night, that I figured, though could not be sure, that what she had said in her broken whisper was, 'I want you to give me back my life.'

Edith wandered around on unsteady legs listening to Youselli splashing water in the bathroom. Standing in the hall saying goodbye, he looked hard and focused, and loose at the same time. Edith studied him with something approaching awe. Her skirt still lay on the floor. She could not be bothered to put it back on to see him out. How insouciant, she thought.

Sounding vaguely ominous, Youselli said there remained only one thing left to do.

'What's that?'

'Move the duck.'

'Don't,' she blurted when he shifted the yellow rubber duck several inches. She took it as a sign of bad luck.

'Now you'll remember today as the day we moved the duck.' He gave her a smile she did not return, perhaps because he seemed so determined to extricate himself with no mention of what had just passed between them. After he had gone she found that, apart from a vague tingling sensation and a pleasant soreness, it was as though nothing had ever happened.

As it was still before midnight in Los Angeles, she decided to phone Susan, on the number left in her message. She lied, saying she had been out when Susan had called.

'Are you all right, mother?' Susan asked sharply.

Edith surprised herself by asking, 'Do you think it's wrong for me to have a sexual relationship with someone much younger?'

'What?' Susan dragged out the word and Edith tried to decide if this was a new mannerism.

'I think I'm being very foolish.'

'Tell me,' said Susan excitedly.

Edith did, more or less, leaving out Youselli's name, which only created more questions.

'It doesn't matter who,' said Edith defensively. She and Susan had never previously discussed her sexual needs.

'How long has it been going on?'

'Hardly at all.'

It occurred to Edith that without Susan's initial call she would not have given herself to Youselli. How twisted, she thought, the blames and resentments of blood relations. They had both led such solitary lives in recent years which no doubt made it harder to accept changes in each other.

Susan told Edith she was having an affair with a stuntman. Ever the practical mother – the spoiler, Edith thought, with a scoop of secret pleasure – she asked Susan what she was going to do next.

'Harry's getting a job on this film which he thinks he can get me on too.'

'What film?' She was still hoping Susan would come to her senses and return home.

'Some remake thing to do with angels.'

'Angels?'

Susan sounded amused. 'Yeah, those things with wings.'

'Be careful, Susan,' said Edith without knowing why.

CHAPTER THREE

Another letter was waiting at the Dakota. It provoked the strongest feeling of *déjà vu* in Anjelica. She was surprised to remember how casually she had treated the arrival of the first letter. The postmark on this latest was a week old, which told her roughly how long McMahon had been gone. She tried to ignore it. But then it was in her hands, with her having no recollection of tearing the envelope, only a lingering trace of dizziness, like she was in a high place about to fall.

—I am so sorry, you can't believe how sorry.
Forget everything I said, except that I love you and
we will be together, sooner than you think. I get
so frustrated with this Lazarus thing. My mind and
body are in a turmoil these days. Sometimes I want
to call and hear your voice. Writing gets so lonely.
I say things I don't mean. Sometimes it all gets
hopeless and I stop believing. In us and myself.
You know in your heart something is meant to
be but your mind says otherwise. I was looking at
the palms in the setting sun and it was this most
beautiful, incredible sunset, but all I could think
of was the rats hiding in the trees. Rats are taking

over Hollywood, which is a joke when you think
about it, and I think I know which is the superior
breed.

The angels of Los Angeles would make a good
title for something. Maybe for your next record.
Could you write a song about them? I knew
someone called Engel which is German for angel
and I was so jealous someone could be called that
for real. I thought of using it as my work name but
decided not to. I am serious when I say this place
is Babylon. It is a desert city just like all those ones
God destroyed. We know it'll destruct one of these
days. I know when. Yeah, the big shift but I'll be
long gone – a cabin in Colorado, maybe up in
Nova Scotia with you to keep me warm. I'm tired
of the heat. I want warmth. The loneliness of
waiting gets me down. I packed my bag last night,
I was really desperate to see you. Patience. I was
reading this book about why men and women are
different. Which we know anyway. It was dumb
but it told me one thing I was doing right. Love
letters. Letters are the way to keep a relationship
alive. So this is another love letter to you. I know
it's hard for you to write but I wish you would.

Later in the day, which was spent in a fruitless search
for McMahon, Anjelica experienced a frisson – of fear
or pleasurable excitement, she wasn't sure – when she
realized whose voice the letter reminded her of. Her
own. It was like an uncontrolled version of the one
that ran continuously in her head, for her ears only. It

drew her back to reread the letter countless times
during the course of the day. She was curious to know
how it would feel to let go so completely. She felt
envious of this woman's obsession and wondered what
she was missing. Leah was tapping into some void in
their lives. Anjelica could imagine the thrill of writing
this stuff. The recognition spooked and excited her.

CHAPTER FOUR

On the Sunday night I moved to a chalet, making sure the desk would reroute calls.

'Why did you move?' she asked.

'You'd like it here, it's a better room.'

'I don't want this to end,' she said in a small voice.

'What to end?'

'Like it is now.'

Night and day bled together, marked by her calls, often several in the space of an hour. She kept them short like she was worried someone might be trying to trace her.

She remembered France a lot better than I did, up to a point, after which she had no recall. She brought our affair vividly back to life. It had been languid and hungry at the same time, symbolized by the vampire-like fang of her canine molar lazily nipping my flesh then growing greedier. She reminded me how I had told her I could not get enough of her tight little slit, and how carnal she was.

'Was I the best?' she asked.

'Always.' I laughed but meant it. We grew comfortable talking about the past, her reminding me of little things I had forgotten. Between calls I worked on a song, something I had not done since Mickey's death. Past and future receded and all that mattered was the now and the connection, plus the delight of her voice – timbre, pitch, inflection – the way she used words, and how her laugh ambushed me and gave me that rarest feeling of it all clicking into place.

'What's the song about?' she asked.

'Two people.'

'Are they in love?'

'I think they're falling in love.'

'Did you love me in France?'

'I see now I did. France was too complicated.'

'Remember how we used to fuck outside at Mickey's in the hammock, hidden in the tall grass.'

The memory of it hit me hard.

'Maybe we should find an orchard to meet in, instead of some hotel room. Would you like that?' she went on, her voice very close. 'Or maybe go back to France, the two of us.'

I said if that was what she wanted. She did not answer and asked instead, 'Did you know how confused I was?'

'We were not good people to be around.'

It sounded again like she was crying as well as laughing. 'Remember how insecure I was about my breasts.' I had forgotten that too. 'Compared to Mom's. And what did you say?'

'What did I say?'

'"Yours don't sag."'

'I said that!' We both laughed, a step closer.

'Say it to me,' she said.

'I love you.' There was a long silence, then she whispered thank you and hung up.

Once or twice it crossed my mind that the illusion we were cherishing was a dangerous one.

She made me go over how it had been my idea to approach Astrid about France because I knew she was giving Mickey a hard time about taking a babysitter. This was so we could carry on seeing each other in secret because of Donna. In those days you always had a regular old lady because the thing you were most scared of was being alone. How casually we arranged other people's lives.

'You did like me?' she asked. 'More than just a fuck.'

'I liked being with you. I should have had more faith in us.'

'It must have been hard with all those girls throwing themselves at you. I remember Mickey saying how easy it was to wipe his dick on different girls.'

Our calls edged imperceptibly closer to the fateful day of the accident.

'We're going to have to go back in the room,' she said. 'I need you to tell me what happened.'

She sounded definite, but then grew scared as though revisiting the past would make it happen over again. I told her I was there to help her.

'What, like last time?' There was a sneer in her voice. It was the first time she had been openly nasty and she apologized straight away, afraid I might hang up. 'Please, don't go. I am so sorry. It's because I don't want to go back in the room.'

So it went, ducking and diving, circling closer and pulling away, she growing more impatient and scared, and aggressive with it.

'When are you going to tell me what happened?' she would ask, then accuse me of not saying how I had felt. 'Maybe you felt nothing because you were relieved. "Oh, well, she won't be coming back."'

'Of course I felt bad.' It came out sounding lame.

'Hey.' Her voice was sharp. 'So far we have been skating on the surface. We are going to have to go deep down on this if we want to make the other side.'

It sounded vaguely ominous. 'The other side?'

'The future. Us.'

'Is that a bright future?'

'That depends on what happens between us.'

I put my next question carefully. 'So there is a battle being waged here?'

'You know there is.' She said it with real feeling.

'Who are you?' I asked, knowing she would not answer.

'Your dream come true,' she said quickly, teasing her way past the question. 'You better believe it. You want it enough you can have it, but you got to want it. We have to move out of that dark room into a brand new morning.'

She sounded artificially bright, like she was selling a TV product. With her mood switches it could be like talking to different people in the same conversation. Her voice would subtly alter too.

I made her a deal, that I would talk about what had happened if she came to me.

'Uh, okay,' she said, like we were discussing the blandest of dates. 'Soon.'

I felt the shiver go down my spine. Was she the angel of death after all? So far the experience of talking to her had been like the light scary feeling you get fooling round with the Ouija board. But now it seemed we were entering a more troubled area, one with a sense of infinite possibility, a vast space beyond the immediate membrane. Crossing a line beyond which there were no more left to cross and through which there was no way back. My surroundings fell away until I was barely conscious of the room or of anything outside us and the telephone line. She began to spook me with her memories of France, until there was no possibility of it being anyone except her. We were moving beyond the game, back to where it had all started.

'I didn't want to fuck Mickey,' she said, sounding upset. Mickey had been besotted but she had not been interested, she said, until I rejected her. After Donna had gone she wanted to move in with me and bring Paolo. I had said no, thinking I was making an effort to stand on my own feet for once.

'Is that how you saw it?' she asked, and I had a flash of how whiny and accusatory she had been, how ridiculously young.

'You know what I wanted? I wanted you to save me from the malfate.' She was crying now. 'You're the only one who can undo the malfate.'

She did not say how and moved on to bad memories of being fucked by Mickey with Astrid joining in and how lost she became in their maze, unlike with us when it had always been clear, which was true. It had been. There had been no games between us. For all the air of malignant intrigue that had hung around us that hot summer we had been strangely uncorrupted, not separately but together. Going over old ground made me realize the extent of that lost love, denied since. The abiding memory is of her coming to me through the tall grass in a white dress that dazzled in the sun, carrying her straw hat so she could feel the heat of the afternoon. Maybe it was her childish innocence, purity even, and her refusal to play games with me that broke her. Once I had dumped her so casually and unthinkingly she tarnished fast.

'Do you remember watching me with Alex?' she asked, reminding me of an incident I had no wish to remember. 'Did you tell Alex to move on me and take some of the heat off you? I always wanted to ask you that.'

'Absolutely not. Why did you take him to *our* place?' The aggressive question was because I had been relieved at the time by Blackledge's move though I had not specified it.

'I wanted to hurt you for what you had done to me,' she said, her voice weird and sing-songy, and for a moment I saw that we were walking close to the edge of the black pit, and had been all along. I knew where her siren lure could lead us, how the hand offered in forgiveness could disguise another that held the weapon.

She knew about the platform in the trees. She had found it too. Until then I had no idea if the others had been aware of its existence because I never told anyone. It was a space about eight feet square, around twelve or fifteen feet high and reached by a ladder. I used to go there when I wanted to be alone. Blackledge was doing some filming and sniffing around, and from up there in the tree I watched the two of them cross the meadow into the orchard and over towards the hammock. I could tell that this was their first time. I watched Blackledge, solicitous at first, worm his way inside her, then proceed to fuck her every which way as I had done, even when she resisted. It was crude possession, and possession was power. In his cruel calculations I saw the extent of my own degradation and decided to stop being the person I had become. I resolved to change, and I was going to. I was. But you can't rearrange reality.

But. Cut to so many years later. Maybe you can. I told her I needed to see her. I wanted to tell her what happened in the room.

There was a long, long silence, as long as the moment when it had all turned around, after the time and distance from the bullet leaving its housing and point of impact.

'If I come,' she said slowly, stopped and started again. '*When* I come, you know we can't be sure how it is going to be.'

I knew what she meant but made her spell it out.

'When you have been hurt as bad as I have,' she began and faltered.

'You get angry, I know,' I assured her. 'I read the

205

letters. We are going to work on that anger, take that anger away.'

I was on the edge of laughing I felt so confident that I could defuse her. Expose her, the sneaky, calculating and unbelieving part of me was thinking. Did she guess there were two of me like there were two of her? She could come as love or she could come as destruction.

'I am talking to my angels,' she said. 'They are telling me I am wrong to trust you.'

Oh fuck, baby, I thought, and realized how crazy we both were.

'I love you,' I said. 'I need you. I need to tell you what happened.'

There was another long silence.

'Don't chicken out on me now,' I tried making a joke of something that was no longer funny. But she was gone. There was only the empty silence of the unhung-up phone and whatever space she had been in. Far away, another life away, I remembered saying to the cop, you don't like it you can always leave. He had not. All I had to do was walk out the door, be gone when she came. I waited. Some things you have to know.

Early one bright sunny morning she agreed to come, after we had talked on and off through the night. I could picture the cleaners walking past the window, at the start of their rounds, housecoats unnaturally white against the shrubbery, the 'Do Not Disturb' sign hung on the door.

This time I was certain she would come. After fifteen minutes I found myself incapable of anything except listening for her footsteps. After twenty-five, time started to drag. I stared at the phone willing it to ring, then at the door, waiting, thinking she was wearing soft shoes so I wouldn't hear her coming.

My restless pacing did nothing to quicken her arrival. Footsteps came and went, and my spirits rose and fell, until at last far away I heard high heels that sounded so familiar and right, so perfectly poised. They paused, approached, stayed outside the door, then moved on. I had been so sure.

Then she came back. This time there was a knock. Now it was my turn to hesitate. It had to be a let down, I thought. My hand grasped the handle and swung open the door. I did not dare look up and started with her shoes, then heard the wrong voice.

Anjelica stood in the doorway and stared, wondering what was going through his head. He opened his mouth to speak but nothing came out, only empty astonishment. He stayed like that a long time, wild-eyed and staring, incapable of speech until at last he managed in a cracked voice to say, 'You're not her, you can't be.'

Anjelica's heart sank. She had thought her husband's binges were a thing of the past. His eyes were blood-shot, and he was blinking like he had not seen daylight in a week and he stank of drink. It was eight in the morning and McMahon was pie-eyed. He looked spooked too. Maybe he was tripping, she thought.

In the gloom of the room she could see his laptop on the table, the bright exploding fireworks of its screen-saver. It confirmed her worst suspicions. McMahon was in trouble with the book and she felt even more guilty about having gone away.

'How did you get here?' he eventually managed.

'I've come to take you home,' Anjelica said. 'Aren't you going to ask me in?'

She was not sure if she wanted to step inside but it seemed preferable to everybody watching McMahon having his nervous breakdown on the doorstep. She was feeling not far from collapse herself being exhausted after too much flying and too many time changes.

McMahon moved back to let her in, behaving like everything was in slow motion and under water.

'We have been looking all over for you,' Anjelica said. 'Nobody knew where you were.'

It was Youselli who had suggested checking old haunts, after tracking him to Los Angeles through the airlines. Thinking of her collapse in Zurich, she wondered if McMahon had been going through something similar. There were tears of what looked like confusion in his eyes and when she instinctively reached out and stroked his hair he flinched. She gradually coaxed him into lying on the bed, and found herself crying too, remembering her loneliness in Zurich. Where would they be in a year's time, she wondered. Would she have the strength to leave him as planned? Anjelica felt the resolve draining out of her. She was torn between leaving him and staying and looking after him. The book had been something of a last chance because he had not written a song in years and everything, for as long as she could remember, had been a case of judicious recycling. Now with their collapsing reserves it seemed that the ending might be coming even faster than she had thought.

CHAPTER FIVE

When the telephone rang Edith hoped it was going to be Youselli and was annoyed for wanting it to be. It was Susan. Edith was beginning to think her calling so often was a sign of bad conscience. Sitting in her dark hall, she had a flash of muddy brown waters and treacherous undercurrents, a reflection perhaps of her true, unacknowledged relationship with her daughter, once they got past all that surface niceness.

'Your man McMahon has a growing file,' said Susan referring to her internet searches.

Susan had become mildly obsessed with Edith's famous client. To humour her, Edith supposed, in the absence of regular film production gossip. Her initial interest had been sparked by a casual remark of Edith's about McMahon owning an apartment in the Dakota. Because of that Susan wondered if he had a deathwish. It was also Susan who told Edith about McMahon being in Los Angeles. She had heard him on the radio. She also confessed to a teenage crush, which had surprised Edith who thought of her daughter's musical tastes as more traditional. Susan had replied that proved how little Edith really knew about her. She was beginning to wonder. The boyfriend

Harry was a stuntman, which did not sound like Susan either.

The overall changes to Susan's circumstances left Edith feeling disarmed: the relocation, the new man, the lack of certainty about whether she was coming back. Whenever Edith broached the subject of Susan's house standing empty the conversation turned sour and left her feeling like a lonely nag. On anything not involving them, Susan remained relentlessly cheerful.

'There's a guy called Alexander Blackledge who is pretty interesting in all of this,' she said brightly. It sounded like she was eating another apple, one of several dozen she had chomped her way through in the course of their calls. Susan was on an apple and broccoli diet.

'This is true, what I am about to tell you,' she said. 'Harry was in Hawaii in 1980 on a film the summer before John Lennon got shot outside the Dakota. He ran into Alex Blackledge who knew some people on the production. He was guest teaching a film course, okay? Plus he makes these films with all this heavy magic stuff. And guess who one of his course students is?'

Edith sighed as Susan stitched together the details of her conspiracy, based on Blackledge's apparent cultivation of the troubled young man about to turn killer. The shooting, Susan was convinced, had to be taken as Blackledge's revenge on the English singer after being crossed in a disagreement over music for a film.

'You have no proof,' said Edith

'Mother,' said Susan impatiently. 'Harry was there. The man makes satanic movies, he cultivates a relationship with this kid and see what happens. We are talking cause and effect here. And he knows McMahon, who lives in the Dakota, *and* they have fallen out too.'

Susan was speaking so fast now she was tripping over her words in her excitement to tell Edith how there had been an argument over a Blackledge film commissioned by McMahon about life on tour, but whose release he later suppressed. The move left Blackledge claiming McMahon had ruined his career and it was now difficult to raise even the modest sums he needed for his projects. Sensing her mother's silent disapproval Susan gave a deep-throated laugh. 'Enjoy, Mother, enjoy!'

CHAPTER SIX

It was the first time Youselli had seen McMahon since
the trip to Aaron's and he was shocked by how gaunt
he had become. He was slopping around the apartment
in a robe like he was sick, which maybe he was as the
wife had told him he was checking into a clinic.
Youselli wondered if it was to dry out because he
could smell drink on him. It had taken several attempts
to fix a meeting because the wife kept stalling, saying
McMahon was fragile. From what he understood,
McMahon was undergoing some kind of crack-up to
do with his book. He thought Anjelica had looked
stressed too as she let him in.

He found McMahon in the room the wife called
the library, sitting listlessly, doing nothing. He wore
fancy braided slippers with no socks. Youselli could see
a plaster stuck to the top of his foot which made him
seem even more vulnerable.

'What happened in LA?' he asked, trying to make it
sound casual. He was embarrassed seeing McMahon
again, and was still mad at him for jumping off to Los
Angeles.

McMahon shrugged to say it was none of his
business. Fine, thought Youselli, reaching into his

jacket pocket. He lobbed the cassette to McMahon who fumbled before catching it, glaring with annoyance at having things thrown at him.

'Movie time,' said Youselli flatly. 'Where's your machine?'

McMahon pointed towards a built-in cupboard below the bookshelves and looked at the cassette. He asked what it was because it had no markings. Youselli said it was a surprise and cued.

The first pictures were almost abstract, distinguished by grubby lighting and bleached colour. As the camera moved wider, it became clear that they were looking at a woman getting fucked in a three way set-up. She was skinny and washed-out and very out of it.

'Daria?' asked McMahon. He was standing close to the screen after inserting the cassette. He sounded bored.

'Rough cut of her last movie.'

'Did anyone locate her yet?' he asked vaguely.

Youselli ignored him. 'You can see where they didn't cover up the track-marks on her arms with make-up. You ever do any of that junk?'

McMahon turned away from the screen. 'That's not her.'

'Well, that's Daria,' said Youselli, 'making screen history. And I'm pretty sure she's Leah too.'

There was little resemblance to the photograph of the plump teenager he had been shown by her mother. Youselli rubbed his teeth with a finger. He felt a buzz like he had been taking drugs. Maybe seeing McMahon so enervated was giving him a rush.

'Is that it?' said McMahon dully. 'Is that what you wanted to show me?'

Youselli was irritated that McMahon was treating him like history. Maybe he was embarrassed after all by what happened at Aaron's and was intent on putting a distance between them.

Youselli picked up the remote, aimed it and said, 'We can skip the chugging cock. There's one more scene I want you to look at.'

Neither spoke as the machine fast forwarded. Youselli wondered what had happened in Los Angeles to spook McMahon so badly. He found the scene. Daria was talking dirty on the phone. McMahon glanced at it and said decisively, 'That's not her.'

'Why not?'

'She sounds wrong for a start.'

'She not the woman you talked to?'

Youselli could see McMahon knew what he was referring to, and he did not hide his delight at having the drop on the man. 'You left a trail as clear as a slug. TV, radio, phone-ins.'

He froze the image of Daria and went up to McMahon, deliberately standing too close. 'I'm disappointed, you running off like that. I thought we were working this one together, had ourselves a nice little ass-tight situation as your old buddy Aaron would say. What would have happened if she had turned out a psycho, sliced off your dick? Would you have called out my name, for me to come and rescue you? You are my client. You go off and get yourself in deep water, it reflects badly. Already I am in trouble with your wife. Unthinking behaviour, my friend.'

'Well, here I am,' said McMahon sarcastically. 'Home safe.'

'You going to share the content of your tête-à-têtes?'

McMahon's wouldn't-you-like-to-know look snapped at Youselli's patience. 'What you talk about, how she blew her brains all over the fucking wall?'

McMahon stared at him like Youselli was trampling on something precious. 'It was her.'

'How do you know, did you see her?'

Youselli was starting to shout and McMahon sensed a weakness. 'Hey, you're jealous.'

Youselli stabbed his finger at McMahon's chest. 'The desk said you did not have visitors, you did not make calls out but the same woman kept phoning in.' He pointed at the screen. 'It was her. Little Miss Spaced.'

McMahon shook his head. 'I told you, the voice.'

'That's not her voice,' he said dismissively. He liked seeing the uncertainty in McMahon's eyes. 'They add the sound after. Daria did not voice that scene. She had already been fired. She was revoiced by a well-known straight actress. It's true. Actresses hit thirty, the parts aren't there any more but they got a lot of post-synch experience. Some big names do this stuff, I tell you.'

Youselli stuck his hands in his pocket and grinned unpleasantly. Something about the man brought out the worst in him.

'Since you got back there have been no more letters. Not a squeak. For over a week, and when did a week

go by without something from her? So, what I con-
clude is something significant happened.'

Youselli cocked his head, watching McMahon shift
uncomfortably. He crossed the floor, making the most
of his moment. 'That significant something is she's
dead.'

From the other side of the room McMahon looked
like he had shrunk, suddenly appearing tiny and
hunched.

'Daria has gone and done the big *adiós*,' Youselli
went on, his confidence rising with each sentence.
'Gomez checked Jane Does. They found her in some
room. She had been dead a while. The timing of the
death is interesting from your point of view. Approxi-
mately the time of your exit from Los Angeles.'

McMahon insisted again it was not Daria he had
been talking to.

'You pathetic, deluded fool,' said Youselli. He said
it nice, almost with affection, the better to sharpen the
sting of what he was about to say. 'What did you do,
give her dope money? She would have been happy to
go along with your game, pretending she was her
sister. Talk to Paolo. He thinks she was a set-up from
the start, give you something to put in your memoirs.'

McMahon clenched and unclenched his fists.

'Fantasy's over. Daria's cold.' Wanting to goad him
further Youselli added, 'Was it something you cooked
up between you, or did you latch on to her?'

McMahon shook with anger as he opened his
mouth and shouted for his wife. Anjelica rushed in and
McMahon pointed a shaking finger at Youselli and

told her to take him out. Youselli held up his hands in mock surrender, pausing on the way out to make his last point.

'Either you were in the room with Daria when she was fixing up and she overcranked it and you ran away. Which is your style. Or, she did it by herself when she found out you'd sneaked back home. What happened? The game get a little rough? Either way, how I see it, the end stays the same. Without you, Daria and her sister could still be alive today.'

Stung, McMahon rallied. 'I don't give a fuck for your dumb cop explanations. I never talked to Daria in my life.'

'Yeah, well,' said Youselli giving his best smile. 'It ain't me going to the clinic. Happy landings.'

He brushed past them and walked out without looking back. He was waiting for the elevator when the wife called after him.

'You forgot this,' she said handing him the tape.

'I don't think we will be needing that any more.'

'I want you to take it away. It has upset my husband.'

Youselli pocketed the cassette. 'What happened to him out there?'

'He won't say except he swears he was talking to her.'

Not for the first time that day, Youselli thought the man's stubbornness made no sense.

'You don't think she and my husband were in it together?' Anjelica looked nervous and Youselli decided her question was the real reason she had come after him. He shook his head.

'I was giving him a hard time back there for which I apologize, but he has been less than straight with me. You want my opinion, for what it is worth, Daria grew up with an image of her sister knowing this famous person, and as her own life went into freefall it became the only fantasy outlet available to her. It's sad really. I hope your husband gets better.'

He held out his hand for her to shake. Maybe because things were turning out all right after all. Betesch had hit his wife's lawyers with the threat of heavy artillery and Paolo's with a counter suit for bodily harm, since when they had heard nothing. Maybe all Paolo needed was standing up to. Now the case was over normal service could be resumed.

After telephoning to report Daria's death, Youselli decided to put Edith Weber on hold while he made up his mind if he wanted to follow up on her. He had no problem fucking someone older, witness Daria's mother. He had taken to consoling her. Mrs Geffen had, to his surprise, been upset by her daughter's death, which Youselli uncharitably read as sorrow at her carelessness, losing both children and a husband. He spared her the sordid details and made no mention of Skye Blu. Mrs Geffen wept noisily, from grief or self-pity he could not tell. He found the experience unexpectedly erotic and thanked his good fortune he had a handkerchief and a clean one at that. The drying of tears led easily to physical consolation, and from that to lying down in the bedroom, minus the pooch, which he made sure stayed outside. On the bed he moved slowly, inching her towards arousal, a process that took more than an hour. He made sure she remained oblivious of his seduction, letting her think she was making the moves, which she eventually did while protesting at the inappropriateness of her feelings. Five minutes later she wasn't complaining, thought Youselli, as she wrestled him on top and went at him with a fury, working herself into a lather of guilt that became indistinguishable from her abandon. His patience was rewarded with an orgasm that rated with the best.

Afterwards he wasn't sure how he felt. What she told him was not something he had ever suspected, and he was riled by the information. McMahon had been there before him albeit a long time ago. During his involvement with Leah, he had been seeing Mrs Geffen too. Even though she would not admit as much, Youselli went away with the strong impression that McMahon had fucked them together, maybe even in the bed he had just been in. On leaving he aimed a kick at the dog which skittered across the shiny parquet flooring.

Edith found it hard to cope with Susan's late-morning breeziness in the dying light of her own afternoon. She was fighting a deteriorating mood brought on by indecision over whether to call Youselli. California was bright and sunny, as Susan kept insisting. 'It's a beautiful day, Mother!'

Edith had more or less stopped listening. Susan was still feeding material on McMahon, regardless of being told on several occasions that the matter was closed. Edith was wearied by her daughter's relentless keenness, this time pointing out some obscure connection between McMahon and the actress Mia Farrow, and wanting congratulations for her exhaustive research uncovering a trail connecting Blackledge to a bizarre religious cult called the Church of Mephisto.

The name meant nothing to Edith, nor that of Marcus Del Ray, its founder. Edith thought Susan's description made it sound completely crackpot, with Del Ray presiding over ceremonies in plastic horns with naked women on altars pretending to be witches.

'Tack-y,' said Susan and laughed. Edith didn't. She was staring at the dictionary, trying to remember how it had ended up in the hall and why she would have needed it there in the first place. Her forgetfulness was starting to worry her: tiny irretrievable blank spots were forming over her life. She leafed idly through the pages while Susan droned on. She randomly noted the meaning of centrifugal as 'moving away from the centre or axis; and, using centrifugal force: a force that appears to cause a body that is travelling round a centre to fly outwards, off its circular path'.

The word caught something of her own anxiety. Even with Daria gone, taking with her the ghost of her dead sister, Edith was left with a sense of gathering momentum. In the light of what Susan said next, she found she could only look back at that moment as a terrible and unwelcome premonition.

'Del Ray preached something called the malfate.'

Edith was brought up short. 'The what?'

'The malfate. Sometimes they spell it with an extra

"e". Maelfate, which makes it sound like the trouble you get with men. Maybe that's what I have.'

Susan laughed an irritating laugh that sounded recently acquired. Edith failed to recall how her usual one had sounded. Darkness seemed to have fallen outside without warning, and seeing her own reflection in the window unsettled her. She had not expected to hear of the malfate again, particularly from such an unexpected source. Edith did not want to know any more but found herself incapable of interrupting Susan who was reading extracts from the church's teachings.

'This is what it says about the malfate. I summarize. You will be happy to hear most of us are lucky enough to escape the malfate, which, as I understand it, is a kind of negative version of our lives which is played out in some shadow world. There seem to be moments of coexistence when things could go one of two ways: good or bad. Or bad to worse maybe.' Susan sounded brisk and cheerful. 'According to this, there is an evolutionary thing attached and some are more vulnerable than others.'

Edith felt suddenly anxious at the thought of the dark and empty rooms that surrounded her. However little she liked where Susan was taking them she did not want the call to end and be left on her own. Reluctantly she let Susan talk on. She presumed Blackledge had picked up the notion of malfate from Del Ray and passed it on to McMahon who had told Leah.

While Susan was talking Edith was able to objectify the coincidence of her own daughter reintroducing her to the malfate, except for when she experienced a roll of fear as Susan read out a quotation she recognized:

'Our lives hang by the slenderest of threads every minute of every day.'

After the call she went to her files. In Leah's second letter she found the same stark sentence. Written down it looked like a warning addressed directly to her.

Yet only a short while later she felt oddly buoyant as she picked up the telephone, reflecting on the irony of Susan giving her the excuse she needed to contact Youselli. She gave a terse smile as she called his number and told herself she did not believe one jot of the rubbish Susan had dug up.

She did not manage to reach Youselli until late that night and then he told her to fax him. He sounded cold and his tone said she was wasting his time. As in their one previous call he made no reference to their date and Edith hung up crushed.

She berated herself for not standing up to him. Part of her wanted to jolt him out of his indifference, to infect him with the uncertainty Susan's call had caused regardless of her reasoning. In the end she obediently faxed him, saying there was evidence to suggest McMahon was in danger and that Blackledge, whom she believed to be the source of that danger, was due in New York to attend a film festival showing his work. She silently thanked Susan for being such a busybody.

Youselli called back not long after. He sounded friendlier.

'There were things on my mind when you called.'

Edith did not trust herself to speak.

'My message service says someone keeps ringing in and hanging up.'

Edith felt a flush of dizziness. 'Why would anyone do that?' Her voice sounded very small.

'Because they are crazy or desperate, or both. It will be my wife. I tell you these are strange days.'

Now he was on the line he seemed happy enough to talk, Edith thought, while wondering at her own behaviour. At first it was urgency that had made her call his number so often, then curiosity at what it was like to indulge in such irrational behaviour. She had a flash of Leah's obsession, and was surprised it left her with such a warm pleasurable feeling, almost of contentment. There had also been her anger at Youselli's continued unavailability.

She was relying on his continued interest in Leah. When he had called to tell her about Daria she had sensed his disappointment. Her one crucial piece of information came from Susan. Leah was listed among those who had appeared in a Blackledge film, shot partly in France in the summer of her death.

CHAPTER SEVEN

Watching the fuzzy weirdos troop into the dilapidated movie-house Youselli decided he had to be crazy giving up his evening for a freak show. One Gothic couple stared hard at him and he leered back at the woman who stuck out her tongue. The awning which sheltered him from the rain announced the Flaming Creatures Film Festival. Edith Weber was ten minutes late, which added to his discomfort.

He saw her arrive by cab. Watching her pay he was struck by how tall and elegant she was. She smiled when she saw him and quickened her step. Youselli was not sure how to greet her but Edith fluently offered her cheek like they were old friends.

'You look good,' he said, and she did in her English-style raincoat. 'We got ourselves the Addams Family for company.'

He already had the tickets and they made their way through a crowded foyer. Youselli glimpsed the silver head of Blackledge surrounded by a small crowd and tried to remember the last time he had been to a movie theatre without his kids.

They walked down a long corridor smelling of damp with carpets climbing half way up the walls.

Edith wrinkled her nose with fastidious distaste. The auditorium was an unmodernized rat-hole and Youselli steered them to seats on an empty side aisle, away from the freaks.

Some minutes passed. Youselli spent them trying to decide whether Edith's silence was an uncomfortable one. Then a young man with a goatee came down to the front of the hall to introduce a programme devoted to the 'counter-culturalist' Alexander Blackledge who would be on stage after the screening of the first film they were about to see, his longest and most ambitious work, made over twenty years, and only recently completed. Youselli felt they were digging in for a long evening.

Once the lights were down the place became full of the scrape of matches and the noise of popping cans. Soon the heavy smell of dope was hanging in the air and smoke wafted lazily in the beam of the projector. Youselli tried to concentrate on the scratchy black and white images. They looked nothing like how he imagined France and featured a gloomy castle-type place on the shores of a lake and scenes of people with painted faces in flowing robes delivering incantations to the accompaniment of tinny music. Youselli was soon bored and sensed the crowd getting restless. Edith squeezed his arm and apologized for dragging him along. Her hair brushed his face. Catching her perfume left him with an inappropriate urge to spend the rest of the show necking with her.

Edith thought the audience was right to laugh. The film was risible. Yet she found herself disturbed by its malevolent and insinuating decadence. It was the work of a man who had seen too much, which fitted what she knew of Blackledge's history. After a period of painting British society portraits he had mysteriously disappeared to the Far East. Edith pictured his story as one of post-colonial hangover and Conradian corruptions – emphasised by his shadowy role as a go-between in the making of *Apocalypse Now* – with the too-ripe stench of the tropics never far away. She imagined him inhabiting a world of erotic submissions. Appropriately it was a piece of French commercial pornography, which he had worked on as a location finder, that had first bought him to the Philippines.

Youselli found himself being nudged awake by Edith. 'What's happening?' he mumbled.

'I don't know,' whispered Edith. 'But this looks like France.'

He saw another castle-type building, white not grey, and a field with tall grass and trees with a hammock. Youselli grunted and struggled to stay awake. Nothing in the film made sense to him. Nevertheless it began to exert a fascination: anyone dedicated to producing something so bad had to be serious. The only things that looked real were the blood and the sex. Blackledge was obsessed with scored female flesh and delicate razor cuts. For ten minutes a masked couple fucked for real in a room of velvet drapes. Youselli fancied it was Mickey and Astrid. The story, if there was one, seemed to refer to conjuring a spirit from the dead. *Speed* it was not.

A squawking white chicken held by the legs was banged down on a table and almost before Youselli could take in what was happening blood was pumping from its severed neck. The camera stared remorselessly as the headless chicken continued to be held down in its death throes. As the furious kicking began to subside, the wretched bird was set free to die. This it did by staggering to its feet, blood still gushing from the neck, and blind-lurching towards the edge of the table, wings flapping in panic until it managed to rise and fly headless for a few feet before crashing down dead.

Youselli sensed Edith's intense disapproval without having to look. The rest of the audience seemed stunned, its sniggering apathy replaced by a sense of shock which increased when it became apparent that the beheading had been witnessed by a young child who ran forward to pick up the dead bird and hold it above his head, tilting his face until it was bathed in blood, and smiling all the while.

'I don't believe it,' Youselli whispered to himself. He recognised Paolo, grinning even then.

The film ground on for what felt like hours with no further glimpse of the white castle or the sunny orchard. Youselli wondered if Leah had been one of several hooded female nudes in an earlier scene.

A landscape came up he had not seen before, showing a stream overhung with trees, dappled by bright sunshine. Edith nudged him and pointed out what he had not yet seen: beneath the surface lay a naked female torso, its slim shape blurred by the stream's current. Youselli leaned forward, sure this was Leah. He did not understand the shot. Despite the summery feel, the water looked cold and she was doing a good job of keeping still. At last the camera moved to her face, which was turned a little sideways. It stayed tight on her mouth and closed eyes. She was clearly beautiful but the water's movement made it impossible to say how she really looked, except in some intense, unreal and dreamlike way.

Edith thought Blackledge's appearance afterwards an act of bravado, given the combination of hostility and stoned indifference that greeted the film, which she had loathed. Against her will she found him fascinating in person. Hooded reptilian eyes gave him a fathomless look, sometimes ancient, sometimes boyish, with a clear trace of former beauty. His fine silver hair flopped youthfully forward to be tossed back with feminine grace. He bristled, sniffing the air, soaking up the negative energy of the crowd. Edith was grudgingly impressed with his unrepentant manner and the look of superior amusement. His had a narcissist's sullen eyes, she thought, and an air of patrician sloth guaranteed to rile.

Right up to the moment when she put up her hand Edith had no conscious intention of asking a question. Out of the corner of her eye she saw Youselli looking at her in surprise. She had decided, watching Blackledge's performance, that there was something so profoundly negative about the man that she wished to state her opposition. She stood, though it was not necessary, and saw how out of place she looked in that audience.

She asked about Marcus Del Rey, which earned her a curious look from Blackledge who responded that Del Rey had appeared in several of his films.

'Do you know Marcus?' he asked archly, earning a laugh at the expense of her conventional appearance. Edith was aware of Youselli shrinking down in his seat.

'By reputation,' said Edith. 'Tell me, has he been in any other films?'

'You would have to ask him that,' said Blackledge, turning away to show he was done with her. Youselli sensed that Edith had made Blackledge uncomfortable. It was also clear she was no pushover.

'I understand,' she went on, her voice firm and louder, 'he also made an appearance in the film *Rosemary's Baby*.'

'I believe so.' Blackledge sounded bored.

'As what?'

'I beg your pardon?' He cupped his ear, pretending he couldn't hear, or that her question was too boring to answer. The audience dutifully laughed.

'As what part?' repeated Edith.

Blackledge rallied. 'As the Devil, what else? Now perhaps we can let someone else have a turn.'

'I haven't finished yet.'

Blackledge rolled his eyes. 'I can't see how this is of any interest to the rest of these good people.'

Edith replied sternly, 'I don't give a fig what they think. My question is, do you think if the film *Rosemary's Baby* had not been made the director's wife would be alive today?'

Youselli could see the question had thrown Blackledge, who stalled. 'I should explain here, for the few of you who may not know, that the director's wife was murdered soon after by the followers of Charles Manson.' He gave Edith a worldly look. 'I have no idea if there is a connection. You sound like a conspiracy theorist.'

A few in the audience sniggered, but most remained intent, Youselli noticed, sensing they were witnessing the unfolding of an argument as old as time, between light and dark.

'I am an analyst,' said Edith lightly. 'Which may amount to the same thing. Would you ascribe the murders in Cielo Drive to the malfate?'

Blackledge looked at her sharply. 'Your analysis has taken you into some very unlikely areas.'

'I have a particular case where the malfate is implicated. Am I right in thinking what we have just seen is an interpretation of the malfate, an attempt to render visible the invisible?'

Youselli was amazed by Edith. He would rather face down an armed punk than stand up and argue his case before a room full of strangers.

'My film is about many things,' Blackledge announced with an air of mystery.

'All of them bullshit,' muttered Youselli.

The goateed MC tried to move the questions along. Edith ignored him. 'But the film is particularly concerned with magical properties.'

Blackledge conceded with a wave of his hand and turned away to block her attempt to ask another question. A hand in the audience went up and Blackledge quickly pointed to it.

Edith sat down agitated. Youselli felt she was

annoyed with him for not supporting her. Blackledge avoided looking their way for the rest of the session which consisted of innocuous questions from admiring young women beguiled by superior looks and a British accent. Youselli wondered if his hostility toward Edith was because they were the same age. It would put her outside his usual range, he figured. Blackledge seemed to hit on younger people. He was at least fifteen years older than McMahon, and when Leah had been sixteen he would have been in his forties. Youselli decided he was watching a man who had learned to move through a world of easy pickings.

They lasted ten minutes of the second half before Edith announced she had had enough. Blackledge was sitting in the foyer, as though waiting for them. He was flanked by a couple of silent young women, dressed in black and looking exotically beautiful in a masochistic way. Youselli was surprised how exhausted Blackledge appeared, wounded even, as though his performance had taken everything out of him. Even so there was no denying the power of the man. Seeing him sitting there Youselli was reminded of a dragon guarding the exit in some old childhood story.

Youselli was for walking away but Edith had other plans. She marched up to Blackledge. Youselli hung back watching Blackledge, who remained seated, saying nothing, ignoring her. Edith stood her ground until he deigned to look up.

'I repeat my question,' she said. 'Do you think there is a connection between the making of *Rosemary's Baby* and the events at Cielo Drive?'

Blackledge gave her a weary look. 'What I will say is the film touched on dark and powerful forces and those involved perhaps took their responsibilities too lightly, thinking they were involved in making mere entertainment.'

'Not a mistake you would make, Mr Blackledge,' said Edith tartly.

Blackledge sat there, staring at his nails, riding the insult. 'What I will also say,' he continued without looking up, 'is that the black aura surrounding *Rosemary's Baby* – and film by its nature is a chemical if not alchemical process – could have influenced other events.' He gave Edith the full benefit of his mesmeric blue gaze. 'To a layman like yourself,' he went on with sinister quietness, 'I would say the ground is treacherous and full of pitfalls—'

'How might it have influenced other events?'

'There are processes of initiation,' he said mysteriously. 'Tread carefully.'

Youselli was confused by Edith's persistence. She said nothing and appeared deep in thought.

'Tell me, Mr Blackledge,' she eventually said, 'The girl in the stream, who was she?'

'I forget. It was a long time ago,' he said insincerely. Youselli wanted to expose the lie but found himself unable to intervene.

'Would it have been Leah?' asked Edith.

Blackledge shrugged. 'I am always bad at names. Often people were only around for a day or two at a time.'

'Where is she now?'

Blackledge refused to be drawn. Edith took a step forward. Even then the women on either side paid her no attention and radiated a profound boredom.

'We both know perfectly well what happened to her.'

Blackledge regarded her with indifference. 'Tragic.'

'She is not alive.'

'Sadly not.'

'Then perhaps you can explain why there have been times when I believed she was still alive.'

Blackledge stared, astonished for a brief second until the mask slipped back. But in that moment Youselli had a clear glimpse of the excitement and fear in him.

'Do you believe that possible?' For the first time Blackledge sounded engaged.

'Everything in my conditioning and training tells me it is not,' said Edith.

He stood up, animated at last, plucking at her sleeve. 'We must sit and talk about this. I have been wondering too.'

'No, Mr Blackledge, my sense of moral outrage at what I witnessed in your film would prevent me from sitting down with you. What I will say is that for someone rumoured to have sold his soul to the Devil you make very dull films.'

Youselli tugged at Edith's sleeve while Blackledge glared, his venom at last apparent. The seated women watched more keenly now, with excited eyes.

'I am sure you know the saying that in the land of the blind the one-eyed man is king,' Blackledge said. 'You would do to remember it when death comes to yank open your mouth. Which won't be long now.'

He made a configuration with his left hand like some kind of sign of the cross. 'May the malfate be with you.'

Edith walked away without waiting for Youselli who found her on the street in a state of agitation.

After that the evening deteriorated. Edith felt that her forthright questioning had disarmed Youselli. She wanted to tell him it was uncharacteristic. The encounter with Blackledge had left her deeply restless. She had no idea what she wanted except that Youselli take charge but they drove aimlessly in his car trying to decide what to do. In the end Edith made him take her to the restaurant they had been to on their date and immediately regretted it. What she should have done was go home, except Blackledge had left her with no desire to be on her own. Youselli's mood deteriorated along with hers and by the time they arrived at the restaurant they were silent. The evening had become ridiculous, she decided, because her real motive had been to use it as an excuse to see Youselli.

They distracted themselves with the menu. The place was dispiriting in its emptiness and the staff, sensing their mood, kept a distance. In contrast to his earlier indecision he now contradicted her orders with suggestions of his own. But Edith stuck to her choices, to his visible annoyance, and he brusquely told the waiter not to put too much vinegar in the dressing. Edith noticed for the first time that he sometimes had difficulty pronouncing his 'r's and was ambushed by a wave of tenderness. She wanted to take his hand and say what she really felt, that even if he only came to her once in a while it would be enough. After the waiter had gone Youselli put his hand on his stomach and said, 'I think I am getting an ulcer.'

She took this for a rehearsal of a later conversation about feeling too ill to come in. Well, thought Edith, you shan't be asked. Having decided that she felt more in control, but sad, and made an effort to engage him. They talked about McMahon's flight to Los Angeles. From Youselli's dismissive manner she sensed a rivalry between them, though he now saw himself as having the upper hand.

'You want to hear my theory?' he said. 'Mid-life crisis.' He grinned to show how far it was from being his problem, his impending ulcer apparently forgotten.

'You think he was running away from something?' asked Edith.

'Except I don't think he realized it.'

'Would you describe him as paranoid or delusional?'

'Paranoid, yes. Delusional, I don't know. What was all that about back there, with you and Blackledge?'

'I am interested in understanding why McMahon believed he really was talking to Leah in Los Angeles. Either he was, which we know to be impossible, unless she is alive—'

'Or he believes she is.'

'Or he has been led to believe she is.'

'By Blackledge. But why?' he asked.

'All I know is that the building where McMahon lives has a history of bad luck, shall we say, directly or by association, and if you look at any of the points of intersection—' Edith made a right-angle of her hands '—who do you find?'

'Blackledge.'

'Precisely.'

She re-ran the connections for him, starting with Blackledge's history of feuding, his cultivation of John Lennon's killer in the period prior to the singer's death.

'But where does the stuff about *Rosemary's Baby* fit?' asked Youselli.

Edith could see he was humouring her. He was no doubt relieved to keep conversation away from their night together. She asked if he remembered the film, then felt stupid when she realized he would have been about five when it came out. Before he could say anything she blurted, 'It was filmed in the Dakota. Mia Farrow had a child by Satan in it.'

Youselli whistled through his teeth. 'You think Blackledge did it?'

He was laughing at her and Edith was surprised she was so upset. It was not as though she actually believed what she was telling him, though since confronting Blackledge she felt a new anxiety. She ploughed on, passing on what Susan had told her. How on arriving in England from Poland in the 1960s, the director of *Rosemary's Baby* had been befriended by Blackledge. They were thought to have worked on a number of projects, none of which had come to fruition.

'So they quarrelled?' asked Youselli. Edith nodded. 'And what happened to the director? Are you going to tell me he's dead too?'

Edith shook her head slowly. 'No, he is still alive.

He is a survivor. As a child he spent the war in hiding in Poland because he was a Jew.'

She had been struck by the fact that she and the director would be more or less the same age, and by the subsequent adventurousness of his life compared with the timidity of hers.

'I'm not a fanciful person,' she went on carefully. 'I take the world for what it is. I don't believe in anything after. There's us and our bodies, and our family and friends, and these make up countless social units, and we live our span and then we leave.' She shrugged. 'I don't believe in God – either one of benevolence or of wrath – nor in angels or devils. Yet part of me remains superstitious. And I am unsettled by what I am about to tell you because of the way it hints at invisible patterns.'

Edith suspected the real reason she was talking like this was as a prelude to seduction: there was nothing like a whiff of mortality to quicken the carnal appetite.

'You have nice hands,' she said and Youselli looked surprised, then pleased, and Edith smiled, thinking: I'll have you yet.

'You know what happened after *Rosemary's Baby*?'

'The director's wife was killed.'

And now, Edith thought, my daughter is living in more or less the next street.

'But what's to tie Blackledge in with that killing?' Youselli looked sceptical.

'Del Ray. Blackledge was close to him. Del Ray was a major consultant on *Rosemary's Baby*, and one of his witches was among those who carried out the Cielo Drive killings.'

Youselli pushed his plate away. 'Do you believe any of this?'

'It's not what I believe. I am trying to explain how a situation might come about so McMahon would believe it.'

'That he was talking to the real Leah, that's a pretty big step.'

Edith nodded. 'Except Del Ray's teachings are based on a fundamental assumption it shares with Christianity. That it is possible to raise people from the dead, the difference being that they are returned to this earth.'

Youselli did a slow double take, done for comic effect. 'Well, that explains it. And you think that's what Blackledge was telling McMahon.'

'I suppose,' said Edith, remembering the look of fear and elation she had seen on Blackledge's face when she had challenged him. 'I have no desire to dwell on any of this when there are more important things for us to talk about. Yet I do. I find myself constantly being drawn back against my better judgement. I feel so sorry for that child. She would be the same age as my daughter and I can't help thinking how much Leah has missed.'

Edith felt the tears pricking. Youselli looked concerned.

'Hey, it's over now,' he said. 'There is nothing to go back for.'

'I still worry about the girl. She's still very much on my mind.'

'You seem disappointed she's gone.'

Edith tried to keep her voice level. 'I don't want to be on my own tonight.'

239

Youselli smiled. 'What made you think you were going to be? You want me to stay with you?'

Edith nodded.

'Sure,' said Youselli. 'I'd like that.'

Edith insisted on paying her share and on the drive home the silence between them was easy. Youselli reached for her hand. It had been raining and the streets were slick and bright with reflections. Edith told herself not to think beyond that night. She felt a pang at the thought of his body.

They pulled up, Edith relishing the pause between arriving and getting out. Youselli appeared to remember something and reached for his cell-phone and rapidly punched a number.

'You can use the phone in the house,' Edith said.

He shook his head and said he was through already. Edith could make out the tinny voice of his machine relaying his messages. She wanted him to start making love to her in the car. He seemed to read her thoughts and leaned over and kissed her on the mouth while listening to his machine. He kissed her again, harder, running his tongue against her teeth and Edith placed her hand on the back of his neck and tentatively offered him her tongue and felt him tense. He pushed her away.

'What did I do?' she asked, bewildered.

He was still gripping the phone and even in the dark she could see his face was unnaturally pale.

'What?' Edith asked, panicked.

Youselli switched off the phone. He looked scared, she thought, but more excited than he had all evening.

'She's back.'

CHAPTER EIGHT

—I am sorry I have not been able to write. My sister died, I expect you heard. Yes. I am back (from the other side). I could have loved you again, did love you.

Some days I get so scared that I will not be able to control my anger. Control my angel. They overwhelm me. Words spill out, blood from a cut. I know I should not feel so angry after we got so close, but the way you left makes it hard to trust you ever again. I have a justified reason to be mad, but I feel I am on the edge of doing something I will regret. Nobody said coming back would be so hard.

I see now. I have been too long under your spell. All I ever wanted was to make things better. I would do anything for you.

I bet you thought you would not be hearing from me again. I have been checking flight times. Some days I believe this thing between us has to go to the end. Some days I fight so hard to break from you, cut you out of my life because I know you are bad for me and have been ever since you let me fall in France.

I want to make you see how much I really loved you and how much you really hurt me.

CHAPTER NINE

Youselli drove to the clinic where McMahon was, feeling a rush of exhilaration, laced with trepidation. Things were moving. *All I ever wanted to do was make things better*, she wrote. He could sympathize with that. Edith had told him the latest letter signalled a new phase, of struggle within and an almost certain violent ending. She had seemed scared and dispirited by the letter. When asked what the matter was she replied that she had courted the malfate.

'Don't you see? We are all bound by it.'

Youselli did not see it like that at all. He felt above it. He felt close to being able to make an intervention. McMahon's influence was on the wane.

What interested him most about her return was the emotions she was stirring up in the others. Anjelica had been mad at him because she had thought there were no questions left to answer. To which he had replied, Talk to your boyfriend. His knowing about her affair with Blackledge only made her madder. Youselli's emerging image of Blackledge was of the man never to be found in the frame: absent from the picture of Mickey's funeral, not in the photographs in France, presumably because he had been taking them.

Youselli reached Blackledge on the telephone at his hotel. He had sounded unsurprised, no doubt because Anjelica had forewarned him. Typically, he was on the point of leaving town and, just as typically, he claimed responsibility for Leah's return without asserting it outright.

'Certain things that happened then are coming to fruition now.'

When Youselli had asked if that was a roundabout way of saying Blackledge was performing some fancy trick to fuck with McMahon's head, Blackledge responded enigmatically. 'I am sure if you went to Los Angeles and found her it would be her. I was in no doubt she would return one day. This is not to say, however, that I am not alarmed by what I might have unleashed.'

You old bullshitter, Youselli thought, then he was not so sure. He thought he could still detect the same mix of excitement and fear he had witnessed before in Blackledge at the notion of Leah's return. Then Blackledge dropped a real zinger, announcing that he had film of Leah shot on the day of her death.

'I thought you did not get there till the next morning,' Youselli said once he was over the shock.

'I think you will find McMahon has been playing you for a sucker. He was in the room when it happened. We should talk more about this next week when I get back.'

He had hung up before Youselli could press him further. The news about McMahon neither surprised nor bothered him as he had always suspected that his version of events was endlessly deferrable. But the film was something else.

Youselli had arrived at McMahon's vampire clinic to find him playing tennis with Paolo. This at first had surprised him, then seemed quite in keeping with the strangeness of the location, with its dreamlike lawns so emerald they could have been painted. McMahon was in whites and had worked up a sweat.

'I am a different man,' he said with a smirk. 'I had my transfusion.'

He seemed keen to put distance between himself and the business of Leah and expressed mild concern that Youselli was getting too involved. Compared to Youselli he looked fit and chiselled. He was playing a lot of tennis, he said, and doing the book.

'I hear she is writing again,' he said vaguely, patting his face with a towel while Paolo practised a kicking serve in the background. 'Do you play?'

Youselli was thrown by the question and McMahon smiled showing white teeth, the first time Youselli could recall him doing so.

'You have gotten so intense,' McMahon said. 'Relax. You work too hard. You should check in here except you could not afford it. A pity. If you had been nicer I would have paid your bills. I am generous to those who are loyal.'

When Youselli tried to talk about the latest letter McMahon merely smiled and placed his hands over his ears to show the subject was no longer of use or interest. Whatever his previous involvement, he was now cured of Leah. When Youselli mentioned the film referred to by Blackledge McMahon dismissed its

existence, maintaining that it was Blackledge's way to
spread rumours.

'It may not be over,' said Youselli. 'She is going to
come for you.'

He meant it to unsettle but McMahon continued to
look serene. Youselli wondered about his medication.

'First she has to find me,' he said. 'You take care
of it. I got to play another set.'

He leaned forward and kissed Youselli on the
mouth, whispering, '*Ciao, caro*! I was hoping you
would come and see me.' He laughed at Youselli
involuntarily wiping his mouth, and added softly,
'Now you caught her bug too.'

Youselli had been there barely five minutes, but
that was fine by him. He had found out what he had
come for. McMahon was out of the picture. His way
was clear.

CHAPTER TEN

—The way I had imagined was pretty much the way it went. We met. We talked. He was charming and I forgot myself. I was feeling sad anyway – angry to be honest – because I was having a bad day regarding you. One of the down days when everything seems so hopeless. He had a cute accent. He suggested we drink champagne. I don't really like to drink daytime, but he insisted. I caught him trying to look up my skirt and we smiled at that. Does this make you jealous? It should because he got me tipsy and I fucked him for the job. We were sitting opposite each other in soft chairs in some suite and I put my legs up on the arm of his chair and smiled at him over the top of my glass, and he ran his hand up my leg. Then I knelt on the floor and unzipped him, pretending it was you. He started making a whistling noise, lying back, eyes shut, and it was easy to imagine it was you, and for a moment I forgot I hated you for leaving me. So I felt good/bad about this guy. It was not you. It should have been you. 'Come here, baby,' he said when he could not stand any more. I did not want to fuck him to his face, so I made him do it from behind which turned him on, so there we were, kneeling on the floor, him with his trousers in a pool, me with my skirt hiked round my waist and my panties round one ankle, believing he was someone else. He had me grabbed by the hips and was thrusting away unaware of me working myself, making myself come before he did. Afterwards I could honestly tell him how good it was because I had not been fucking him at all.

Later I did feel bad. Because I had fucked an asshole, and because the asshole fucked me and did not give me the job. So I'm going to have to cause a scene. Send the angels round. See how he likes that when they cut off his feet and pitch him into his own swimming pool. See how the blood blossoms in water. Hear how pathetic his strangulated Scottish cries sound so far from home under a California moon.

CHAPTER ELEVEN

Susan told Edith that the angels film was due to start preparation in Los Angeles, but she was still waiting to hear about working on it, as was Harry. The film was to star some actor Edith had vaguely heard of who was a regular in a television series. 'The director is from Scotland,' said Susan.

While Susan droned on Edith tried to collect her thoughts. There had been a reference to the Scottish director in the latest letter. Susan had already discussed with Edith the possibility of Leah, with her angel obsession, contacting the angel film production company. Edith had decided Leah was probably an actress because of her skills of impersonation and empathy. She had passed these observations on to Youselli, who, since the letters had begun again, had been increasingly difficult to reach.

'Wouldn't it be weird,' Susan had concluded, 'if she and I were on the same production?'

Edith had recently begun to acknowledge that deep beneath the surface of her relationship with her daughter lay an antagonism neither had admitted. For all their professed closeness and assertions of love and mutual support, it was all acting, Edith realized. She

248

wondered crudely if Susan had fucked the director for the job and been rejected, wondered too if her daughter was the sort to give sex for favours. The hostility, she was sure, was also there on Susan's side, and as strong.

Edith felt thoroughly shaken. What she had been thinking, she realized, was not necessarily that Susan was Leah. The idea was ridiculous. It was that Leah could be *anyone*. Evil in her memory wore a uniform and she had always thought – naively, she knew – she would recognise it when she saw it again.

The thought of her deteriorating relationship with Susan left Edith wracked with guilt, and drove her to spend many hours re-studying the letters for some missed clue to the identity of the writer. In one of the most recent letters she noticed a sentence she had previously attributed to Daria. *I thought of using it as my professional name.* She had assumed Daria had been talking about her life as an actress. Rereading it, Edith recalled her earlier misgivings about Daria as Leah. To her mind the writer was older than Daria had been. She read on. *I knew someone called Engel which is German for angel and I was so jealous someone could be called Angel for real.*

The name nagged. It had not registered properly before because she had carelessly assumed the reference was fanciful. Now, out of desperation perhaps, she thought she knew it from somewhere, maybe from one of a couple of thousand case histories she had read up during her professional life, whether in general or criminal psychology though she had no idea.

Youselli was not answering messages, so Edith called

Linda Gomez in Los Angeles and explained what she needed. Gomez's efficiency made her think how old and hesitant she was starting to sound. Gomez said 'uh uh' a lot, then, 'Here's what I'll do. I will have Dwight run Engel through the files, see what comes up. No clues? Dates, background, location.'

'I assume it's local to you because of her reference to the angels of Los Angeles. To be honest I have no idea, I'm probably clutching at straws.'

'We will do our best,' said Linda with a briskness that made Edith feel foolish.

CHAPTER TWELVE

—This is how the angels do it. The man lives up on
Scenario Lane off Beverly Glen. It is after dark but he
does not draw the drapes. They are blinds I discover
later. At night he pads round the house barefoot – so
considerate of him to have removed his socks and
shoes seeing what is about to happen – drinking
something and tonic, his script open at the page he is
making notes on, and when the phone rings he props
the receiver under his chin, keeping his hands free. I
got one of his earlier movies out on tape the other
night.

Our Scottish friend is a bit of an adultery man on
the side. I know because I heard him talking to his
daughter. He was sitting out on the deck, just above
my head.

'Hi, sweetie! It's Daddy,' he cooed. And then he
talked to his English wife, saying how much he loved
her and missed her. And I thought, if I was a bad girl,
I would get the number in England where the little
wife lived. Most in the world what I want is to wait
till the middle of the night in England and phone, and
when the sleepy voice answers I say, 'Ask your husband
where his dick has been.' And when she says, all

annoyed, 'Who is this?' I answer, 'An acquaintance of your husband's nasty little dick.'

I got the number anyway. He is the kind of man who does not like to spoil the shape of his clothes so he puts the keys under a stone when he leaves in the morning, figuring it's safe up there, tucked away in the hills.

Other people's space fascinates me. They are like movie sets around which you can construct whole stories. I rearranged a few things discreetly so he might come home and think, I do not remember leaving that there. In the end I had the smartest idea. Maybe phoning home was the last call he had made. So I hit redial and listened to the numbers singing away, then the moment of void before they hook up.

She sounded like she was still up. 'Hello, hello,' she kept saying in her prissy British accent. 'Who is this?'

Next time she spoke to him – at least the next time I was listening under the deck – she made no mention of me, to go by his end of the conversation.

'I'm fine, a little tired,' he said, sounding totally strung out. 'This is such a hard movie,' he went on, sounding like he wanted sympathy. Yeah, I thought, with your trousers round your ankles.

So, the angels—

'What are you doing here?' he asks sharply when he sees and recognizes me.

'You left your door open.'

'What do you want?' He sounds guarded and I make out I have been doing nothing except think of him since, going around in a state of permanent excitement, and I am ready now and not wearing underwear and, look, I show him, watching his Adam's apple jump. He is nervous and I say, 'Don't you want to do it again?' And I come on to him and he says feebly, 'I think you better go now.'

'Fuck me, first,' I say. 'Please.'

He nods and says he needs the bathroom. Needs to make a call is what he means. I step aside like I am going along with it and when he walks past, *thwack*! He goes down in a heap, cracking his head on the metal corner of the glass coffee table, which is going to leave him with a scar, except he is not going to be around to worry about it. Ballbearings in a Gap sock, in case you are wondering. After that the angels get to work on him. They lay him out beside the pool, arms outstretched like he is on the cross, a dish towel stuffed in his mouth to stop him crying out. Music helps. A tape I bring. One of yours. The sound will carry to the next houses, but only just as they are some distance away, and they will think it's a party. There is nothing below or behind, just the reservoir on the other side of the hill. Clean cuts, surgical amputation. Why the feet, I often wonder.

The guy's bug-eyed. It's fifty-fifty whether he is going to die of shock before he drowns. Snip off his dick and post it to his wife. What angers me most is the way he pretended to be you and used that as a way of getting to fuck me, catching me with my guard down, and that's not all! I say that to show you I still retain a sense of humour about all this. The oldest trick in the book and I fell for it − fuck them for the job, no job.

CHAPTER THIRTEEN

'The name Engel came up,' said Linda Gomez calling Edith back. 'In Wisconsin.'

'Wisconsin?'

Gomez had accessed a centralized computer directory containing a catalogue of names relating to any homicide in the United States from the last twenty-five years. Included was one Hannah Engel, victim, aged nine. Gomez added, 'Does the name Stella Ritter mean anything?'

It took Edith a moment. 'My God,' she said.

'That's what I said. You remember?'

'Not in detail.' Edith would need to refresh her memory because the case was nearly twenty years old, but what she could recall was chilling enough. 'Could it be Stella we are looking for?'

'If it is it certainly changes everything.'

'Don't the Wisconsin authorities have a record of where she is?'

Wisconsin did not have any record of Stella's current whereabouts. Linda said, 'She's out there somewhere. She was released five years ago, relocated and got a job in a library with a new name, Nancy Merryweather. Fanciful, don't you think?'

'She'd had long enough to think of one,' ventured Edith. Linda laughed and Edith supposed she had made a joke. She asked how long it had been since the disappearance and was told three years. She was also thinking that Stella, or Nancy as she now was, would be about the right age for Leah.

Edith spent the rest of the day working on the case of Stella Ritter, consulting the sources available at short notice, including a faxed transcript of psychiatric interviews. Stella was an only child, born nearly thirty years previously and initially raised in the state of Mendota, Wisconsin, where her father ran a general store – her earliest memories were of its dry bean smell – until she was five when he upped and moved on, leaving behind only the mystery of his disappearance, never referred to by Stella's feckless mother. This, and the confusion of too many subsequent moves, left Stella friendless and vulnerable. As a result she developed a fantasy world and around the age of six had started to introduce real children into her previously innocuous games, enticing them into cupboards and other enclosed spaces to ensure they did not leave, as her father had.

When I was a girl there was a best friend I used to keep in a drawer, Edith remembered.

The facts of the fatal afternoon towards the close of 1979 were simple. Stella Ritter, aged seven, Judith Rose Grabowski, also seven but nearly a year younger, and Hannah Engel, nine, had played outside in the tranquil, well-to-do suburb until bad weather had sent them indoors to Stella's house, a large building of grey weatherboarding. Mrs Ritter was out. Stella had told

Judith Rose she envied the Engel girl her name and happy family, and she wanted to be her.

According to Judith Rose, Stella had involved Hannah in a game with her invisible friends. Tea was taken, conversations had, and Stella had suggested she and Hannah make a blood pact and swap last names, an offer which Hannah had declined. In Judith Rose's version, Hannah was sceptical of the existence of Stella's imaginary friends. Stella and Hannah had then taken a bath together, watched by Judith Rose who had refused. Edith tried to imagine the scene. Three children in a grown-up space, pretending to behave like adults. After the bath the three girls lay down together, with Hannah a willing accomplice. In so far as Judith Rose's testimony was reliable, sexual curiosity seemed to have been expressed by both Stella and Hannah, with the latter more curious.

They had then played hide and seek with forfeits – more sexual overtones, thought Edith, who had learned never to underestimate the complexity of a child's world. When Hannah said she had to go Stella pleaded with her to play one last game.

In Judith Rose's statement, Stella asked her later to say Hannah had gone. The two girls watched television until the return of Mrs Ritter.

Later that afternoon Stella told Hannah's mother on the phone that Hannah had left more than an hour before. When Hannah had still not appeared by nightfall Stella was questioned again, this time by the police who had no reason not to believe her story and mounted a fruitless search of the surrounding area.

Hannah's body was discovered only when it started

to decompose. It was Stella who first noticed the smell and alerted her mother. She denied all knowledge of what had happened and again was believed. Hannah's death was thought to have been the result of a terrible accident, until it was noticed that both clasps on the trunk had been locked.

Hannah Engel had been locked in a trunk that had once belonged to Stella's father and left to suffocate.

Linda Gomez talked to the Scottish film-maker whose name was MacGregor. He reminded her of a pocket-sized version of the tennis player Boris Becker, with red eyelashes so pale they were almost invisible. His milky, freckled skin made him vulnerable in the hard California sun. She found him difficult in manner. Once his initial curiosity had worn off he made it plain he was too busy to deal with any distractions.

They were in an open-plan office with a dozen or so people showing signs of frantic business, phoning and pointing at things. Gomez was always amazed at how little really went on in film productions, contrary to appearances. Her father had worked in set construction and she remembered him saying he had never seen so much disorganization and incompetent leadership outside of the army as on a film production. They were like temples to useless activity. To prove her point, a woman came up and interrupted MacGregor to ask if he preferred red socks or yellow ones. Mac-Gregor blinked like a man confronted with a life or death decision. 'Definitely the yellow.'

Gomez reckoned he did not have a clue. The

woman with the socks left nodding as though Mac-Gregor had uttered some profound truth. Someone else arrived to take her place and hovered.

Gomez said, 'It would be better if we could talk somewhere private.'

MacGregor sighed. She figured he was not much past thirty and saw him burning out long before his movie was done. She wondered what he used to keep going. He snapped at the hovering attendant, 'Not now,' and showed Gomez to a small office with a glass window overlooking the main work area.

'Where did you say you were from?' he asked, closing the door.

He looked blank when she told him and asked if that was part of a private organization. She realized anything outside the film was off his map.

'This is police business and it concerns your safety.'

MacGregor blinked at that and looked at her sceptically.

She said, 'We intercepted a letter that talks about a relationship with a Scottish film director—'

He interrupted to name several other Scottish directors working in Los Angeles.

'We are sure it's you.'

She told him what the letter said and he strenuously denied having sexual relations with anyone, adding pompously, 'I love and miss my wife.'

'Then is there anyone you have had dealings with who has reason to feel aggrieved?'

He shrugged. 'I turn people down every day, but they are people who understand it's the nature of the job.'

'Any actress strike you as neurotic?'

'Show me one who isn't.' He gave her a hard look that betrayed his chauvinism. 'Now if you will excuse me.'

She could see he was not interested but decided it was her duty to warn him. 'If I were you I would get the production company to move you to another house, as a precaution.'

'You think it's that serious?'

'She may be a fantasist, but better safe than sorry. She seems to latch on to famous people.'

He looked pleased at being called famous. See if I cry, Linda Gomez thought, if she comes and gets you.

His father looked surprised to see Youselli. It was not one of his regular visiting days.

'Hey, Pop, I am not going to be able to come for a while,' he said.

'Are you in trouble, son?' his father asked shrewdly.

'Not so you would notice.'

They sat making small talk, drinking weak coffee. His father was wearing a blanket over his knees. He needed new slippers Youselli noticed. The realization hit him that he probably would never see his father again.

'Lousy weather,' said Youselli. He felt his eyes fill with tears and had to turn away. His father looked at him, saying nothing, his fingers working distractedly at his blanket. They had passed beyond the stage of filling in the silences.

His father finally spoke. 'Now I'm dying I find

myself thinking about what happens next. They shut the lid, it stays shut. I'm still trying to figure a way round that one. Eternity is starting to look like an awful long time. The worst thing is the idea of not being me. Not that I ever liked myself particularly. I was a bigot. I treated your mother bad, and if I had my time over again I would probably do it the same way because, the way I see it, nobody did me any favours.'

'Maybe there is something else after this.' Youselli did his best to sound reassuring. 'I am dealing with such weird shit at the moment I am starting to believe there could be.'

His father snorted in disbelief. 'That's women and priests' talk. Next you'll be telling me you're taking it up the ass.'

Youselli was offended by the old man's wheezy laughter. 'Hey, come on.'

'Come on, yourself. Let a dying man have his laugh.'

Youselli could see the fear in his father's eyes and reached out for his hand, which was frighteningly cold to the touch. 'It's going to be okay. It's going to slide away nice and easy.' Ill-equipped for the sombreness of the occasion, he fell back to joking. 'Fuck, it's not as though lots of people didn't do it already, and did you hear any complaints?'

'So take my place,' his father replied, trying to return the joke, but his heart was not in it.

'No, no, that's okay. Besides, you would not want to be dealing with the shit I have landed myself in. Fuck-ups all round, Pops. On top of that I am stuck with weird stuff I don't know what to believe any more. If it's some kind of evil like the Church teaches or if it's all bullshit.'

His father stared at him. 'You're not about to go soft on me?'

Youselli shook his head impatiently. 'There's this woman, writing letters from California, and they are as clear as daylight, and I am thinking this is somebody I would really like to know. I am in love with her and I never met her.'

'Hey, wait a minute,' his father said. 'She writes you letters and you don't know her.'

'It's complicated.' He cast around for some plausible explanation, then gave up and shrugged. 'She's dead.'

'Suffering Jesus!' His father coughed so hard Youselli had to thump him on the back. Then he saw his father was laughing helplessly too. 'Are you trying to kill me!' he finally managed to say.

Youselli was glad to see his father momentarily cheered, but as for himself he was confused and approaching incoherence. 'I know I am not making any sense, but I find myself wanting to believe it is her, not somebody pretending. And seeing you now, I'm hoping there is something for you after this. You know, with the job we see the street and the street is what we see and I thought that was all there was to it. I am me and we have our time and then I am not me—' He was vaguely aware of someone saying something similar recently.

'Thanks for reminding me.' The old man looked gloomy again and Youselli felt guilty for wanting to be away.

'I am on the high board, Dad, and I think I am about to jump off. It's too late to go back down.'

'Fuck them!' his father said with unexpected vehemence. 'Do what you have to do.'

'What's going to happen after? Nothing makes sense any more. Hundreds of thousands of years of civilization and we still don't *know* what happens next. Maybe we are the tip of the iceberg because I think I am dealing with something right off the bottom.'

'Sounds like you got to go with it.'

It was the first piece of encouraging advice Youselli could remember his father giving him.

'You are right,' he said. 'I want to put an end to it. But I have a bad feeling, so maybe I'll be seeing you sooner than you think!' He pointed upwards.

'I'll be waiting,' his father said and loosely bunched his fists, to show that he would go down fighting.

Now that the moment of parting had come Youselli felt nothing, certainly none of the triumph he had spent most of his life anticipating. All those years of hatred and now he felt sorry for the old man. When the moment came he did not have the courage to say goodbye.

'So long,' he said. 'Take care.'

His father made a pistol of his finger. 'You bet.'

He looked back once as he walked to the car. His father was sitting in the window, looking terrified. The last thing he had said was how as a kid he had always been afraid of the dark. Youselli raised his arm in farewell but the old man did not respond.

PART III

CHAPTER ONE

Youselli got an extra drink from the stewardess and
toasted himself, murmuring, 'Rogue cop.'

He was by a window and could see Denver 35,000
feet below. It was a good flight. There were plenty of
spare seats. Even the little coaster which the stewardess
had served with his drink pleased him.

He thought back to his visit to his father and
decided it was the right decision to forgive his old
man, whatever reasons he had for hating him. It had
been so long he could no longer remember exactly
what they were. The old man had squeezed out a
couple of pathetic tears when Youselli told him he
loved him, and said it was the first time any kid of his
had. 'Nobody said that before, not even Amy.'

Amy was Youselli's mother. He had to resist spoiling
the old man's little glow of contentment by pointing
out that Amy would have to have been certifiable to
love anyone who had treated her the way he did. Line
management, his father had called it. He slapped her,
she hit the kids and everyone knew their place.

When he got back home Youselli had found a
message from his father, saying to take his old service
revolver, which his colleagues had got nickel plated for

his retirement. Youselli had it tucked in his waistband, which had meant showing his badge to airport security.

Daria's grieving mother he had dumped, more or less, saying he would call when he got back, which he would not. It was a pity you could not fuck a Martini, he thought, she would be happy then.

Linda Gomez he had told he was on a fishing holiday near Albany. She had sounded surprised. He had no idea if there was fishing in Albany. As for the department they thought he was on a week's leave.

Only Edith Weber remained on his conscience. He had meant to tell her *adiós* too and gone round the night before but found he could not. There was nothing so poignant as the possession of beauty lost. She was a dignified and gracious woman whose unstinting giving of herself left him feeling less soiled than normal. Even the way she slowly rolled off her stockings – she still wore stockings and a suspender belt which drove him crazy with desire – had a natural elegance. When she took him inside her he felt cared for.

With her he had the occasional glimpse of how a relationship ought to be. Most of the time with women it was like looking into a thick mist. With her he realized there might be a whole landscape hidden in that fog. She was too old of course. If he had more heart or courage he would say he wanted to spend his time with her, but then he thought of his colleagues. In the department of emotional risk he knew he was faint hearted.

★

Edith had been surprised by Youselli turning up on her doorstep, saying he had been driving by. Seeing how preoccupied she was he had suggested they went to a quiet bar a few blocks away.

He apologized, saying, 'I should have called before.'

Once they were settled in a booth and had their drinks, Youselli made her go over the story of Stella Ritter several times. She sensed the tension and disappointment in him as he kept asking if she was sure. Edith could see his jaw working, and felt increasingly uncertain about her findings.

'I worry that many of my assumptions are wrong,' she said with an air of helplessness. She saw by his frown that he was uncertain of her drift. 'We live in a time of acceleration and change, you would agree?'

Youselli nodded.

'Years ago I remember watching some murder mystery on PBS where the detective said, "Perhaps there are new kinds of despair unknown to us," and getting angry because this was already a century of unimaginable horrors, and here was this piece of entertainment—' She faltered and trailed off. 'I'm not putting this very well. I did not agree with the remark. In fact, I vehemently disagreed. But I remembered it not long after, when I started to read about the Aids virus.'

Youselli nodded. '"This is not the worst so long as we can say this is the worst." Shakespeare.'

Edith was impressed. Youselli didn't look the quoting type. He smiled ruefully. 'My old man used to say it when we had sausage for dinner.' She missed the joke, so he pushed on. 'You were saying.'

'I think I believed human consciousness and experience had boundaries, and though we did terrible things to each other there were limits. Now I am not so sure. I also believed behaviour was readable and that there were usually mitigating circumstances, which did not excuse the deed but went some way to explaining it.'

'You mean like child abuse.'

'Yes. We learn through example.'

'But now you are not so certain.'

'Why shouldn't there be new strains of psychopathy? We have learned to do everything else better. We run faster, we develop better technology, we have machines the size of thumbnails that can out-think humans. Why shouldn't we get better in other ways, or worse?'

Youselli looked at her carefully. 'You mean develop as psychopaths and criminals?'

'Psychopaths without the usual signs. People who are unreadable because if you go into their pasts you will not find any of the familiar clues to their development. They will have had perfectly blank, uneventful childhoods – no abuse, no alcoholic parents, no splits, no signs. I suppose I mean *imaginative* psychopaths.'

Youselli considered. 'And you think this is like a clinical development?'

'In a way, yes.'

'And the reason?'

'Well, I think in one way it is probably a uniquely American experience, brought about by rootlessness, mobility and geography, combining to produce a corresponding lack of conscience. But it could also be described as good old-fashioned evil, which is perhaps something we try too hard to deny.'

In the silence that followed, Edith made a fist of her hand and Youselli saw she was on the point of crying. He reached for her hand.

'Tell me,' he said gently.

'My fear is that realizing this will—' She had to stop and start again. 'That by acknowledging it I am exposing myself to it.'

'You cannot know that.'

'I have been hiding all my life, pretending there is nothing nasty outside the cupboard.'

He failed to find anything comforting to say.

'This malfate thing, it's like a virus,' she whispered.

'It's just a superstitious thing.' He said it with more conviction than he felt, remembering McMahon's parting kiss.

She was shaking her head in disagreement when she surprised him with a burst of near-hysterical laughter. 'You meant *wurst*.'

'That's correct,' said Youselli, feeling foolish about the joke. Edith laughed too long and apologized for her brittle state. Youselli told her not to worry but he looked glum, she thought.

'So now you are thinking Stella was Leah all along?' he asked.

'I don't know. We told ourselves it was Daria and it wasn't.'

'How do you figure it's Stella?'

Edith took a sip of wine and considered. 'Daria and Stella became friends, and she learned that Daria had a dead sister. I can see Stella becoming obsessed with Leah. Stella lost a life too, spending all those years locked away. Through Daria she could have learned about Leah and fantasized about making her come back again, as a way of reclaiming her own past. Maybe Stella had a teenage crush on McMahon too, which would make him a point in common, and an obvious conduit.'

'Let me ask a question,' said Youselli. 'What happens when she gets found out?'

Edith frowned, not sure what answer Youselli wanted.

Youselli said, 'In her own mind she's Leah, right?' Edith nodded and he went on. 'Then someone comes along and exposes the lie.'

'Rather than face the truth she would destroy and move on,' said Edith.

'Destroy and move on,' he repeated.

Like you, she thought, or me come to that. She sensed he was already gone. She wanted to tell him that he was the biggest mystery: the man seated opposite her was no longer the same man she had invited into her house.

She was surprised when at the end of the evening he asked if he could stay, and was secretly pleased but it left her saddened too because she knew he would break her heart.

CHAPTER TWO

For several days, every time Edith's telephone rang she wanted it to be Youselli, but it never was and she wondered if she was punishing herself by refusing to call him. This time when she picked up the receiver she did not recognize the voice. It was a man who sounded about her age. He gave her name its German pronunciation, which unsettled her. It turned out he was the local newspaper reporter who had covered the Stella Ritter case, a man named Behm now retired. Edith had been trying to reach him and had left a message via the paper asking him to call.

She thanked him for getting back to her and he dryly announced that he was happy for any distraction from watching grass grow. In a reedy, distant voice he went on to tell Edith about the immediate response to the murder of Hannah Engel and how there had been an understandable local consensus to play it down. Furthermore, the accused's mother had influence, in the shape of the ear of the mayor – and more besides according to the gossip – so the case had been dealt with hastily and its circumstances barely released. Behm's editor had been coerced into covering up the whole business as far as possible and Behm complained to Edith that he had not been allowed to report the story in any depth. If the killing had happened in a working neighbourhood it would have received a lot more exposure.

'The thing everyone felt bad about, but would not admit,' continued Behm, 'was that the Engels were not liked. They were newcomers and he was pushy and responsible for local businesses going under. So when this terrible thing happened most people felt a sense of relief that it was the Engels' child rather than someone else's.'

Edith asked if anti-Semitism had played a part.

Behm chuckled ruefully. 'Which came first, the chicken or the egg? Saul Engel drove a hard bargain and he saw how the retail market was going before anyone else. If he had not, someone else would, but I can't put my hand on my heart and say that a gentile would have been socially rejected the way he was.'

Edith asked about the severity of Stella's sentence, given the ambiguity of the situation. Stella had spent nearly eighteen years in institutions, until she was twenty-five.

'I think the punishment was a reflection of the bewilderment everyone felt,' Behm replied. 'None of what I am saying now was clear then. There was a stunned sense of this awful, incomprehensible thing having been visited upon a peaceful community. I am not saying Stella was the scapegoat, but there was a strong feeling of everyone wanting to forget. Nothing remotely like this had ever happened in these parts. Of course, much later on another version emerged.'

'Which was?'

'That Stella had in advance cruelly and deliberately planned the death of the Engel girl.'

Edith had been initially surprised by the fact that Stella's victim was two years older and assumed Stella must have been very intelligent and manipulative, though this did not appear to be so judging by what she had read in various assessments. It was a puzzle.

'Where was the evidence for that?' she asked Behm.

He told her it came from Judith Rose, the third girl present on the afternoon of the Engel girl's death.

'At the trial?'

'She was never called. Being nearly a year younger she was generally thought to have gone along with whatever Stella did, and was not considered bright. Some years later she started putting it around that Stella had confided to her about wanting to kill the poor girl and the different ways she intended to do it.'

'And what was the reaction to that?'

'Nobody wanted to know. Judith Rose was a handful by then and Stella was history.'

'Did you talk to her?'

'Yes, she sought me out. I have to say I thought she was attention seeking, but one thing did strike me.'

'What was that?'

'There was nothing backward about Judith Rose. She struck me as very smart.'

'Do you know where she is now?'

'You got me there. She got troublesome in her teens. I think I remember hearing she walked out and left for Chicago.'

★

Youselli had not realized how hard it was to get hold of a busy movie director. He had obtained the production office number from his hotel desk clerk who was too polite and actor-handsome, and resting between assignments, he confided, before listing his television credits. Youselli phoned from a pay-phone with a view of the studio gate. A woman PA with a cheerful voice that had no trouble saying no told him his chances were remote as he did not have an appointment, and even that was no guarantee.

'Right now Mr MacGregor is one of the busiest people on the planet.'

'I've come from New York, I am a police officer and it is a matter of personal concern to Mr Mac-Gregor,' he said and could tell she did not believe him. 'Just ask him, please.'

Sensing he was not about to give up, the woman flipped him over to the waiting music. Youselli endured several minutes of jaunty classical and felt his temper rise several degrees.

The PA came back and announced in clipped tones, 'Mr MacGregor's safety has already been discussed with a member of the Threat Management Unit. I suggest you contact them. Thank you.'

Thanks for nothing, he thought. He could not think of a way to call Linda Gomez without alerting her suspicion, but did anyway.

'How's the fishing?' she asked.

'It's good. Fish are biting. Listen, I have been thinking, that Scottish film director, do you have a contact number?'

'Sure.' She gave him the number he had just called.

'Any others?'

'Nope. That's the only one. I don't even know if he took my advice and moved. You want me to talk to him?'

'It's okay. It's probably not important.'

'Go catch fish, forget about it.'

'You're right.' He was glad she was not in an inquisitive mood.

'Lot of traffic,' she said as he was about to hang up.

'Busy road,' he said hurriedly.

He went and had a coffee and Danish in a diner over the street and watched the studio security barrier going up and down for the cars. He could wait all day if he had to and follow the guy, except he did not know what he looked like, though he was willing to bet he'd drive a Saab convertible. If MacGregor had moved he could well be staying in one of half-a-dozen smart hotels. Youselli could trawl his way through those, or he could schmooze the gate man. In the end he did it the easy way and paid his handsome hotel clerk to find out MacGregor's hotel. It cost fifty dollars, which was good money since it probably took no more than a couple of calls. The description he got for free.

'He's short and thin and very pale for LA with red hair. I would get to him while you can,' the clerk said conspiratorially.

'Why?'

'Word is he won't be around much longer.'

'I thought he was in the middle of a picture.'

'A little birdie says they're talking of bringing in another director in time for principal photography.'

'Does he know?'

'Heavens, no. They are like wives, always the last to know.'

The handsome clerk stated that his name was Carl and asked if he could do anything further to oblige. Youselli wondered if it was routine in California to state one's availability quite so openly.

He phoned the director's hotel at intervals during the evening and was told he was out. Around eleven he decided to go over there and found a table in a mezzanine bar that looked down on a marbled lobby.

The director showed up at five to midnight with a woman. Youselli nearly missed him because he had company and wore a cap, which he had on backwards as an indication of his asshole credentials, as did his baggy shorts worn with Timberland boots. It was his pale legs that alerted Youselli.

He got down to the lobby in time to intercept them on their way to the lift. Close to he could see the red hair and freckles. The woman was dressed scruffy too, but there was no denying her looks. Without his movie there was no way she would have been with Mac-Gregor, Youselli reckoned. He flashed his badge and said he needed to speak with him briefly, on account of a client who was being threatened by a woman almost certainly known to MacGregor. Youselli spoke low and fast, allowing no interruption, and kept moving forward, crowding MacGregor's space. He was pleased when the woman took her hand from his arm.

Youselli wondered if she was a hooker. He realized he was homesick.

The director wanted to tough it out. Youselli thought of flattening him for the hell of it. Their stand-off was broken by the woman saying, 'Tell him what he needs to know and give me the key, I'm going to bed.'

MacGregor looked like his day had just been spoiled. After sulkily watching the woman enter the lift, he made no move to sit down though there were lobby chairs nearby.

Youselli said, 'My client is being harassed by a woman. It has come to our attention you might be associated with the same woman.'

MacGregor's eyes strayed in the direction of his vanished companion. Youselli was surprised a man so fair could pale the way MacGregor did.

'You fucking her?' asked Youselli.

MacGregor swallowed and nodded.

'Let's go talk to her.'

MacGregor looked dazed and let himself be led into the lift.

'Long way from home, huh?' said Youselli grinning as the doors closed.

'What is this?' asked the actress, doing angry like she had been taught in class. If this performance was anything to go by, thought Youselli, she was lousy. When they had walked in the room the television was on but Youselli figured from her jerky behaviour she had been doing more than watch television.

'What's your name?' asked Youselli.

The woman glared and MacGregor answered, saying it was Katherine. Behind her, twenty floors down, the lights of the city spread away to a distant horizon. The phony opulence of the suite seemed to be making all of them nervous. The television was showing a rerun of *McHale's Navy*.

'Are you in his movie?' Youselli asked.

She nodded tersely and he turned to MacGregor. 'It's not her. The woman I want fucked you and did not get the job.'

'Who is this asshole?' the woman asked, making it sound like a line she had rehearsed too often.

MacGregor looked at Youselli expectantly and Youselli said, 'Tell her she can take her bath now.'

She glared again and Youselli said, 'Run along if you still want to be in his movie.'

MacGregor suddenly looked exhausted, like a switch had been thrown or his drugs had worn off. Youselli wondered if the rumours about him being on his way out were true.

'Did you fuck anyone else?'

'I'm not a monster.' He said it without any real conviction.

'Date someone and turn them down for the job?'

'I told the other woman already, I spend my life turning people down.'

'Anyone you remember, anything unusual?'

'I get hit on all the time.' He said it in a surprised voice. 'It seems to be the basic currency in this town.'

Youselli satisfied his curiosity as to what the girl-friend had been doing. Under an open magazine left hurriedly on the coffee table were a couple of lines. He dabbed some on the end of his finger and tested it and pulled an appreciative face.

'Better than you get in Scotland?'

'I wouldn't know,' MacGregor said archly.

Youselli gestured at the lines. 'May I?'

'Be my guest.'

They did a line each and *McHale's Navy* got a lot funnier. Youselli asked MacGregor about his lead actor who had been a TV cop. MacGregor said he was a nice man in a tone that suggested it did not matter either way.

'I always thought he did a pretty good cop. Realistic,' said Youselli.

They watched the television. MacGregor, shaking his head and laughing at the same time, snapped his fingers and said, 'A woman came up to me in a bar.'

'What was she like?' They were in tune now.

'Quiet, intense. She said she was a cutter.'

'A cutter?' He liked that. He had a flash of a knife tracing its delicate way across MacGregor's hairless chest and knew he would happily watch.

'Cutter, editor. She wanted to cut my film because she knew about angels.'

'She's the one,' said Youselli excitedly. Everything was clear now to the end, the sharpness of his mind like her cutting. The two went together.

'She came up to you in a bar?'

'Yuh. She was quite polite. Nice smile.'

'What did you do?'

'I told her to see the production manager.'

'Then what happened?'

279

'The production manager told me she had the wrong experience.'

'What, not enough?'

'She cut the wrong kind of movies.'

'Her name?'

'I don't remember.'

'Did she call herself Leah?'

MacGregor said he could not be sure. 'I meet too many people.'

'And you never heard from her after that?'

'I saw her.'

'Saw her, where?' Moving closer all the time, Youselli thought.

'A couple of times in public places. I had a feeling maybe she was following me, but that's not unusual on this picture. It has attracted more nuts than I know what to do with. Half the religious freaks in the city hang around the office.'

'Anything unusual happen recently?'

MacGregor laughed. 'This is LA! I can't believe what I'm seeing half the time.'

Looking at him with his glittering eyes and his silly cap, Youselli figured no one in town would remember him in six months. His moment would have gone. He wondered if MacGregor sensed it too because he looked lost all of a sudden.

'Someone called my wife and hassled her,' he said. 'A woman.'

'What did she say?'

'She said I'd been sleeping with her.'

'What did you tell your wife?'

'I denied it and she believed me.' MacGregor shot him a sneaky grin.

'Do you have any suspicion who could have made the call?'

'I figured someone I turned down for a job. The women I have been seeing would not make that kind of call.'

'Women, plural?'

MacGregor looked pleased with himself. 'Katherine would not do anything like that and the others, well, they were professional. Do you know anything about Scotland?'

'Apart from kilts, no.'

'Lots of depression and not much sunshine. I figured I might as well enjoy it here while I can.'

Youselli asked if MacGregor had any idea how the caller might have got his wife's private number.

'My personal assistant has it but she would not give it out under any circumstances. Maybe someone hacked into her files. Though—' He broke off, looking thoughtful. 'Sometimes when I got back to the house it felt like someone had been there while I was out.'

'This cutter woman, did she seem in any way dangerous?'

'We met in a bar for two minutes. She didn't come with flashing blue lights.'

'Good looking?'

'What's that got to do with it?'

'Because you are the only person I know who's seen her.'

MacGregor nodded. 'Trim, attractive but not in

your face. She looked like lots of people. What I remember was not so much the way she looked, it was her stillness, like she watched things for a long time. She had a trick of making herself not noticed.'

'And you did not fuck her?'

MacGregor shook his head.

'You can tell me,' Youselli cajoled.

'She never asked. Had she asked I would have. Then again, maybe not because I work sixteen, seventeen hours a day. I don't even think about sex any more.' He nodded in the direction of the bathroom. 'And she expects me to stay up screwing her half the night. It's all right for her, she can lie around all day learning her ten lines.'

Youselli was on the point of leaving when MacGregor frowned, looking like he was trying to remember something. 'She did say one strange thing.'

'This cutter woman.'

'That was exactly her point. She made like it was a joke but now I am not so sure. She corrected me when I referred to her as an editor. She said she was a cutter and it was her job to cut out the bad bits.'

Next morning Youselli had the cutter woman's name and number, which turned out to be an answer service. A copy of her work record had been faxed through by one of MacGregor's PAs. She had been in the movie and television business for six years, but with a lot of moves, including Chicago and Denver. Several wildlife programmes were listed. Since Los Angeles things seemed to have been more of a struggle – a few films cut for students and lots of gaps. He looked at the name she worked under – Elizabeth Stoller. From Leah Geffen to Elizabeth Stoller. He wrote both names down and decided he liked them equally.

MacGregor's production manager was in meetings all morning and when Youselli finally reached him he sounded impossibly busy and abruptly announced he had no idea who Elizabeth Stoller was. Youselli was trying to remind him when he found himself on hold while another enquiry was dealt with, leaving him to fume to the same bit of classical music as the day before. How dumb, he thought, playing the *Four Seasons* in a city that doesn't have any.

'Yes, how can I help?' said the production manager without apologizing for the interruption. Youselli explained but the man refused to be prompted, saying he had already met and forgotten hundreds of people in the course of this production.

'Mr MacGregor said you would give me every assistance,' said Youselli roughly. The man sighed heavily but did not hang up and Youselli emphasised that the woman had been referred to the production department by MacGregor. Sensing the man bristle at MacGregor's name, Youselli threw in a question. 'Is it true he isn't going to make it through the picture?'

'You heard that?' The production manager sounded surprised, even gratified.

'They are looking for a replacement is what I hear.'

'Well, put it this way,' he said, lowering his voice and sounding eager. 'I've worked for a lot of steady Eddies who do it by the book and turn in pictures as dull as ditchwater, but these are the guys who get hired because they don't shit on anyone's shoes. I have worked for one or two gifted directors who create magic out of chaos. Then there's this guy, pure chaos. First big picture he thinks all he has to do is sit back and let it happen.'

When he finally remembered the woman, Youselli was sure he had all along. 'She came in, she was quite up front, said she was meant for the job. Her angels told her so.'

'I would have thought that was pretty memorable.'

'That's not even footnote material. I got a woman trying to see me says she's Joan of Arc. Anyway this woman made it seem like it might be some kind of sophisticated joke. Maybe she is a good cutter, but she cut the wrong kind of pictures and it wasn't my choice. The job is going to the producer's girlfriend.'

'What kind of wrong films did she cut?' Youselli was sure he already knew.

'I got nothing against someone who cuts X-rated movies,' said the production manager. 'Dramatic pro-grammes and movies are the hardest thing to break into. A lot of cutters do X-rated to get the work experience. Thirty years ago they would have done B pictures, now they do X.'

Acme Films, Youselli was thinking. That sent a tremor through him. But five minutes and a phone call later his elation had gone flat. Acme had no Stoller, or an Elizabeth or a Leah, or a Stella. From the tone of the woman answering Youselli gathered she took a lot of crank calls.

He decided to drive over there. On the way he figured it out. Remembering that Daria had worked as

Skye Blu, it was obvious why there was no Elizabeth Stoller at Acme. At the end of Daria's movie he had noticed how the credits were made up of joke names. Two he remembered were Carlton Cum and Vanessa D. Ream. When he arrived at Acme he apologized to the receptionist for his earlier call and proceeded to charm her, teasing her first by saying he was willing to bet she'd thought he was from the IRS. He explained who he was looking for and made up some story about how he was making inquiries on behalf of Daria's parents. 'It's not an investigation, you understand, more a kind of *in memoriam* thing. They asked me to speak with people who knew her.'

'That sounds like Kitty,' said the receptionist, trying to sound helpful. She explained what Youselli had already guessed, that everyone at Acme was called by their professional pseudonym. Kitty's picture credit was Kitty Kut.

Youselli could see the editing rooms in the corridor behind the receptionist and asked if they might take a look. She looked dubious.

Youselli said, 'I have come a long way for this.' He gave his best smile. 'It's for Daria.'

That appeared to make up her mind and she motioned him through with a conspiratorial wave of her hand, telling him to hurry because she was not supposed to leave the desk.

He followed her to the end of the corridor. They slowed before an open door. Youselli took a deep breath and thought about how far he had come. As he stepped into the room the receptionist said, 'I guess she's not here.' She said it with the same dumb smile she had used to introduce herself. 'She probably went out the back way to get a sandwich. I expect she will be here in a minute. She usually works lunch.'

Having psyched himself up for the moment, You-selli felt the disappointment in the pit of his stomach. He even staggered a little.

'Are you okay?' asked the receptionist.

'A bit faint is all.' He felt dizzy as though with a caffeine overdose. 'Is it all right if I sit down a moment?'

The receptionist looked doubtful. He said, 'I can wait in the lobby if you prefer.'

'Are you okay?' she asked again. 'You have gone white.'

He said he would be all right if he could sit there a while.

'Can I get you anything?' she asked, sounding confused.

'I'm okay.'

She departed uncertainly. With her gone, Youselli felt better. He looked round with a surge of glee. Less than twenty-four hours and he was in her room.

There was no personal touch to say anything about its occupant. It was like a cell. There were gray walls, a tiny window high up with no view, plain shelves full of boxed tapes and a desk and chair with a computer and a couple of monitors. The machine hummed and the screens showed frozen images of close-up screwing. He wondered how she felt cutting this stuff.

Each time he heard footsteps he braced himself but they either stopped or walked on by, so he nearly jumped out of his skin when a voice said, 'I hear you're looking for Kitty.'

Youselli spun round. The man in the doorway was barefoot and wearing a suit. He regarded Youselli suspiciously. 'Are you a cop?'

'Private inquiry.'

The man looked unconvinced. 'We run a legitimate business here.'

'Your business is none of my concern,' said Youselli, still recovering from the shock of the man's arrival. He was annoyed at having his wait interrupted. It was more than a wait, he decided. It was a vigil.

He told him what he had told the receptionist and the man seemed to relax and introduced himself as Duggie saying that Daria had been like a daughter to him. 'It is a common misconception that this business is a fast track to abomination. This is not true. We're a family here. We look after each other. It is a refuge for battered souls. Most of them come from backgrounds so scarred you would not believe. Daria, for instance, suffered the terrible indifference of rich parents. She told me many times.'

Yeah, thought Youselli, while you had your dick in her. When Duggie questioned the parents' sudden interest in their daughter, Youselli decided he was a pompous smartass.

He gestured at the editing desk. 'What about her?'

'Kitty?'

'What about her?' Youselli repeated. 'Where's she from?'

'Kitty has always been a bit of a mystery.'

Duggie grinned a knowing, possessive grin and Youselli went for him. Next thing he knew he had the man pinned to the wall by the lapels of his expensive suit and saw the darting fear in his eyes. He was happy to let Duggie feel his strength.

'Tell me.'

Duggie opened his mouth but nothing came out and Youselli saw the man was too scared to talk. He slapped Duggie's cheeks a couple of times – enough to make him talk. It was funny, he thought, it reminded him of a scene from Duggie's movie, slapping buttocks to loosen up an asshole.

'Come on, baby, don't go dry on me.' He laughed at that but after the laugh sensed panic rising: he was getting in too deep. At the sound of footsteps he hurriedly let go of Duggie, and turned to see who it was. He felt another kick of disappointment when he saw it was only the receptionist, mouth wide with surprise at Duggie sliding down the wall.

'He's having some kind of asthma attack,' said Youselli deadpan.

She looked from one to the other, shaking her head at so much drama. 'Kitty came back,' she finally managed. 'And she turned round and walked right back out.'

'You told her I was here?' asked Youselli.

She looked scared, like he might hit her. Duggie's head was lolling like a castaway's.

'How long ago?' asked Youselli moving past her.

'Not even a minute,' she said, sounding fearful. 'What did you do to him?'

But Youselli was already running.

CHAPTER THREE

Because of Daria things have gotten messy. I went out of my way for her, but her path through my life was marked by unsisterly cigarette burns and rings from sloppy coffee mugs and wineglasses. The times I wanted to scream at her I blamed myself because she was the free spirit I would never be, borne aloft on the wings of our love. I told her that. She hugged me and said it was the nicest thing anyone had ever said to her.

After all those years she still had my things. The book hidden in the lining of the suitcase, along with the photographs, looking like they had not been touched since that hot summer's day so many years ago in France. How strange it felt coming across these souvenirs of a world I had willed myself to forget, of hurt and degradation and suspicion of a kind that forced me to make a secret of the diary in the first place. There was even a note to that effect: *I must be careful that these people don't find this. My thoughts are my own. This is perhaps the last thing they have left me. A. above all wants total possession. I have never met bad people before and I don't know what to do.*

How young and naive I was, how ripe for exploitation! And I have gone and let it happen again!

Believing in you a second time, letting myself be seduced by the sound of your voice.

Daria's problem, as I discovered when she came to stay, was she had turned into a doper, and that stirred bad memories of France. I berated myself for not being more forgiving but she was so messy and she showed no gratitude when I got her work, and if she used the car she never replaced the gas, and my patience was exhausted by so many used needles. I helped her some-times, slapping the vein to make it stand up. She was my sister after all and I still loved her. Each time I said it was the last time and she did not believe me. Even when I helped her move she thought I would change my mind. I saw her only the once after that when she came to the house, strung out and mad as hell, screaming abuse. I felt a burning shame as I uttered the words of rejection, 'You do not deserve me for a sister.'

'You're crazy,' she kept repeating, and when I wept I wept for us both.

Now, because she is gone, the man has come. When I heard about him I felt the special anger of those betrayed. My fear all along was that it would not be you I met at the crossroads, but some agent of yours, some black angel. I was offering freedom, but you prefer captivity. And now you have sent your agent to destroy the purity of my love.

I shed tears for the future we will not have. The sun burned the freeway white and I tried to imagine this moment seen from another time, a long way in the future, when both of us would be dots of nothingness in the overall scheme of things. But this thought did nothing to take away my grief.

I pray to the angels to ask if there is any way I can allow you one more chance, to see the error of your ways, to prove forgiveness is all. They say no, definitely no.

They say I must go to you.

Maybe that was my mistake all along. I was waiting for you when it should have been the other way round. Now it is your turn to wait.

CHAPTER FOUR

Youselli caught a glimpse as her car skidded out of the Acme lot; not enough for a positive identification – dark glasses, hair cut to the neck and flicked out at the sides; hey, isn't that Natalie Wood, except she drowned.

He drove the neighbourhood hoping to catch sight of her car, except he was not even sure what make it was, even the colour was nondescript shit, Japanese probably. Why couldn't she be in a Mustang? If this was his movie, that's what he would have her drive, wind in her hair, sun glasses on, nothing under her dress.

The next time he went past Acme there was a patrol car. The angrier he got at losing her the faster he drove, making the tires squeal on corners.

Then he stopped looking and just drove, he didn't know where. He was in the middle of Los Angeles – except Los Angeles had no middle, everybody knew that – and he did not have a clue. From the looks he was getting from other drivers he figured he must be talking to himself.

He could not remember when he had last cried, but he did on the freeway, squeezing out the tears, savouring the novelty. 'Man,' he said, inspecting himself in the mirror, 'You are one fucked-up bastard, you deserve to weep for the gross fuck-up that is your life, you deserve to weep at how close you were. You were in her space and she was in the building.'

He wondered why he was really there. Maybe it was something about the way she gave voice to her feelings. That was what he wanted, he decided, to understand the secret of her voice, and the way it came through to him as clear as a local call.

Driving down the moving coffin of the freeway he realized for the first time that nobody had ever taken the trouble to listen to him, except Edith perhaps but that was because she was lonely. The times he had tried to confide his real feelings people had laughed. It was like all his life he had been yearning for a voice to call his own. He had grown up talking in voices he never felt were his own. His home voice was a defence against his father mostly. He had always thought maybe he would find the right voice at the next stage, or the voice he knew he harboured inside him would speak up. There had been his school voice, his husband voice, which sounded worryingly like his father's sometimes – 'Shut up, bitch!' – and his cop voice, which was even tougher. Teach me O Lord to find my real voice, he should have prayed when he still believed all that shit.

As the excitement of just missing her wore off, it occurred to him that maybe there was no missing voice. Maybe they were all his voices and his real voice amounted to no more than a man in a darkened room grunting, 'Shut up, bitch!' He had always made excuses for himself until now. Justifiable behaviour.

You want to know where someone lives, you check the last place anyone would think to look. There she was, nestled between Stollar and Stollery. Never did an address look so sweet. Seeing it gave him what they called wood in the X-rated business. He tore the page out of the phonebook, coughing in case anyone heard, like he had seen some joker do in an old movie. The audience had laughed then. Youselli thought, I catch anyone laughing at me, they join Duggie in the lifeboat, and wondered what the lifeboat had to do with anything.

He drove by her place a couple of times, trying to stay concentrated on that feeling of excitement and tight expectation and to ignore the fact that he was close to falling apart, thanks to Los fucking Angeles. Finding the address had been one thing, locating it quite another. There had been no one to ask directions from. Valuable time was wasted driving around trying to find someone. In the end he had gone to a gas station and bought a street plan. He was on one page, so far as he could tell, right in the crack, and she was way off on another page, also at the point where the pages joined, which was always the way. 'Story of my life,' he thought.

An hour later he was still on the same page after a disastrous freeway excursion. Thinking he was driving north, it was only when he saw the late-afternoon sun to his right that he realized he was heading towards Mexico.

It had taken four hours and countless stopping to consult the map to find the house. Once he had negotiated his way into the canyon it did not get any easier because the roads turned so squiggly it was impossible to tell what was connected to what. One point he found himself right on top of a hill before working out that the street he wanted was at the bottom.

After searching for so long he was disappointed by his initial drive-by. It was just a house, wood frame with a porch and a bit of nothing grass in front. In fact he missed it the first two times because he was expecting more.

It was almost evening. There were no cars parked on the street. Not wishing to draw attention to himself, Youselli decided to drive round till nightfall, find somewhere to park and walk back. He would know from the lights if anyone was at home. Shit, he thought, what if there was a husband? All that way to find some dick standing in the way.

There was a store with some car space a quarter of a mile down the road. He parked there and realized as he set off back up the hill that he was subscribing to the old joke about no one walking in Los Angeles. The absence of any sidewalk testified to the truth of the cliché.

Like magic a light switched on in the house as it came into view. Fortune favours the brave, Youselli thought, marching up to the front door. There was no point in skulking in the undergrowth.

His nerve went before he could ring the bell. Figuring it was dark enough to move without being seen, he slid round the side.

The kitchen was in the back, lit up, and someone was inside. He heard her humming before he saw her, back to the window, standing at a chopping board, he could tell by the staccato tap of a knife blade on wood. He thought how perfect that in his first vision of her she should be cutting. She had a bottle of red wine open and nearby a large glass she kept reaching for. Youselli had not figured her for a drinker.

She finally turned. His first reaction was one of disappointment followed by a swift reprimand. If that was her then that was her.

She looked neat and wore her hair in a bob and moved like a dancer, lithe the word that came to mind. He felt good after all, being in the right place at the right time. One or two cars went past and in the sky there was a crescent moon. A night bird hooted, and she was in the kitchen, waiting for him, not realizing. Once or twice she seemed to peer out of the window searching the darkness, wondering who was out there in the broad reaches, who had been hunting her that afternoon. 'Only me, babe,' he whispered.

The humming was not contentment as he had first thought. It was nerves. Time to ring her bell.

She came to the door. There was a screen door as well. She was eating something, and opened both doors with no sign of suspicion. She looked at Youselli without any fear, one arm resting against the door jamb.

'Yup.'

He saw she was drunk, enough at any rate not to be cautious. He tried to reconcile this dark-haired woman with how she had always appeared in his mind's eye: palest skin and wild red flyaway hair.

'Hey, momma,' he had always been going to say at this point, 'Daddy's come home.' It was going to be a good-humoured moment of recognition, the kind of remark people make when they know each other, which he felt he did. He opened his mouth and nothing came out, and it was like he had turned into Duggie. The woman laughed at his embarrassment.

'Are you all right?'

There he was lost for words and she was laughing. Youselli felt himself redden like he was seventeen.

'I wanted to ask you,' he eventually managed, 'about Daria.'

'Who?' said the woman, frowning.

'Daria?' He was handling this so badly. 'She called herself Skye too.'

'Is that a sequel?' She was humouring him and he knew he should have responded in kind instead of continuing to burn with embarrassment.

'Tee, double oh,' he said lamely. He should have known from her letters she would be sharp with words.

He realized how unprepared he was. He had thought that just by finding her his endeavour would be rewarded. Now he saw how far there was still to go.

'What's this about?' she asked, more serious.

'I'm a philosopher,' said Youselli showing he could play light too, but the joke was lost on her. He hurried on. 'And a cop, except I am not a cop at the moment. I came from New York on vacation to see you.'

'To see me?' She was puzzled. As well she might be, thought Youselli floundering even more.

'Why do you want to see me?' she asked, starting to back away.

'Because of what happened.'

She was shaking her head, no longer amused. Youselli wished he could go away and come back and start over. The woman frowned, and her mouth opened in perplexed recollection.

'But that happened years ago,' she said.

It was Youselli's turn to be confused. 'What did?'

She was shaking her head. 'I think you should go.'

'I have come thousands of miles. I need to talk to you in a way I have never needed to talk to anyone else.'

She scanned his face, seeing his desperation. She started to laugh again, a big whooping laugh like he had said something really funny.

That was her first mistake, hooting at him. He had read her all wrong, he saw. She was just a tease. She did not exist in the way she had in his imagination. In reality she was like all the rest. He wondered if Edith Weber would have laughed at him in the same situation.

The woman was saying, 'You're crazy, mister.'

She could have run back in the house but she was too smart for that. She tried to dodge past him instead, into the open space that beckoned beyond, but he was too fast for her. She was about to scream, so he had to clip her, making her teeth slam together. She tottered backwards, taking them both towards the house, with Youselli thinking, 'We are crossing the line together.'

His anger was directed more at himself. What had he been expecting? That she would welcome him with open arms? That she would even admit who she was? That she would see him for what he was?

The cruellest irony was that in the ABC of it, everyone had their obsession, but the object of obsession did not necessarily respond. She had kept writing McMahon saying it was all as plain as paint to her. And now here he was, come all that way to explain how he, not McMahon, was the one for her.

He liked the house. He could be comfortable there. There was no beer in the refrigerator, only some fancy wine. He helped himself. It was cold enough to chill the glass, and he held it against his forehead. The house was on one level and mostly dark wood which gave it the feel of a retreat or a lair. As well as the kitchen and bathroom there was a bedroom and a den with a divan, plus two reception rooms that had been made into a single space. Youselli padded around, looking through drawers, smelling perfumes, and admiring the neat racks of clothes hanging in the closets. In the bathroom he used her toothbrush and wondered about spending the night there. She had the same habit as him of not throwing away toothbrushes. He inspected himself in the mirror, baring his gums, pleased they were pink and healthy, and rinsed out his mouth with wine.

He had not wanted to restrain her, had not wanted

to stuff a towel in her mouth. When he went through to the living room where he had left her she was flipping up and down like a fish, trying to loosen her bonds. She glared at him and guttural animal noises came from her throat. He was supposed to be fishing, he thought, an observation that did not strike him as funny under the circumstances.

He had to straddle her to quieten her. 'I am not here to hurt you,' he said. 'I came a long way for this.'

She was tossing violently from side to side like she was having a nightmare.

'Don't be scared,' said Youselli, though as he did he experienced a wave of something akin to terror, as though he had opened a door into a huge cathedral full of turbulence. All his life he had suspected that in the fragile vessel of his body were emotions and spaces far larger than could be contained by its physical limitations. He felt like his head would burst and spill open, scattering black seeds.

Then it hit him how dumb he was. He had been a bad detective, he had misread the clues. He should have realized. Those most innocuous household objects – the additional toothbrushes – should have told him.

He went back to the bathroom. At least two brushes were in use. He knew the difference between a used toothbrush and a dead one. He sat down heavily on the toilet seat and wept for no reason he could understand, his thoughts fizzing. He wondered if this was how philosophers felt, wrestling with their big ideas, feeling they were in a dark room, sensing rather than seeing the light under the door, which made the dark all the more despairing.

He should leave, walk out, quit before it was too late. No one would trace him.

He thought of all the crime scenes he had witnessed. It was an undeniable fact, his job was to turn up after the party. He wondered whether his penetration of women wasn't a counter to the vacuum he found at a scene of crime. It depressed him, always turning up late, having to picture the act in his mind and those pictures always stuck however hard he tried to rinse them away. What excited and unsettled him most about these fantasies, he realized sitting there, was the way crime elevated the everyday and intensified the mundane: how a previously undramatic room became full of significance, a depository of dangerous feelings. He remembered seeing Jerry Lee Lewis, with the maddest eyes and a profanity of voice. It had made him think that if homicide had a parallel expression it was exhibited in that man's performance. Homicide was as American as rock and roll. Homicide was the last great private act.

'There is a grandeur to all this,' Youselli said, testing how it sounded while suspecting there was not. He had got the wrong woman. He had hit on the second person sharing, whoever she was. She was not Leah.

He stood up and composed himself, trying to remember where he had put his jacket. His father's gun was in his waistband. He could do the honourable thing and use it on himself. The number of cops he knew or heard of who ate their gun did not bear thinking about.

He went through to where she was lying. She was dozing or pretending to and that sent his anger shooting up. How could she when he was in such torment? He pulled her to her feet and ripped the tape from her mouth, not caring if it hurt, and removed the towel, telling her not to yell. He asked who she was, but when she opened her mouth it was to scream. He hit her, and uttering the fateful words of the man in the darkened room he saw the edge and the malfate grinning below.

'Shut up, bitch!' he repeated, knowing already it was too late.

You animal, he thought to himself, you deserve to die in hell, then he remembered that the point of hell was you never died. He had to clench his teeth to stop the giggles, like the time they smoked and drank the holy wine behind the altar, still dressed up in their cassocks and cotters. This was so bad it was funny. This was as forbidden as it got. No crossing back over this line now. He was way ahead of McMahon. He regretted McMahon not being there. He would have liked seeing his skinny panic.

His own panic kicked in like somebody had smashed down a door. He had to hug himself to stop the shaking. He had hit her to shut her up, that was all. He had not meant her to crack her head on the way down, had not meant her to end up lying so still.

Lord forgive me, he said, I have transgressed. All his life he had held back from anything seriously bad. He considered himself a better man than McMahon. He had scruples about using Edith Weber, if not the grieving widow. He visited the sick, gave succour to his old man who was a real bad hat and had been on the take for years, yet there he was dribbling safe in his home with nothing like this on his conscience. Fuck the woman on the floor, it was her fault for getting in the way.

The panic went as fast as it had come, leaving him feeling purged and super calm, with a sense of wonder and exhilaration. He took a glass of wine out into the garden where the night was sharp and everything clear. He toasted himself. For once he had got to the party early. At that moment he believed crime was sacred, the ultimate private violation. It stayed sacred till you got caught. Many times he had looked into the eyes of killers, wanting to know how it felt at the moment of perpetration, before the shame came down. Change the letters of sacred round, you got 'scared'. He hadn't seen that before. He would be all right, he decided. The house would keep its secret for the moment. He thought ahead to the mess and interruption of the investigation, but he would be long gone.

CHAPTER FIVE

The job on the angels film Susan had wanted had not materialized but she gave no sign of coming home. It left Edith feeling doubly abandoned. There had been nothing from Youselli. She had not expected to miss him. Her initial feeling was one of relief that life could return to what she thought of as normal, an emotional mid-gray. According to his office he had taken leave at short notice. She rather hoped it was family related, some ordinary explanation that would mean he would call in his own time.

'Hi, it's me,' Susan said and Edith hid her disappointment. Susan now spent most of her time sticking her nose into Edith's affairs, when she wasn't nude sunbathing on her deck; Susan whom Edith had always thought of as being so buttoned up.

'Remember that Stella Ritter case you told me about?' asked Susan with barely concealed excitement. 'Well, I found her.'

'In Los Angeles?' Edith asked.

'Up near Seattle.'

Stella Ritter, it seemed, was living a life of probity in the clean air of Washington State, working as Nancy Merryweather, the name she had taken on release.

Edith sighed. She felt worn out all of a sudden, and incapable of any enthusiasm for Susan's detective work. She wished Susan would go back to being the Susan she remembered.

'You don't sound very interested.' Susan sounded cross. 'Don't you want to know how I found her?'

'Sorry. There's a lot on my mind. Tell me.'

'Through the association of librarians,' Susan crowed. 'I almost missed her as she wasn't listed among regular members, but then I saw a separate entry for area secretaries, and there she was! Representative for the North-west.'

Susan had discovered that Nancy née Stella was married to a man called Walter, owner of the local garage. Edith asked how she knew this.

'In a minute,' said Susan. 'Nancy lives in a small community where everyone knows everyone else down to their children's names. Stella's are Jesse and Rachel. The family attends the local church and three days a week she works at the library in a nearby town. She also gives private lessons to dyslexic children.'

Susan's news appeared to rule out any connection between Nancy-cum-Stella and Leah. With first Daria and now Stella eliminated they were no nearer to finding Leah. Who on earth was she? wondered Edith. She thought back to her confrontation with Blackledge and her last conversation with Youselli; the impossible solution was the one that made the most sense. Edith shook her head and asked again how Susan knew all this.

'Because I talked to her,' said Susan triumphantly.

'You what?' asked Edith sharply.

'I made out I was doing a survey and asked her lots of questions.'

'You called her home?'

'Oh, Mo-ther, you're starting to sound annoyed. Yes, I called her home.'

'How did you get her number?'

'It was listed in the librarians' association index, for heaven's sake. I think she secretly wants to be found! If I'd known you were going to be such a grouch I never would have told you.'

'Susan,' Edith said, 'you know case information is confidential. You can't go phoning people up under false pretences.'

'Mo-ther, for goodness sake show some gratitude for once! I found her. I'm trying to help, so why are we having an argument?'

Because you are being unethical, thought Edith. Neither gave proper voice to their anger until Susan asked if the real reason for their disagreement was Edith's resentment about her being in California and having a good time.

'We were always so close. I miss you, that's all,' said Edith, trying to repair the damage.

'Mo-ther, you smothered me. For as long as I re-member I was supposed to be your grown-up little com-panion. I wasn't allowed a childhood. You wouldn't let me out of your sight.'

'That's not true,' protested Edith.

'It is, and you know it. You made a prison of my childhood.'

'My God,' whispered Edith, horrified by her daugh-ter's wounding remark. Of all the things she could

306

have said, this was the most damaging. To have had her own family perish the way it did, then inadvertently to create a prison for her own daughter was a thought too terrible to contemplate.

Susan said, 'You know I'm not coming home, Mother, so this is goodbye. I'm making arrangements to sell the house.'

'Susan, please! I need you here.' She did not care how selfish she sounded.

'I've lived with your guilt too long, Mother, and I no longer aspire to your intelligence. I always thought it took brains to figure out how to be happy. Thanks to Harry – who's not over-endowed in *that* department – I now know this is not the case.'

Susan sounded so shrill. Edith saw the extent of their animosity, deeper even than she had suspected. For her own part, she had deluded herself over the years into pretending to love the daughter she had never wanted. Since failing to go through with an abortion, she had forced herself into believing that having Susan was a matter of choice and her birth was in commemoration of her own dead brothers and sisters. This she now saw for the lie it had been all along.

Edith cut Susan out of her life, taking down her photographs and throwing out the rubber duck which still sat in the place it had been moved to by Youselli.

The weather took a turn for the worse and hard frosts left cold, clear days that sharpened her resolve. A first snow helped bury her feelings further. When

Susan threatened to sneak into her thoughts Edith told herself that deep down she had always been alone and was better for recognizing it.

Youselli called at last, with no apology, sounding faraway. Edith asked if it was a long-distance call and he said it was local. His father had died.

Edith's struggle over Susan had left her too tired to deal with Youselli and she did not trust herself to speak beyond uttering a few platitudes of condolence. They talked for only a few minutes. She told him about Nancy Merryweather and from his terse silence gathered his mind was on other things. They made no move to meet, though at one point he said he wanted to talk. But Edith made her excuse, punishing him for his silence and herself for being a fool. He sounded strained but that was hardly surprising, she thought, with the funeral to arrange.

'Goodbye,' she said, meaning it. He was gone before she could hang up, leaving her staring at the empty receiver and feeling utterly bereft.

Was it malice, Edith wondered, or plain old nosiness that made her dial the number after looking up the code for Washington State, or the need to pass on her misery to someone else.

She spoke to a breezy sounding woman at the library and asked for Nancy Merryweather.

'This is Nancy,' said the woman brightly. 'Can I be of assistance?'

'You don't know me,' Edith said and she could tell

from the chilled silence that this was the call the other woman had been dreading.

Nancy quickly said, 'I will call you right back from the office. We are busy right now on the desk.'

Edith said she would telephone again in five minutes, adding, 'This is not a hostile call.' She said her inquiry was on behalf of the New York Police Department.

She waited, watching the sun slant through the window and wondered how she would fill her time after the next call. She had no plans, no more calls to make. Stripped of its distractions she saw how absurd life was. Having so effectively hidden from it, she felt she was in the final stages of becoming invisible, after severing her few remaining ties. She wondered what Susan was doing, then firmly drove her daughter from her thoughts. She remembered the boy who had broken into her bathroom and asked herself how long it would be before he came back.

Nancy sounded breathy and frightened when Edith spoke to her again. Edith explained how she needed to know if anyone in Los Angeles was acquainted with Nancy's past, on account of references to Hannah Engel in a letter that had come to her attention. Edith experienced a furtive pleasure listening to the intake of breath at the mention of Hannah, and wondered who she should call next.

The woman said that only her husband knew of her past. Edith thought she sounded quite different from the irritatingly bright person who had first picked up.

'There's no chance he told anyone?' she asked.

'Walter is the kindest, most supportive man.'

'There is no such thing,' Edith said abruptly, surprising herself with her bluntness.

'I beg your pardon?'

The sanctimonious tone in Nancy's voice was so irritating that Edith was compelled to ask, 'Why were you stupid enough to use a name that could be traced through the library system when all you had to do was list your married name?'

The woman's speechlessness gave her an enormous kick; that and the recklessness of asking an unguarded question after a life of check and deliberation.

'Who is this?' Nancy demanded, her voice rising.

'And does your daughter know,' Edith went on, the words spilling out, 'whom she is named after? Is that a motherly thing to do, naming her after the child you killed?'

Edith wondered what nasty person was saying this. She was getting in a terrible muddle and was quite mistaken thinking this Nancy or Stella woman, or whatever she was called, had named her child Hannah. It was Rachel.

'I'm going to end this call now,' said Nancy, her voice irritating and whiny. 'And I would appreciate it if you didn't call again. I don't believe for one minute you are from any police department. You are just an evil person.'

'Me, evil! Don't think you can walk away from this,' said Edith, her voice cracking. 'You are the one who needs reminding.'

The woman sighed. 'I will have you know Hannah Engel was an unscrupulous, unpleasant little child and she made the lives of others hell, mine most of all because I was forced to spend eighteen years in correctional institutions for a crime I did not commit.'

Edith was barely listening. She was speechless with shame at what she had done. She hung up quickly, hands shaking.

CHAPTER SIX

It was a big funeral, lots of retired cops, speeches, men sweating with the booze, toasting the memory of Big John. His mother was a tiny figure at the centre of it, secure in her grief, knowing for once she had finished ahead and seen the old bastard off. Youselli worked the room, bad conscience buried, testing his resolve against the hard-edged bonhomie of his father's ex-colleagues, a bunch of one-time petty tyrants run to fat.

Being in church again, the first time for as long as he could remember, he felt no guilt, no sense of being watched from on high. Most of the time, Los Angeles was someone else. He had practised his story till he was comfortable with it, believed it.

His only outstanding worry was that he had been seen. He had mistimed his exit, hoping the road would be clear down to where his car was. By then there was little traffic. But he had only just passed the end of the drive when a car came round the corner, lights on full, catching him in their glare before sweeping past.

Their eyes had locked, not long enough for him to see her properly, but enough to take in her look of closed-off determination, face bluish-pale in the dashlight. She had looked scared and intent and the way she nailed him with her eyes, even in that briefest of moments, had given him goosebumps. In the first instant he had thought she was just some driver, but, even before the car turned into the house, he knew. Her face was a perfect match for the voice he had heard coming out of the letters.

He had wanted to protect her from what she was going to find, but that would have meant taking care of her too, so he carried on running, cursing his bad timing. Twice they had missed each other by *that much*. He ran, trying to think of all the other people he might have missed by the same margin. All the women walking into bars as he was leaving, the ones he had never met who would have changed his life. He found his brain could not accommodate the concept because then that life would not have been his, and he would not be where he was now, in deep shit.

He checked the news, East and West Coast. Over the course of snail-like days he persuaded himself that she had not reported it. She must have lit out too, which meant weeks could go by before anything was discovered, and by then it would be a local news case with no follow-up. Anyway, he was a different man now, the son in mourning.

The only bombshell since getting back was Edith telling him about Nancy Merryweather sitting in her library in the Great North-west, which put her out of the frame. It had been a difficult enough call to Edith without that. He had missed her and wanted to see her but he knew since Los Angeles the gap from his side had grown wider, however much he wanted to cross back. Maybe when everything else had faded he could think about seeing her again.

As for Leah, he consoled himself with the fact that at least he had seen her. He had been privileged with a glimpse. He had seen where others had not. 'It means she is still out there running free like some creature of the wild that cannot be caged by man's imagination,' he said solemnly to his mirror. He had taken to inspecting himself for any signs of change, any manifestations of the bad thing he had done, accident or not. He felt a little guilty because if anything he was looking better with losing weight from worry. The whole sorry incident was something he'd meant to talk to his father about, figuring it would bring them closer, give the old man something to take his mind off the door closing on him.

Seeing him being lowered into the ground, Youselli wept with the realization that now there was only himself left to hate.

The story was that his father had died peacefully, but he had overheard one of the nurses saying he had gone squealing like a stuck pig. It was funny, Youselli thought, how someone who had despised life, and spent his time shitting on it, should protest so loudly at it being taken away. Even the ground seemed not to want him. There had been talk of the funeral being postponed because of the trouble the mechanical digger was experiencing cutting deep enough into the frozen earth.

At night on his own Youselli figured to sweat out

HAPTER SEVEN

of coffee and a long shower, Youselli
y drunk when he arrived at the studio,
l felt it and knew he would be riding a
n. McMahon was back and recording, he
e telephone, and sounded very up.

terrible,' said McMahon, who did not.
. the clinic had left him rejuvenated, and
mpany of Paolo who hovered like some
ian. They both wore smart dark suits that
i feel even more of a mess.

erked his head in Paolo's direction. 'Why
me now you got him?'

l McMahon, with mild chastisement. 'We
now how you were, touch base and all
porting metaphors.'

re standing in a lobby area outside the
red leatherette furniture, a water dispenser
: plant that reminded Youselli of Acme in
McMahon was remote and self-contained,
selli with a clear understanding that what-
here had once been between them no
ed. McMahon had moved on. Even his
Youselli seemed spurious.

what was left of his guilt like a fever. Trickiest of all
was a phone call from Linda Gomez who got him at
home and came on sounding office-normal, which to
him was like calling from another planet. She asked
about his holiday and he said, 'What holiday?' which,
to his relief, she took for a joke.

'We got a body,' said Gomez.

'Who?' he asked.

'A Judith Rose Grabowski.'

It had been sloppy not to check. 'Judith who?'

'Judith Rose Grabowski. The third girl in the Hannah Engel case. Are you okay?'

'It's asthma. What she die of?'

'Some kind of fall or from being hit. She was
restrained too because there was chafing on her wrists
but she wasn't tied when she was found. She's been
dead over a week, so don't hold your breath. It looks
like another stone-cold homicide. You sound really
bad, you want me to call back?'

'I'm all right,' gasped Youselli. 'You got a suspect?'

'We figured at first it was an intruder, but given her
disappearance it could be someone called Elizabeth
Stoller.' Youselli gripped the phone tighter. 'Judith
Rose was living in the house with her and Stoller looks
like she left in a hurry. She hasn't been seen at work
since. I did some checking. This Stoller woman ties in
with Daria. She worked at Acme Films. She must have
been in the building when I was there. I even walked
past her room.'

It felt strange, secretly knowing the places Gomez
was talking about. He liked the simple way she made
her connections, after all the confusion of the case,

making everything sound logical and inevitable. His own intervention had left the surface unruffled. It was neatly tying up.

'This Judith Rose thing,' he said, trying to make it sound like he was working an angle. 'Could it have been an accident?'

'Not from what I was told. Why?'

'No reason. Maybe because of Daria being accidental.'

'Or made to look like it.' Gomez sounded excited. 'So there you got it. Stoller knows about Leah from Daria, and about Hannah Engel from Judith Rose, so it looks like Stoller was your letter writer.'

'You have no idea where she is now?'

'It crossed my mind she could surface in New York, given her obsession, so I thought I'd better keep you up to date.'

Youselli thanked her.

'One other thing,' said Gomez. 'You remember the Scots film director?'

Youselli gulped and squeezed the receiver even harder.

'I spoke to him again and he said someone claiming to be a cop had been asking questions.'

Youselli felt his guts go and thought he might have to excuse himself. But listening to Gomez relate his own description he realized she had no idea what he looked like. He spent so much time talking to her, fantasizing about what she looked like, but they had never met.

'What's your reading?' asked Youselli, feeling bolder.

'Who know
Gregor went h
'I thought he
'He got fired
Youselli felt
barely aware of
what was so funn
After hanging
shouted out, 'I a
inviolable.'
All was well, he
same dream, that
crowd instead of M
and not knowing
baying crowd roare

After a gallo
was not visib
though he st
hangover soc
had said on t
'You loo
His stretch
still in the c
malign guar
made Youse
Youselli
do you nee
'Hey,' sa
wanted to
those other
They w
studio, with
and a rubbe
Los Angele
leaving Yo
ever links
longer appl
concern for

'You should not let yourself get so run down,' he said, sounding vague.

'What I do is my own business,' said Youselli. He was wasting his time, he decided, and had only been dragged there for them to gloat. He wanted a drink.

'How did you enjoy Alex's show by the way?' McMahon asked, like they were making tea-party talk. 'The woman you were with, she's quite a lot older than you.'

'She's the psychiatrist who was working on the case.' Youselli tried to make it casual but it came out sounding tight. 'Who told you – Alex?'

'Alas, Alex is in my bad books. I have to say that, given what he is doing with my wife. No, Paolo. Paolo was there. Paolo was most interested by your companion's questions. And so was I, come to that.'

None of them had sat down. Paolo fetched two paper cones of water from the dispenser, one of which he handed McMahon who sipped delicately.

'You said you had something you wanted to discuss,' said Youselli.

'We are discussing it,' said McMahon airily. 'I want you to pay Alex a visit.'

Youselli looked at Paolo and said, 'The shot of the girl lying in the stream, that was her, right?'

Paolo shrugged a fraction. In that shrug Youselli realized why she had been lying so still. 'Alex made the shot with her dead, didn't he?'

Paolo looked at him levelly. 'I don't remember.'

Youselli turned to McMahon, who smiled back. 'He wanted to refresh her soul, he said.' He sounded like he was discussing events a world away that had nothing to do with him. 'The time has come to put all that to rest. Alex must get his comeuppance. You know what he's trying to do?'

Youselli was aware of a dull hammering at the base of his skull, the start of a big headache. His eyes felt like they had been rubbed with sandpaper. He hated McMahon for the way he walked untouched through the battlefield, without so much as a backward glance.

'He's trying to conceive a child.' McMahon's voice rose with sudden hysteria. 'With my wife. In my apartment. Now why would he want to do that?'

'Maybe he loves your wife,' said Youselli but the sarcasm was ignored.

'The Dakota is a site for his occult power. That's why he needs to take my place,' McMahon went on, his eyes dancing at the significance of it all.

'Oh for heaven's sake,' said Youselli.

'It's true,' McMahon said. 'Your companion's questions put us on to it. Alex wants a child with magic properties.' McMahon giggled. 'Alex wants to father a little devil. Let's hope they find him a good school.'

'I'm through with this,' said Youselli stony faced.

'Not quite,' said McMahon. 'There is one more thing.'

'With you there always is.' Youselli turned to go.

'Okay, go. I'll have Paolo fetch it.'

'Fetch what?' Youselli asked without meaning to.

'See. I knew you'd be interested,' McMahon crowed, letting Youselli see he had won the point. 'Film. A can of film, of her.'

McMahon held Youselli's gaze and raised an eye-

what was left of his guilt like a fever. Trickiest of all was a phone call from Linda Gomez who got him at home and came on sounding office-normal, which to him was like calling from another planet. She asked about his holiday and he said, 'What holiday?' which, to his relief, she took for a joke.

'We got a body,' said Gomez.

'Who?' he asked.

'A Judith Rose Grabowski.'

It had been sloppy not to check. 'Judith who?'

'Judith Rose Grabowski. The third girl in the Hannah Engel case. Are you okay?'

'It's asthma. What she die of?'

'Some kind of fall or from being hit. She was restrained too because there was chafing on her wrists but she wasn't tied when she was found. She's been dead over a week, so don't hold your breath. It looks like another stone-cold homicide. You sound really bad, you want me to call back?'

'I'm all right,' gasped Youselli. 'You got a suspect?'

'We figured at first it was an intruder, but given her disappearance it could be someone called Elizabeth Stoller.' Youselli gripped the phone tighter. 'Judith Rose was living in the house with her and Stoller looks like she left in a hurry. She hasn't been seen at work since. I did some checking. This Stoller woman ties in with Daria. She worked at Acme Films. She must have been in the building when I was there. I even walked past her room.'

It felt strange, secretly knowing the places Gomez was talking about. He liked the simple way she made her connections, after all the confusion of the case, making everything sound logical and inevitable. His own intervention had left the surface unruffled. It was neatly tying up.

'This Judith Rose thing,' he said, trying to make it sound like he was working an angle. 'Could it have been an accident?'

'Not from what I was told. Why?'

'No reason. Maybe because of Daria being accidental.'

'Or made to look like it.' Gomez sounded excited. 'So there you got it. Stoller knows about Leah from Daria, and about Hannah Engel from Judith Rose, so it looks like Stoller was your letter writer.'

'You have no idea where she is now?'

'It crossed my mind she could surface in New York, given her obsession, so I thought I'd better keep you up to date.'

Youselli thanked her.

'One other thing,' said Gomez. 'You remember the Scots film director?'

Youselli gulped and squeezed the receiver even harder.

'I spoke to him again and he said someone claiming to be a cop had been asking questions.'

Youselli felt his guts go and thought he might have to excuse himself. But listening to Gomez relate his own description he realized she had no idea what he looked like. He spent so much time talking to her, fantasizing about what she looked like, but they had never met.

'What's your reading?' asked Youselli, feeling bolder.

'Who knows?' said Gomez. 'Anyway, Mr Mac-Gregor went home.'

'I thought he was making a movie.'

'He got fired.'

Youselli felt the laughter well up and let it out, barely aware of Gomez sounding puzzled as she asked what was so funny.

After hanging up Youselli punched the air and shouted out, 'I am armoured, I am protected, I am inviolable.'

All was well, he believed, except he kept having the same dream, that he found himself out in front of a crowd instead of McMahon, saturated with stage-fright and not knowing the words to the songs while the baying crowd roared back its hostility.

CHAPTER SEVEN

After a gallon of coffee and a long shower, Youselli was not visibly drunk when he arrived at the studio, though he still felt it and knew he would be riding a hangover soon. McMahon was back and recording, he had said on the telephone, and sounded very up.

'You look terrible,' said McMahon, who did not. His stretch in the clinic had left him rejuvenated, and still in the company of Paolo who hovered like some malign guardian. They both wore smart dark suits that made Youselli feel even more of a mess.

Youselli jerked his head in Paolo's direction. 'Why do you need me now you got him?'

'Hey,' said McMahon, with mild chastisement. 'We wanted to know how you were, touch base and all those other sporting metaphors.'

They were standing in a lobby area outside the studio, with red leatherette furniture, a water dispenser and a rubber plant that reminded Youselli of Acme in Los Angeles. McMahon was remote and self-contained, leaving Youselli with a clear understanding that whatever links there had once been between them no longer applied. McMahon had moved on. Even his concern for Youselli seemed spurious.

'You should not let yourself get so run down,' he said, sounding vague.

'What I do is my own business,' said Youselli. He was wasting his time, he decided, and had only been dragged there for them to gloat. He wanted a drink.

'How did you enjoy Alex's show by the way?' McMahon asked, like they were making tea-party talk. 'The woman you were with, she's quite a lot older than you.'

'She's the psychiatrist who was working on the case.' Youselli tried to make it casual but it came out sounding tight. 'Who told you – Alex?'

'Alas, Alex is in my bad books. I have to say that, given what he is doing with my wife. No, Paolo. Paolo was there. Paolo was most interested by your companion's questions. And so was I, come to that.'

None of them had sat down. Paolo fetched two paper cones of water from the dispenser, one of which he handed McMahon who sipped delicately.

'You said you had something you wanted to discuss,' said Youselli.

'We are discussing it,' said McMahon airily. 'I want you to pay Alex a visit.'

Youselli looked at Paolo and said, 'The shot of the girl lying in the stream, that was her, right?'

Paolo shrugged a fraction. In that shrug Youselli realized why she had been lying so still. 'Alex made the shot with her dead, didn't he?'

Paolo looked at him levelly. 'I don't remember.'

Youselli turned to McMahon, who smiled back. 'He wanted to refresh her soul, he said.' He sounded like he was discussing events a world away that had nothing to do with him. 'The time has come to put all that to rest. Alex must get his comeuppance. You know what he's trying to do?'

Youselli was aware of a dull hammering at the base of his skull, the start of a big headache. His eyes felt like they had been rubbed with sandpaper. He hated McMahon for the way he walked untouched through the battlefield, without so much as a backward glance.

'He's trying to conceive a child.' McMahon's voice rose with sudden hysteria. 'With my wife. In my apartment. Now why would he want to do that?'

'Maybe he loves your wife,' said Youselli but the sarcasm was ignored.

'The Dakota is a site for his occult power. That's why he needs to take my place,' McMahon went on, his eyes dancing at the significance of it all.

'Oh for heaven's sake,' said Youselli.

'It's true,' McMahon said. 'Your companion's questions put us on to it. Alex wants a child with magic properties.' McMahon giggled. 'Alex wants to father a little devil. Let's hope they find him a good school.'

'I'm through with this,' said Youselli stony faced.

'Not quite,' said McMahon. 'There is one more thing.'

'With you there always is.' Youselli turned to go.

'Okay, go. I'll have Paolo fetch it.'

'Fetch what?' Youselli asked without meaning to.

'See. I knew you'd be interested,' McMahon crowed, letting Youselli see he had won the point. 'Film. A can of film, of her.'

McMahon held Youselli's gaze and raised an eyebrow. He said the film had only recently come to his attention, after believing it had been destroyed in France until Paolo had informed him otherwise. Blackledge had told Astrid that the film he had burned was of other footage.

'Alex has been holding out on me,' said McMahon. 'I see now that since France I have been compromised and not allowed to achieve my full artistic potential.'

Youselli inspected McMahon for some sign that he was kidding.

'Alex's possession of Leah allowed her to become a bad influence in my life,' McMahon went on. 'And Alex retaining the film I thought he had destroyed has given him too much power over me.' His eyes flicked over Youselli. 'Alex shot a snuff movie, you know that?'

Youselli looked from one to the other. They both stared back intently, curious for his reaction. Youselli found himself unable to speak.

'Of course it was an accident,' McMahon said airily, then suddenly leaned forward in earnest, fixing Youselli with his full attention. 'Fetch that film and bring it to me. It will be in a small silver can, not even the span of a hand. I will show it you – that will be your reward – and after that we will destroy it.'

'Fetch it yourself, or send Paolo. You don't need me.'

McMahon shook his head. 'It needs someone to break the circle. I know you will never be satisfied until you have seen it. Bring it to me and we will lay to rest a lot of ghosts.'

Youselli appeared to consider this and nodded slowly. 'You believe this shit about Alex having power over you?'

McMahon shrugged. 'No harm in taking precautions.'

'This is really about Alex fucking your wife.'

McMahon seemed willing to agree. 'If you say so.'

'You want me to rough him up? No extra charge.' Youselli leered and threw McMahon a hard laugh.

McMahon smiled and said lightly, 'Throw him out of the fucking window if you have to.'

They both laughed at that and Paolo stood there with a tense little grin. Youselli stopped in mid-laugh and said to McMahon, 'It wasn't you who pulled the trigger?'

He returned Youselli's gaze and said, 'She managed that all by herself.' He paused and gave a conspiratorial smile. 'Fetch the film.'

Youselli stuck his hands in his pockets. 'What if Alex refuses or does not have it with him?'

McMahon raised his finger like Youselli had made an important point, then joined his hands as though he was praying. 'Alex has it because Anjelica asked for me. Now the extent of Alex's games has been made clear to her she is – shall we say – keen to keep her options open.'

McMahon stood slightly hinged forward, sure he had Youselli where he wanted. Paolo looked confident and bored, like everything was a foregone conclusion.

'I got a question,' said Youselli. McMahon raised an eyebrow. 'That sled.'

'What sled?' asked McMahon irritated.

'The sled you got as a present.'

'Oh that sled.' He looked uninterested.

'Yeah, *that* sled. It was the meaning of the whole fucking movie.'

McMahon nodded and smiled, indulging Youselli who said, 'What is your sled moment?'

'My sled moment? That's easy.'

He told how he had been raised on army bases in Europe and an early memory was of his mother pointing out a vibrant young man who looked so alive and so coarse that it seemed he was lit up by the light of a million eyes shining on him, and when he smiled his lip curled like he did not quite believe any of it, and at the same time could not believe his luck. McMahon told his story in a quiet, reflective voice, aware that he had Youselli hooked. 'He had a name like I'd never heard before. It was a jewel of a name. Later on I made other words out of the letters of his name: LIVES and EVILS.'

Youselli stood, nodding his appreciation. Even Paolo looked interested. Youselli smiled at McMahon and said, 'It's bullshit, this story, isn't it?'

McMahon grinned and nodded, and they both laughed again. Youselli again stopped first, and poked McMahon in the chest with his finger, angry now.

'Take your film and shove it up your ass,' he said and turned and walked out without waiting for the reaction.

CHAPTER EIGHT

Here I am out on my own in New York, lonely and caught up in events outside my control, my mind so messed about I do not know which of the following statements is true. I am here to give you one last chance. I am here to show that you are the cause of all my anger and despair. Or because we are all in the grip of the malfate.

Nothing has been the same since that terrible Los Angeles day when I saw the running man, and lying on the floor in the house I found what he was running from.

Now I watch your building, but it is not you going in and out. It took me a while to recognize him with his hair gone white. He looks older of course, but not so different once I saw who he was.

He was easy enough to follow because he walked, skirting the park then down to the hotel where he stays. Walking here is one of the few things that gives me pleasure, especially after Los Angeles.

I made my approach in the lobby, simply saying who I was, adding mischievously that I must be the last person he was expecting. He made out he was surprised but he did not sound it and acted more like he had been waiting for me. I figured it was his way to make out he was never thrown.

He stared at me intently, not in disbelief, more like he was inspecting some rare and valuable object.

'You've changed,' he said.

'Not really,' I said. 'It only looks that way to you.'

I offered him a photograph from my pocket.

'This is me,' he said, sounding properly surprised this time. 'Where did you get it?'

'I took it in France. When you were asleep.'

He looked at the picture of himself in the hammock and stared at me again and murmured, 'Can it really be you?'

I smiled and asked for the photograph back. 'I know how rare it is. You never let yourself be photographed.'

He leaned forward and took me by the shoulders, scanning my eyes. 'It must be you. You have come back after all. I cannot tell you how excited and humbled this makes me.'

My old friend, so charming and witty and dangerous. He served English tea in his room and had the impeccable manners of the Devil. This is not being fanciful. He made great play of his wickedness and fussed over me, saying that he had known all along we would meet again. He had never given up hope, had even performed certain ceremonies to bring me back.

'But why should I want to come back, did you ask yourself that?'

He did not miss a beat. 'For revenge, why else?'

He gained more ground with a blandly disconcerting question. 'What are you going to do now you have come to visit us in New York?'

I said I had not decided.

He proposed I shoot you. He made a joke of it but I could tell he was serious. 'It would be perfect, don't you see? It would solve everyone's problems. Are you familiar with the legend of Osiris?'

He told me of the sun gods and of pagan ritual sacrifices, and how they still related to the premature demise of so many public figures whose deaths fed us.

Refined manners hid so much venom. He had grown more dangerous. I measured the distance between myself and the door, knowing I was in the presence of a real and vital danger, the agent of the malfate.

'We must help each other,' he said.

'Why do *you* want him gone?'

'Because it is what he secretly desires and I wish to help him. Nothing is harder to come to terms with than the final stages of a dying star.'

'Dying?'

'As in burned out. He is an impostor. This latest burst of creativity is a sham. The songs he is passing off as his own are not written by him, and the book too. His wife has secretly hired a ghost to take care of that. Oblivion is his only choice.' His eyes grew greedy. 'I can see the ambiguous figure of his fleeing assassin, and here is the twist, she gets away, is never found. This leaves the perfect mystery of identity and motive, an everlasting puzzle to intrigue the empty minds of America. Only I will know the answer. And you. Neat, isn't it?'

He smiled a winning smile. He was quite mad of

course. 'I am close to founding my dynasty,' he went on, 'and once that is done I could come to you and we could do great mischief.' His smile grew thinner. 'Of course if you get caught I will deny everything, but we must make sure you are not. I am far too interested in you for you to fail. You are unique.'

He stood up and crossed to the window.

'What makes you think I will do it?' I asked.

'Because of what I can offer you,' he said. 'What do you want most from all this?'

'I want to be released. What is your offer?'

'A piece of film.'

I nodded. 'I would not have accepted anything else.'

He pursed his lips, seeming to reconsider. 'That film has a special power. Would I be wise to let it out of my hands? It is a talisman, a source of control as long as I have it.'

'Over him?'

'Very probably.'

'But if he is not going to be around much longer—'

'Go on.'

'You'd have no need of it any more.'

'I hadn't thought of it like that.'

'If I had the film with me when I did it, would it give me more power?'

'I suppose it would.'

'Then give it me now.'

'Ha ha,' he laughed. 'What a clever girl you are.'

'Woman, not girl.'

'Excuse me, it's a generational thing, and I'm old

enough to be permitted the odd *faux pas*. If I give you the film now there's nothing to stop you disappearing without keeping your side of the bargain.'

'Is that what we have, a bargain?'

'A proposal, which I'm sure will come to fruition.'

'Show me you have the film first.'

He paused then went to the adjoining bedroom and came back with a silver canister, not much bigger than a large medallion. He held it up and I saw my reflection distorted in the silver.

'That something so small,' he said in an awed voice, 'could contain something so momentous.'

I sensed whatever was in the canister had even more significance than I had thought. I reached out but it was gone before I could touch it, lazily snatched away. He continued to smile, teasingly now. 'We should lie together again,' he said. 'Our physical union will give you strength for the task you are about to perform.'

'No, Alex,' I said using his name for the first time. 'You give nothing as a lover.'

He looked stung before brushing the criticism aside. 'Do what you have to do, then you shall have this.'

He palmed the canister, making it disappear. He added that he had something to give me and went to the bedroom again then emerged hiding something behind his back.

'Shut your eyes,' he said, 'and hold out your hands.'

His skin felt dry as a reptile's.

'Do it now. I can tell you exactly where he is.' His eyes shone again.

★

The studio was twenty minutes' walk. The gun felt heavy in the pocket of my duffel-coat. It was a coat I'd had for years, going back to when I lived in a cold climate. Often in California I had been on the verge of throwing it out but kept it for reasons I could not understand till now. The pocket was made for the gun.

The gun, he told me, he had acquired from the French police, with the help of a bribe.

He watched me holding the gun, feeling its weight.

'This is *the* gun.'

'Does it feel the same?' he asked in a voice oddly tender.

'Heavier, maybe, I don't remember.'

'It hasn't been fired since that day.'

He had given me three silver bullets too.

'Why silver?'

'They have special properties. Of course, I am taking a risk giving you this. You could come back and use it on me!' He laughed. 'But I'm gambling against that because you and I are only at the start of our journey.'

'And you are the silver man,' I had said.

'Exactly.' He had sounded triumphant.

The coat made me invisible. Nobody looked at me.

I had expected clarity by this stage but there was only confusion. I saw Judith Rose lying broken on the floor, and thought of the man I had once loved, still loved, now hated. I asked myself, what if it had been me in the house, would his agent have killed me too?

Judith Rose had only been staying while she waited for her new apartment. Maybe the running man was her malfate. Maybe part of me was secretly pleased because she'd got the punishment she deserved, for what she had done to the Engel girl. Judith Rose was quite open about the whole business. After a couple of glasses of wine and a joint she would hardly shut up about it. Her confessions grew endless, remorseful at first, then, as she got drunk, turned to bragging and she would gloat that another little girl had been blamed for the murder she was responsible for. Her friend had not been the brightest. This was said with a smirk.

Judith Rose could be as sharp as a pin with her tongue and it was not hard to picture her ordering her friend to take care of Hannah Engel because she was too lazy to do it herself. After two weeks of having Judith Rose in the house I started to believe she was incapable of doing anything without asking someone else. Technically Stella did the killing but only because Judith Rose told her. Big fake tears would roll down Judith Rose's cheeks whenever she said, usually around eleven p.m., 'Poor Stella. I wonder where she is now.'

Poor Stella, in the confusion of all those adult questions, ended up believing what they told her about herself. Poor Stella, too dumb to protest. As for their victim, she had made all their lives hell, said Judith Rose, who was never the nicest person when I knew her. But Hannah's nature is not really the issue here.

The angels tell me interrupted lives are the saddest. Leah possesses me. Her story is mine, mine hers. I am her. I have her soul and in the time before my period, when the body is at its most sensitive, I feel the beating of trapped wings against the cage of my flesh. I crave release.

★

I collected the pizzas. Four seemed right. One of the lessons of this life, somebody has always ordered pizza. A doorman stood aside, even opened his door for me when he saw my hands were full. My big worry was the running man. I told myself he would not recognize me because I was wearing the invisible coat, plus he would not associate the woman he caught a glimpse of in the Los Angeles dark with a New York pizza delivery.

I told the downstairs desk I had a delivery in the name of Mac-something.

'Radical Surgery.'

'What's Radical Surgery?'

'Usually they order by the name of the project to avoid confusion.' The desk man looked at me with an old drunk's eyes. 'No uniform today?'

I gave him my best smile. 'No uniform. I'm not even supposed to be here, I'm the manager's sister.'

'Helping out, huh?'

'Brothers, I ask you.'

I could hear him breathing as he dialled a number. Then he said into the phone, 'You order pizza?'

He drummed his fingers while he waited, said 'uh-uh' a couple of times and hung up.

'They did not order them but they will take them.'

'Maybe I shouldn't deliver if they didn't order. It means somebody's going to go empty-handed.' I made a point of sounding interested and helpful, but helpless.

Rummy or not, the desk man gave the impression of being a kind man under his uniform, or maybe he was looking for ways to fill up his day. 'I tell you what, you deliver those, then come back with four more and in the meantime I'll check who made the first order.'

I gave him another smile, like he had just split the atom or something. Treat people right, they can be so helpful. We grinned at each other, me taking care not to be too memorable. I could picture him trying to explain to the police in twenty minutes, 'I told you she looked ordinary. She was wearing this coat like a kid's and had a nice smile. Check with the manager of the pizza place.'

'We did,' they would say. 'He hasn't got a sister.'

The desk man asked if I knew where to go.

'Second floor,' I said.

'Third,' he corrected. 'Turn left out of the elevator, through the double doors, the fourth door on your left is a lobby and the studio is off that.'

Travelling in the elevator I was shaking so much I nearly dropped the pizzas. Whatever Alex had said about using the fire stairs there would not be time to get out of the building before the alarm was raised. It was starting to look like he had deliberately lied, saying the studio was on the second floor. Maybe he had no intention of giving away his silver canister.

I was on my own in the elevator which did not help. It was easier with other people around, then you could play the part, be who you were supposed to be. The walk down the corridor from the elevator seemed the longest in my life. By then I hated the pizzas more than anything. They were starting to bleed through the box. Anyone who ordered these pizzas deserved to die. What happens, I suddenly thought, when the desk man checks with the pizza shop and he finds no delivery was sent out? Twice people came out of doors and swung towards me and I had a split second to decide if they were hostile.

The lobby was empty. I put the pizzas down on the table, then picked them up again, thinking it would look better if I went in carrying them. I was about to enter when a red light went on over the door to show they were recording, so I waited, calming my nerves, not even asking what I was doing there.

The red light went off and I turned the heavy handle that was like the door to a pressure chamber and, with the pizzas balanced precariously, went through.

There were a couple of men sitting behind a mixing table who looked at me with dull curiosity. A woman was sitting beyond them; his wife, I had seen her standing next to him in magazines. She wore horn-rimmed glasses and did not even look round as she issued a stream of technical instructions into a microphone.

One of the men leaned over to her and said, 'Pizza's here.'

She didn't even look up. I could have stood there all day before she noticed. She continued talking into the microphone, reaching down without interrupting herself for her money. She produced some notes from a purse and handed them to the mixing man who passed them to me, telling me to keep the change.

As for you, so close and so far away. You were sitting in a glass booth looking like you were on trial, listening through headphones to a list of your crimes translated by an interpreter. I saw you. You did not see me. You had dark glasses on, which for the moment was what kept you alive. I want you to see me for real when it happens. In the meantime I have the gun, I have the bullets, and I have the time.

No one saw me leave.

Back at the hotel darkness was falling. There was a big commotion outside on the corner with flashing blue lights. A crowd had gathered. I thought of going over but was thinking more about getting my hands on the film, and, anyway, that kind of staring is so morbid.

I told the desk to say I was on my way up and caught their worried glances. 'Are you a friend or relative of the gentleman?' one of them asked.

'No, I'm business.'

He looked embarrassed. 'You can't go up now. There's been some kind of accident in the room.'

That did take me by surprise. Was the malfate here, upstairs?

'Is that what outside is about?'

'Someone fell.'

I gave him my best smile. 'Are you always so careless with your guests?' On the inside all I felt was panic. Now it would be impossible to get in his room.

Back outside the crowd pointed up at a broken window. I tried to imagine the chilly dark as he fell through it and the ground rushing up.

Police and paramedics were taking care of the mess and the crowd had swelled as word went round that there had been a jumper. After all this time and effort, to go away empty-handed seemed so unfair.

As I turned away I backed into a man and we both

stepped aside with meaningless apologies. I recognized him first by a split second. Towering over me was the running man. Now it was my turn to run as fast as I could, his shout ringing in my ear, his pounding footsteps chasing mine.

CHAPTER NINE

She ran ahead, clearly not knowing where she was running. The streets grew darker and more deserted despite her frantic efforts to find a way back to the main thoroughfare. Because of a passing car he nearly lost her ducking down a narrow street and almost missed her again as she slipped into a recessed doorway to hide. He had her trapped. He looked both ways. The street was empty. He moved cautiously forward, eyeing the doorway, waiting for her to duck out. It reminded him of children's games, jumping in front of other kids to scare them.

But she did not move when she saw him slide into view. She stood there quite still like she was waiting for him. He checked, surprised. Then he saw her fear, her face white with it, and he was about to tell her everything was all right, and not what she thought, when he heard a dry cough and for a second he could not work out what was going on, then realized she had shot him.

'What did you do that for?' he asked mildly, like he was criticizing some minor misdemeanour. He still had not properly taken in what had happened and decided she must have shot him through the pocket of her coat.

'Keep away,' she said, still visibly frightened but her

voice calm. She was boxed in by the doorway. 'Don't do to me what you did to Judith Rose.'

'That was an accident. She hit her head as she fell.'

She looked confused. 'Why were you chasing me?'

'I was not. I was trying to catch up.' He was still breathless from running. 'I am here to help.'

She stared for a long time. She was shorter than him, but the right height he thought.

'I know who you are,' he said. She frowned at that. 'I read the letters.'

'Why were you in Los Angeles? In my house?'

'Because—' He could not find the words. He opened his jacket. He had to twist his head to see where the bullet had gone in. There was only a tiny hole. Small calibre, he thought, no blood yet. He still felt strangely calm but had to prop himself against the wall with his arm.

'You should get to a hospital,' she said.

'Later,' he said. 'There's time.'

He could read nothing in her face. The coat made her look very young. 'Stay here a while,' he said. 'I'm in trouble.'

'I know you are. I just shot you.' She said it sincerely, but Youselli laughed, his spirits suddenly lifted. He started talking like everything was normal and all right, telling her how he had buried his father who died while he was away and how he had urgently wanted to talk to him one last time to tell him he had done a lot of bad things too.

'I wanted to do it with that sincerity you see actors do, you know, when they turn away and look back, fixing you with their eye like real people never do.'

He showed her what he meant and did it so badly the effect was comical and her face lit up with surprised delight.

He fingered his side again and said in a matter-of-fact voice, 'I was going to save you from the malfate, now it looks like you turned into mine. Where did you get the gun?'

She was still holding it inside her pocket, he could see, but it was too dark to see the hole in the cloth. Two passers-by, seeing her pinned by him in the doorway, asked if she was all right.

'We are having a private conversation here,' she said forcefully, and after they had gone, 'I wish people would mind their own business.'

He asked again where the gun had come from and she told him it had come from the silver man.

'Silver man?'

'Alex.'

Youselli frowned as he tried to work it out. 'Have you been dealing with Alex all along?'

'No, no,' she said. 'I saw him again going in and out of the Dakota.'

'Again?'

'Yes.' She produced the photograph of Blackledge. 'He was a cruel man.'

Youselli squinted at the picture. 'This is from France.' He looked at her and she held his eye. 'But, of course, you were in France.'

She took him by surprise, leaning up and brushing her lips against his cheek. 'Thank you,' she said. 'For believing.'

When she broke from him tears were in her eyes.

338

'The gun Alex gave me is the one from France. He wanted me to—'

'Use it on McMahon?' She nodded. 'And you used it on me instead, which is maybe what was really meant all along.'

He asked to see the gun and she handed it over quite trustingly. 'It has silver bullets,' she said.

Youselli wondered how much longer he had. From the lack of visible blood he knew the bleeding was internal.

'Are you okay staying here a while?' he asked.

She looked around and said, 'If that is what you want.'

He thought about the shots from Blackledge's film of the body in the stream. It was his turn for his eyes to blur, to the point where the white face in front of him started to look how he remembered it from the film.

Despite rejecting McMahon's proposal Youselli had gone directly to Blackledge's hotel. Blackledge had resisted, as Youselli knew he would, but was stronger than he had been expecting. Even as he had used his own father's gun to club Blackledge into submission he had been aware that he had forgiven his father nothing after all. Leaving Blackledge dazed he searched for the film. Even though McMahon had described it, the canister was much smaller than expected.

When Blackledge had seen what Youselli was taking he bellowed like a wounded animal and tried to wrestle the film away. Their struggle was more like a drunken dance than a fight, lurching first one way then the other, locked in a grisly embrace and grunting from the effort until Blackledge broke away with a gasp of surprise and clutched his chest, eyes popping. He tottered back a few steps as his heart started to take its revenge, leaving Youselli wondering if luck might not be on his side after all. He was about to walk out and leave Blackledge to his fate when Blackledge threw himself forward again. Youselli swivelled to check him with his shoulder and pushed back hard, sending Blackledge and his exploding heart crashing through the window and out of the room in a shower of broken glass.

'The last time I saw your silver man he was trying to fly,' Youselli said. The memory amused him so much he started coughing painfully and saw her look of concern, which he waved aside.

'There is nothing judgemental going on here,' he finally managed to say. 'It is going to break my heart to let you go but that is what I am going to do. You must leave here, go away somewhere safe and start over.' Youselli had a metallic taste in his mouth and wondered if it was blood. 'Listen, walk with me to my car, then you can go. I am not sure I can make it on my own.'

She looked at him cautiously, as though anything could happen once they were out of the sanctuary of the doorway.

'You can trust me,' he said. She nodded solemnly.

Youselli took a couple of tentative steps, tottering slightly. He touched the bullet's entry point in his side and found its tiny puncture mark strangely reassuring, a mark of destiny. He was happy with the way things had worked out, he liked the symmetry. He was scared too of what was waiting, but that was later. There was still work to do.

She let him put his arm around her and they walked slowly, stopping once in a while, his hand pressing his side like he had a stitch. They moved back into streets with people on them and lit-up windows, past restaurants with ordinary things going on inside. It had rained at some point because the streets were still partly wet. There was a wind blowing and the night sky was clear. She seemed to understand what her being there meant to him. A couple of times she asked if he was all right to carry on but she did not fuss or say they should call for help. Maybe she was his angel after all, he thought, there to escort him from this world.

'What are you going to do now?' he asked.

'I don't know yet,' she said. 'What about you?'

'I got some business to take care of, a call to make, then I'll get some rest. You know it's over now, the thing with McMahon. You are free to go.'

She did not answer and he emphasized that she had to get away from there, get away altogether. There was no malfate any more.

'It disappeared out the window with Blackledge.'

'I hope you are right,' she said in a small voice.

Youselli paused and placed both hands on her shoulders, an action that caused him to wince. 'You know I am.'

They reached his car. He hoped he still had enough time left for it not to turn into his coffin.

'I got something for you.' He reached into his pocket for the silver canister and saw her eyes widen.

'You know what this is?'

'Yes,' she said.

'I think it belongs to you,' he said. 'You can have it if you give me the gun. You got no use for that any more.'

She thought about it for a moment and said brightly, 'It's a deal.'

Youselli leaned against the car and felt helpless, suddenly lacking the strength he still needed.

'You want me to come with you?' she said.

'No, no, it's getting late.'

He asked her to slip him the gun which she did without fuss. The weight of it felt strange in his pocket, so close to the point where its bullet had entered his side. He watched the canister disappear into her pocket in place of the gun. She leaned forward and embraced him and whispered, 'In another world.'

She helped him get in the car. He was starting to struggle for breath and was more aware of the pain now she was going. He wanted to ask her to stay after all and help him make the crossing. But when she asked if he was okay, her breath visible in the cold night air and fogging his side window, he nodded impatiently and waved her away. When he looked in the rearview for a last glimpse she was already gone, and for a moment he thought he had dreamed the whole thing till he remembered the silver bullet inside him.

He drove carefully, keeping to the speed limit, not jumping any lights. He put on the radio and punched the buttons until he found something light and classical to ease his way forward. The city lights splashed over his windscreen and for a moment he felt he would be happy for this moment to go on forever, her recent parting still a memory to cherish rather than mourn. The turmoil of the last weeks had vanished. Part of him wanted to keep driving, heading north to see how far he got.

He went back to the studio and parked across the street from the entrance which had a green awning. He settled down to wait. It was clear what he had to do.

When Edith's phone rang she decided not to answer but it rang so insistently that in the end she was forced to pick up. It was Youselli. At first she thought the signal was poor, then realized it was his voice that was weak.

'Are you all right?'

'I am fine,' he answered with heavy irony. She could hear the rasp of his breathing and asked again if he was all right.

'I am dying,' he said and she told him to be serious, though even as she spoke she knew it to be true. She heard the questions tumbling out of her as she asked what had happened and where he was.

'None of that matters. I just want to square things between us. I should have looked after you more. The other stuff I do not regret but I do regret that.'

Edith failed to understand what he was on about. 'Where are you?'

'None of that matters,' he said. 'It's too late.'

There was a long silence and Edith feared that he had gone. She called his name and eventually he repeated in a whisper, 'I should have looked after you.'

He would not say where he was in spite of her pleading, insisting that it was too late. He told her how he had the gun Leah had used in France and how Leah had given it to him, along with a silver bullet, and how Blackledge had gone flying, and about the silver canister which Leah now had, and how he had been in Elizabeth Stoller's house and Judith Rose had been there. He coughed and paused, then laughed, saying, 'I guess I'm making everything sound as if it's running backwards.'

Edith sensed time running out. 'Tell me where you are. I want to be there.'

Youselli hedged again and she was forced to shout at him, saying it was what she wanted, not his regrets.

He told her and added, 'You better hurry, because I don't know how long I am going to be here. And, Edith?'

'What?'

'Wear the coat you wore the night we went to the cinema. You look good in that.'

Youselli imagined the blood slowly rising in him like a tide. The door beneath the green awning stayed shut. It started to rain, not heavy but steady, enough to make the idea of leaving the car unpleasant. Whoever came first – McMahon or Edith – would decide what he did. He knew that what he wanted to do to McMahon would only compound the man's legend and inextricably link their names, when what he really wanted was for McMahon to be eradicated, forgotten. He thought about the ties between them and how

complicated they had grown, how what he was drawn
to in McMahon was the softness in himself that he
feared, how in parallel to the impossible love he held
for Leah there was another unspoken obsession for
McMahon. He wondered briefly if this was the real
reason he wished to see the man obliterated. He hoped
not; he hoped he was doing it for her. Anyway, it was
getting too late for any of that to matter now. He
wanted to believe he was the agent of retribution for
what had happened all those years ago. Feeling the
same gun in his hand he could believe that. All he
doubted was whether he had the strength to get out of
the car. He wished Edith would come and save him
from what he had to do, would come and take him
away and fix him up and look after him, and he would
look after her.

It seemed that wouldn't happen because the door
under the green awning opened. Youselli tensed.
Paolo's bodyguard came out. Youselli figured he was
going to fetch the car. McMahon would be out soon.

He forced himself to leave the car and stand in the
open, to clear his head and prepare himself. It took
most of his strength. He braced himself against the car,
feeling the rain fall and the gun in his hand. Everything
was starting to look like it was happening in separate
time – the door beneath the awning opening again,
the car coming round the corner with its lights on,
McMahon stepping into the street, Paolo glued to his
shoulder. All these events happened simultaneously,
but in Youselli's disintegrating mind they seemed to
occur light years apart. He knew Edith was behind
him now and sure enough when he looked she was

getting out of her car. There was a light behind her head and even from that distance he could see where the rain was starting to darken her coat. She looked good. She looked right. He was happy she was there even if she was too late.

He set off across the dark street towards McMahon who was sheltering under the awning waiting for the car. Youselli found it hard walking straight, knew he was lurching. Everything in his vision started to jump like an old movie trapped in a faulty projector. He heard Edith shout after him. McMahon still had not seen him. Youselli took in one last deep breath. He was not staggering any more, he was dancing in the rain, defying gravity. He was in the last ten yards.

*

EPILOGUE

The images are brutal and shocking and made more so by the flickering, uncertain quality of the film as it records the last tawdry episodes in a young girl's life, a scene of needles, forfeits, unnecessary fucking, and an argument whose exact content is impossible to work out because the footage is silent, but it is not hard to guess. Astrid wearing a sarong shoots up, injecting herself between dirty toes, then fixes the girl, sticking the needle in after pulling down tight white shorts. They start to fool around and the girl spreads herself for the camera, her eyes shiny and totally out of it.

Then the camera switches on in the middle of an argument and closes on the girl, who is crying and pleading, nearly hysterical. The film continues relentlessly, probing her alienation and growing panic at her fear of rejection. The gun is picked up almost casually, and aimed first at the camera and fired. The camera ducks but carries on recording. Whatever crushing dismissal is issued by McMahon at that moment is enough to make her turn the gun on herself . . .

The time had come to cut out the bad bits, make everything all right. It was what she was good at, changing sad endings, to make Leah live again, in the picture and in herself.